For Courtney, Sam, and Luke

My heroes

"Heroism is endurance for one moment more."

—George Kennan, American Historian

WORKS BY TOM ABRAHAMS

**THE TRAVELER
POST-APOCALYPTIC/DYSTOPIAN SERIES**
HOME
CANYON
WALL
RISING
BATTLE
LEGACY
HARBOR

**A DARK WORLD:
THE COMPLETE SPACEMAN CHRONICLES**
SPACEMAN
DESCENT
RETROGRADE

THE ALT APOCALYPSE SERIES
ASH
LIT
TORRENT
AFFLICTION

PILGRIMAGE: A POST-APOCALYPTIC ADVENTURE

EXTINCTION RED LINE
(COAUTHORED WITH NICHOLAS SANSBURY SMITH)

POLITICAL CONSPIRACIES
SEDITION
INTENTION

JACKSON QUICK ADVENTURES
ALLEGIANCE
ALLEGIANCE BURNED
HIDDEN ALLEGIANCE

Prologue

MARCH 17, 2054, 9:00 PM
SCOURGE +21 YEARS, 6 MONTHS
ONE MILE SOUTH OF THE WALL, NORTH TEXAS REGION

The lookout whistled. It was clear. Time to make a run for it.

Andrea Cruz was already out of breath. A sheen of sweat coated her face, matting her long obsidian black hair against her forehead. With one hand, she clutched the underside of her belly, feeling the faint movement of the life growing inside her. With the other, she clutched her son's wrist. The six-year-old was quiet, not having said anything for the last hour of the grueling trek.

"I can't do this," she said breathlessly to the guide. "We won't make it. It's too far."

The guide, a man who told her to call him Zorro, shook his head. Even though he whispered, there was anger in his voice. "We go now, or I leave you here."

"I paid you," she said.

"Not enough," said Zorro. "Yes or no? Go with me or stay by yourself?"

Huffing, she cursed the man, wiping her forehead with the back of her arm. "Fine," she said. "We go."

They huddled behind a dark two-story building, on the northern edge of the nameless town, closest to the wall separating Texas from what used to be the United States of America. It was a cloudless night, which wasn't good for trying to sneak across the wall to freedom.

The moon was quarter full, and enough of it reflected sunlight to cast a dull white pall across the landscape. Between the edge of the town and the wall there was little but dead fields and the occasional bunkhouse or guard stand.

"Stay low," said Zorro. "We're going to cross this road, and then we find the field. Once we're in the field, the high grasses will protect us. Stay low."

"*Bueno*," she said. "Got it."

Zorro stuck two fingers in his mouth and whistled. The lookout returned the call. Zorro began running, crouched, as if avoiding gunfire, across the highway and toward the field.

Andrea reached for her son with both hands, grabbed him under his arms, and hoisted him to her hip. She gave chase, hustling toward the grass. Her feet hurt. Her lower back ached. Her son whimpered as he bounced against her, complaining of being hungry.

Exposed on the highway as she was for those brief seconds, she felt naked. There was too much moonlight. Her footsteps, as soft as they were on the cracked asphalt of the highway, pounded loudly in the silent, windless night.

She'd paid Zorro the last of her money to help her escape, to get north of the wall. If she couldn't succeed on this trip, she'd never have another opportunity.

The wall was as much a barrier between freedom and oppression as it had ever been. In some ways it was only the first obstacle toward living anything resembling self-determination.

Years ago, after the Scourge but before the drought had taken root, the government had built it to keep the wilds of Texas contained. Back then, a loosely affiliated collection of gangs called the Cartel had ruthlessly taken control of the region south of the wall.

Then they fell, losing to a group called the Dwellers. They were worse than the Cartel and left a power vacuum, which gave rise to more gangs. Texas was the Wild West again. That hadn't changed in two decades. Not really.

Instead of organized cartels or gangs with structured hierarchies, Texas had become a no-man's-land, a loose affiliation of tribal areas. There were nebulous cells of evildoers intent on enforcing their will on the weak or timid.

The government, or what constituted a close facsimile of one, was essentially a military outfit that enforced heavy-handed laws. And while its primary influence existed north of the wall, it had a strong presence throughout Texas. Its job was to keep the savages at bay, contain them as much as possible, and make sure their anarchical tendencies didn't bleed into what had been the United States.

But there was more than that. There was another reason the government had troops roaming the piney woods, plains, and hill country of the Lone Star State.

After years of virtually no rain, crops and livestock dwindled. The economy collapsed. The government proclaimed there were too many people and not enough goods. That was why Andrea was running.

Reaching the grass, which was more weeds than dry grass, she stumbled, nearly dropping her child as she hit the uneven earth where the blades grew in thick clumps up to her waist. At the last moment, Zorro reached out from behind one of those clumps and steadied her enough to stop her from losing hold of the boy.

"*Gracias*," she said, crouching next to him, her breathing labored. Her chest hurt as much as her lower back now as she lowered her son to the ground. "Thank you for helping me."

Zorro nodded, raising himself above the grass to look deeper into the field toward the wall. He crouched back down, leaning into her, balancing himself on his toes and fingertips. "We're going to run for about thirty seconds and then stop," he whispered. "There's an old cattle trough out there. It's rusted, filled with dirt and dead animals. It's straight ahead. That's where we'll stop."

"A trough?"

"Like a metal bowl," said Zorro, making large circular motions with his hands. "You know, for cows to drink. *Las vacas, si?*"

"*Bueno*," said Andrea. "*Lo intiendo.* I understand. Cows. *Hay agua?* Is there water?"

Zorro offered her a look that told her he thought she'd lost her mind. Of course there wasn't water. How could there be water? It was too foolish a question to answer with anything other than a derisive glare.

He whispered again, "*Andale. Vamanos.*"

Before she answered, Zorro was up again and running like a fox. He hustled through the grass and was beyond her line of sight before she'd leaned into her first step. This time, rather than carry her son, she held his hand and they moved together. The weight of her belly tugged at her back, putting undue pressure on her knees and feet. Every step was painful and arduous. She dragged her son more than led him, the boy's pace not quick enough to keep up. He whimpered again, complaining about his arm. Andrea ignored him and kept running.

In her head, she counted to thirty in her native Spanish. "*Veinte-dos, veinte-tres, veinte-cuatro…*"

Then she spotted Zorro. The top of his head and his eyes poked above a clump of tall weeds. Weeds were the only things that grew with regularity now.

Waving at her with both hands, he motioned for her to hurry. In the pale light, she saw his eyes wide with adrenaline. His face was tense with expectation, urging her toward him. Steps away now, the expression on the smuggler's face shifted. His thick brows curled inward as Zorro turned away from her, glancing over his shoulder as if he'd heard something.

Andrea's breathing, the shuffle of her feet, the whining of her son, the thump of her pulse in her ears made it hard for her to hear anything other than her own efforts. But she heard the lightning crack of gunfire tear through the dry, still air in the same instant Zorro's head snapped back and his body twisted unnaturally. Andrea gasped and instinctively dropped to the ground, tugging her son with her.

The boy cried out in pain, in confusion, but Andrea pulled him close. Putting her full hand over his mouth, she drew him into her body, against her belly, and rocked him back and forth under the protection of the high, dead weeds.

"Shhhh, *mijo*," she whispered, a knot in her throat and tears blurring her vision. "Shhhhh."

Feet from her, through the curtain of weeds, Zorro's body lay crumpled on the ground, his eyes wide open and staring at her. She squeezed her own shut, pressing the tears down her cheeks. Her body trembled, resisting her struggle to stay still and as silent as possible. If she could just stay quiet. If…

Then footsteps crunched through the weeds and dead grass and onto the dirt. Voices, two or three, spoke in hushed tones. Andrea tried listening to them over the pulsing throb in her ears. The blood rushing the adrenaline through her body was too much for her.

Trembling, she put her lips to her boy's ear and whispered deep into it, urging him to keep quiet, pleading with him to stay as still as possible.

"Be a statue," she told him. "Pretend it's a game."

It was too late. One of the voices was above her now. She looked up to see a man offering her his hand, the outline of his body framed by the moonlight. Backlit and in shadow, Andrea couldn't see his face. His voice was surprisingly kind.

"Take my hand," he said softly. "I'll help you to your feet."

Andrea hesitated, tightening her grip on her boy. Blinking past the sheen of tears still welling in her eyes, she shook her head.

"I'm not going to hurt you," said the man. "C'mon. I've got water and some food."

Andrea started to raise her hand to his, hesitated, then extended her reach. His thick fingers were calloused and rough, belonging to the hands of a man who'd worked out in the elements.

He yanked her to her feet and steadied her. "There you go," he said, a Southern drawl dancing across the words, elongating the vowels as if he was taking his time with each syllable.

Andrea held her son with her other arm. The boy clung to her, his legs wrapped around her side and his hands clasped tight at the back of her neck.

Standing, she saw two other men. One of them had a rifle resting on his shoulder. The other, a thin, wiry man who might have been a boy, was pointing at her. Even in the dark, he looked familiar.

"That's her," said the man, his voice high-pitched, matching his thin frame. "She's the one who paid Zorro."

Andrea knew who he was now. Her jaw tightened, and anger supplanted the fear. This was the lookout, the man who'd told Zorro the path was clear.

"What is this?" she asked, her voice cracking. "What's going on?"

The man who'd helped her up planted his hands on his hips. He was tall, broad shouldered, and wore a ball cap on his head. The brim of the cap shaded his eyes, making it impossible to see them in the dark.

"Well," he said, glancing toward the lookout and not answering Andrea's question, "I don't think it'd take a genius to know this here is the woman who paid Zorro. I mean, take a look at her. She's about to pop."

The other two men chuckled. It wasn't funny. Andrea adjusted her boy, lifting him up higher on her waist.

"Who are you?" she asked, her voice warbling with emotion. "What is this? Why did you kill Zorro?"

The man in the ball cap rubbed his chin then extended his hand again, offering it to shake. Andrea shot a glance at it but didn't reciprocate. The man shrugged and lowered his hand.

"All right then," he said. "I get it. No offense taken. You're Andrea Cruz? Don't answer. I know you're Andrea Cruz. And this little one in your arms is Javier. Javi, is it?"

Andrea flinched at the mention of her son's nickname. How did they know this?

"The baby," said the man in the ball cap. "You given her a name yet?"

Her? How did he know she was having a girl? How could he possibly know about her baby girl, her *mija*? How? Even Zorro didn't know that.

"Oh, forgive me," he said, half turning to the other men as he spoke. "I'm being so rude. I don't mean to be rude. It's just a function of the job, you know? I'm sure you understand we ain't much for the niceties out here at the wall. It's rough out here. We kinda lose our manners. No excuse, just an explanation."

The man took off his ball cap, revealing a bald head that reflected the moonlight. Holding the cap at his chest, he bowed. "My name is Warner. This here is Blessing. He's the one who took the shot. Mighty good shooting, if I do say so. That scrawny little bugger over there, the one who told us all about you, is Frankie."

"What do you want?" Andrea repeated. "Didn't you say you had water?"

Warner put his hat back on his head and smiled. "I sure did, didn't I? Blessing, give Miss Andrea some water. Let Javi have a piece of jerky. I bet it's been a while since the boy's eaten anything. How long you been traveling? Four days, is it? You came up from Giddings?"

Blessing stepped forward, and over Zorro's body, to hand her a canteen. It was dented aluminum and he shook it at her before she took it from him. The water sloshed inside.

Andrea eyed the canteen hesitantly, then took it. She unscrewed the top, letting it dangle by the chain that kept it attached to the container's neck. First, she sniffed it, her gaze flitting to Blessing and then Warner before offering it to her son.

Javi put his tiny hands atop his mother's and greedily gulped down swallows of the water while she tipped it back for him. Tendrils of water leaked from the corners of his mouth until she pulled it away from the boy.

Still holding Andrea's hand, he gulped air now, catching his breath. He tried to pull the canteen back to his mouth, but she stopped him. "Not too much, *mijo*," she said. "I don't want you getting sick."

He wiped his face with his hand and sheepishly grabbed onto her. Andrea drew the canteen to her lips and drank. How long had it been since she'd had a drink? Hours? A full day? She let it sit in her mouth, swished it in her cheeks, and swallowed. Closing her eyes, she relished the drink despite who'd offered it.

"Go ahead and finish it," said Warner. "We've got plenty for ourselves. Give Javi some more too if you want. There's no rush."

She lowered the canteen, holding it at her chest, and licked her lips. "You don't look like you're with the guard," she said. "Where's your uniform?"

"Who said anything about the guard?"

The lookout snickered. Warner shot him a glare from underneath the brim of his cap. The lookout stiffened and shut up.

Andrea handed back the canteen, failing to recap it. Warner looked at it and motioned for Blessing to take the container. She put a hand atop her belly, fingers wide, rubbing it as if to comfort the child still inside.

"Only the guard kills people at the wall," said Andrea. "Only the guard...does what it does."

"Fair enough," said Warner. "Let's say I ain't one for uniforms. I'm more of a free spirit."

Andrea motioned toward Blessing but spoke to Warner. "What about him?"

"Blessing?" Warner asked. "He's with me. Good man. Great shot.

Brother Blessing could hit a speck a dust in a rainstorm."

Now it was Andrea who chuckled sarcastically. "Good man?" she said, protecting her belly with her hand. "What the guard does is evil. What *you* do is evil."

Warner raised a finger and wagged it. "Now that's *not* fair, you see. First off, I'm not the one breaking the law here. I'm not the one who tried to sneak across the wall."

He adjusted his ball cap, tilting it back on his head. For the first time, Andrea saw his eyes. They were black. Blacker than her hair. Blacker than night. They almost seemed to suck in all of the light around them. When they focused on her belly, a chill ran along her spine, and she clutched her midsection.

"I'm not the one…in your *condition*," he said the last word as if it hurt his teeth to speak it. "But we both know that, don't we, Andrea?"

A wave of nausea washed through her. Not the kind that came in the mornings during the first trimester. This was one that sent a weakness surging outward from her core to her fingers and toes.

A broad smile spread across Warner's face as he nodded toward Javi. "How you feeling, Javi?"

The boy was sitting on the ground now, his head bobbing as if he couldn't hold it up. His eyes were slits. He mumbled something unintelligible.

Andrea crouched down, putting her hands on the boy's shoulders. "Javi? *Mijo?*"

He wobbled and his chin fell to his chest. His body fell into hers, unconscious. At the edge of her vision, she noticed Blessing waggle the canteen.

The nausea ebbed, and anger welled again. Holding her son, Andrea spat at Warner, bilingually cursing at him. "What did you do? What did you give my son? What was in the water?"

Warner shrugged. "A little something to help him sleep."

It was then Andrea felt the first effects of whatever it was they'd used to drug her. Her vision blurred and her balance wavered. She tried picking up her son. She tried standing but wasn't able to do either. Instead, she plopped onto the ground, the world spinning in jerky clockwise motions around her. The last thing she saw was Warner standing to one side of her, ordering Blessing to do something she couldn't fully understand. Then the world went black.

Chapter 1

APRIL 16, 2054, 3:30 PM
SCOURGE +21 YEARS, 7 MONTHS
CHATHAM, VIRGINIA

Marcus Battle grabbed the shotgun from the kitchen counter and eyed the threat on the wall-mounted display. The image moved from one side of the screen to the other, across the wide-angled field of view from an outdoor security camera hidden in a tree near the edge of the sprawling farm.

Although it was late afternoon and the bright sun washed out the camera's low resolution, it was clear enough to reveal the armed intruder's position on his property. The threat came from the road, on foot, and had about a quarter-mile walk to reach the front door of the modest farmhouse at the rear of the acreage.

Marcus had time to get to his weapon, which he kept in the master bedroom closet. He could have taken the nine-millimeter Glock 19 he kept in the knife drawer next to the Gstove, but he liked the shotgun. He was planning on getting close to the intruder, close enough to look at the man eye to eye before he pulled the trigger.

It had been a few months since any unannounced visitors had wandered onto his land. The intrusions were fewer and fewer these days. The drought had driven people away from the low, dry hills, pushing them towards the lakes or coastlines. In a strange way, Marcus missed the confrontations with misguided or ill-intended souls who crossed his land looking for something he wasn't willing to share. Like an ignored child who craves attention, even negative, Marcus's solitary existence made him crave interaction of all kinds. The shotgun promised that interaction in a way the other less personal forms of self-defense did not.

Pushing his way through the back door, Marcus moved stealthily from a covered area at the rear of the house toward a thicket of woods that ran along the back of the expansive yard, which sloped away from the house. He was barefoot, and the thick carpet of bronze pine needles cushioned his movements as he worked his way amongst the tall, dying and dead pine trees that still managed to give shade to those traveling beneath their canopy.

The tripwires and other booby traps he'd used to fend off strangers had long since done their jobs. He'd been meaning to reset them. He'd been meaning to do a lot of things.

His knees ached and the arthritis in his shoulders flared as he hurried away from the house, arcing east in a wide semicircle. The dry air was warm, and a rivulet of perspiration sweated his brow. He carried the short weapon, a Mossberg Shockwave he'd traded for a couple of years earlier, in both hands and found himself even with the house again. From behind an old, dilapidated barn that was more kindling than structure, Marcus found the perfect spot from which to surveil the approaching threat. Though reading was increasingly troublesome, he could see things far away as clear as a scope. From behind the shambles he eyed the lone intruder.

Marcus scanned the property spotted with the occasional tree stump and partitioned with the remains of wood livestock fencing, but didn't see anyone else on his land. It was a single man carrying a handgun at his side. The man walked with the slouch of someone at the tail end of a long journey. He leaned into his steps, barely lifting his boots as he trudged forward, forcing a wake of dust and dirt along his path.

There was something vaguely familiar about the stranger's gait, how he carried himself, though Marcus couldn't quite place it. There wasn't anyone he knew who'd be coming today, or anytime soon.

Marcus waited for the man to pass him, to get closer to the house, before he moved around the barn and worked his way west. Again, he made a wide arcing path until he was directly behind the man, then quickly closed the distance. By the time the stranger heard his approach, it was too late. Marcus raised the shotgun, holding it chest high. He pumped the weapon and ordered the man to raise his empty hands high. Empty? Where had the man's sidearm gone?

They were feet from the front porch. Marcus had the drop on the stranger and the man knew it. He lowered his head and glanced over his shoulder.

"I've killed a man for less than stepping on my porch without an invitation," said Marcus, the gravel in his voice more resonant with age. As best he could remember, he sounded a lot like his father. At least how his father had sounded a quarter of a century earlier.

The stranger didn't say anything at first. Doing as he was told, he raised his hands above his head and held them there.

"You armed?" asked Marcus. "Pretty certain you're armed."

"Yeah," said the stranger. "Pistol on my hip."

"I'm gonna reach around and take that from you," said Marcus. "You're not gonna move. If you do, I'll end you right here. And it's gonna tick me off 'cause I just swept the porch. You hear me?"

"I hear you."

Marcus stepped back and, holding the short-barreled shotgun with one hand, extended his other to take the pistol from the man. Moving around to the stranger's side, he gripped the weapon and pulled it from the leather holster looped into the man's belt.

"I ain't here to hurt you," said the stranger.

Marcus tucked the pistol into his waistband and leveled the

shotgun with two hands again as he moved around to face the stranger.

"You're right about that," he said, ready to lecture the stranger about coming onto his land unannounced. Had Marcus not softened over the years, the man would already be dead or wounded.

Before he offered counsel, he narrowed his gaze, focusing on the man's face. There was something familiar about it…

The stranger, perhaps sensing that Marcus recognized him, offered a weak smile. He glanced at the old man and then averted his eyes as if staring too long might earn him a trigger pull.

"I'm here about Lou," said the man. "She needs your help."

Marcus felt the sting of a dagger to his heart. *Lou.* He hadn't said that name aloud in years. It had been longer since anyone else had said it. No way she would send some stranger, easy to give up his gun, to do her bidding. No way.

"I doubt that," said Marcus, trying hard to hide his surprise and his skepticism. "If Lou needed something from me, which I highly doubt she ever would, that firecracker would come and ask me herself."

"She can't," said the stranger. "It's too dangerous."

Marcus studied the man's face. It was his eyes that were familiar. Maybe the shape of his jawline too.

"I know you?" asked Marcus.

"Yeah," said the man. "I'm Dallas. Dallas Stoudemire."

Dallas Stoudemire.

Marcus flinched at the name. He *did* know this man. Not as lanky as he remembered him. He'd filled out. The stubble on his chin even had a couple of flecks of gray. Or was it blond?

Still, he didn't lower the weapon. "Why would Lou send you here, Dallas? What have you got to do with her? And what does she want to do with me?"

"Can I lower my hands?" he asked. "They're kinda heavy and I've been walking a while. I'm tired and thirsty."

Taking another step back, Marcus gave Dallas an elevator stare, looking him up and down while trying to measure the veracity of what he'd said. If this guy was the Dallas he remembered, then it was all good. If he wasn't, and most people weren't who they were eleven years ago, keeping the gun on him was the prudent thing to do.

Marcus motioned with the shotgun toward the high-backed wooden rocking chair near the porch's screen door. Dallas followed the direction with his eyes.

"How about you have a seat in that chair over there?" asked Marcus. "Take a load off. We'll talk. If I buy what you're selling, I'll grab you a drink."

"Fair enough," said Dallas. He moseyed the few steps to the chair and sat down, his weight swinging him back and forth on the bowed runners, which creaked against the pine slatted porch.

When he sat down, he started to reach into a jacket pocket.

Marcus stopped him. "Hold on," he said. "What are you doing?"

"Sorry," said Dallas, lifting up his hands palms forward. "I wasn't thinking. Lou gave me something to show you. It'll explain pretty much everything."

"Slow then," said Marcus.

Dallas nodded and opened up his jacket with one hand while reaching into the pocket with the other. He fished out a rectangular piece of paper four inches tall by six inches wide and, with it between his index and middle finger, held it out to Marcus.

"Here you go," he said. "Take a look."

Marcus's eyes danced between the paper and Dallas as he carefully approached. Still wary of the man he used to know, he snatched the paper and stepped back to put distance between him and his visitor.

Dallas rocked in the chair, his toes pushing up and down on the porch. Although Marcus thought him far too comfortable to be a real threat, he nonetheless kept the shotgun leveled at him with one hand while he flipped over the paper with the other. It took everything in him not to lose it. A knot thickened in his throat and he bit down on the inside of his cheek to keep the tears at bay.

It was a color photograph. Glossy. Recent. Marcus ran his thumb across the smooth surface of the picture. "How'd you get this?"

Dallas shrugged, his feet still pushing up and down. "It's mine."

Marcus frowned. "No, how did you get a photograph made?"

"Printer," said Dallas. "I was scavenging one day. Found one in an abandoned farmhouse. Rudy fixed it up. It's not the best, but we got some ink and there's photo paper. It's old. Like, pre-Scourge old. Works though."

Marcus didn't ask why they would use valuable power to run the printer. Or why Dallas was out scavenging. Or what would make him think to take a printer and ink, of all things, from an abandoned house. Things were still a lot different, more primitive, south of the wall. At least they had been. Marcus couldn't be sure what it was like now. He wasn't sure he wanted to know. He was too focused now on the image on the paper in his hand.

There was a golden hue to the photograph, as if it had been taken before sunset. There were five people in it. None of them smiled, not really. It reminded Marcus of that painting, *American Gothic*, the one with the farming couple holding the pitchfork. Both man and wife held dour expressions. The man stared straight out from the canvas. The woman looked to her left, as if something had caught her attention.

In the photograph, unlike the painting, Marcus knew the names of the people looking back at him. To the left was Rudy Gallardo. He was thinner and grayer than Marcus remembered him. Time and drought did that to people, and he wondered how much older he looked to Dallas.

Next to Rudy was his wife, Norma. Incredibly, she hadn't changed much. Still as strong as ever, she stood with her arm on Rudy's shoulder. Her feet were spread shoulder width apart; her gaze was as intense as Marcus remembered.

On the opposite end of the photo was Dallas. Marcus glanced

back at the real-life iteration of the man on his porch. From the look of it, the photograph couldn't be too old. Dallas appeared almost identical to himself.

In the photo, he had his hand resting on the mop-haired head of a young boy. The shirtless child was four or five. He was holding an empty leather scabbard against his olive skin, and his shorts hung loose at his waist despite being cinched as tight as they might go. No doubt he was his mother's son. The kid was the spitting image of her.

On the other side of the boy, at the center of the picture, was a woman Marcus would recognize no matter how long it had been since he'd seen her. Louise.

Lou.

She was older too, her face having lost any trace of the cherubic baby fat that had filled her cheeks even into her late teens. Her hair was shorter, cropped at her shoulders, and she wasn't wearing the omnipresent Astros ball cap in which he'd always seen her.

One of her hands was hidden behind the boy's back. The other was cupped under the protruding belly that stretched the fabric of the floral-print knee-length dress she wore. Marcus drew the photo closer to make sure it wasn't an optical illusion or glare. It wasn't.

Lou was pregnant with her second child. And that was a death sentence.

Chapter 2

APRIL 16, 2054, 4:00 PM
SCOURGE +21 YEARS, 7 MONTHS
CHATHAM, VIRGINIA

"How did this happen?" asked Marcus, immediately understanding the implications of the photograph. There was a reason nobody was smiling.

Dallas stopped rocking and chuckled. "You need me to explain—?"

"No," said Marcus, devoid of humor. "I don't mean how, I mean why. How could she be so stupid? Lou was never stupid. Argumentative, sarcastic, and obstinate, yes. Never stupid."

The smile on Dallas's face evaporated. "That's what you're gonna ask? You ain't seen us in, what, six years? No letters. No visits. No messages of any kind. And the first thing you got to say is that we're stupid?"

There was a distinct resentment barbing his words. Dallas's face tensed. His gaze, which had bordered on warm, went cold with judgment.

Marcus lowered his weapon and crossed the distance to stand in front of Dallas. He made a point of looking down at him when he spoke.

"The first thing I asked was why you were here," corrected Marcus, holding up the photograph. "I guess I got that answer."

"She needs—*we*—need your help, Marcus," said Dallas, his tone softening. "I used what money I had left to get here. I need you to come to Baird. You're the only one who can get us out of this jam."

Marcus huffed. "I don't know about that."

"About which part of it?"

"Any of it," said Marcus. "Not sure I want to cross the wall again. And I don't know if you've noticed, but I'm not the strapping young vet I once was. I'm gonna guess you could find someone else better qualified than me."

"Can we talk about it?" asked Dallas. "Maybe go inside and get that drink?"

Marcus sighed and stepped back, motioning for Dallas to get up. The two walked into the house, the screen door clapping shut behind them as they entered the foyer of the one-hundred-fifty-year-old farmhouse.

It was dark inside. Shafts of daylight filtered in through the windows, dust dancing in the glow. There were bars on the windows, inside and out. The wooden floors, unpolished and uneven, creaked underfoot as Marcus led his guest along a narrow hallway that led past a pair of rooms on either side then into the kitchen in the back.

The kitchen was brighter than the rest of the house. Larger windows faced the midafternoon sun. The white counters, cabinets, and flooring reflected the outdoor light and brightened the space, making it appear almost cheerful.

Marcus nodded toward a circular oak table to one side of the kitchen. There were four matching chairs around the table, all of them padded with fabric cushions affixed to the seats and backs with knotted loops. The pattern on the fabric was of red barns and piles of hay.

"The furniture came with the house," said Marcus. "Not my taste, but I don't entertain much."

Dallas didn't say anything as he pulled out a chair, its feet scraping against the white tile floor. He plopped down into the seat and leaned on the table with his elbows. There was a mason jar of honey at its center, a brittle comb trapped inside like it was frozen there.

"I chose the place because it's private, isolated, and pretty much nobody knows I'm here," he said. "Chatham didn't fare so well once the drought took hold. I think I'm maybe one of two or three people still living here. The government leaves me alone."

"This place is bigger than the last one," said Dallas. "How long you been here?"

Marcus reached into his refrigerator, which rumbled as much as it hummed, and hefted a clear plastic pitcher from the top shelf. It was half full of water.

"Moved here from Lynchburg maybe seven years back?" said Marcus. "Maybe longer, maybe less. It all runs together, to be honest."

Plucking two glasses from the cabinet next to the fridge, he placed them on the engineered stone countertop with a clink and then filled them both. Leaving the pitcher on the counter next to the shotgun, he carried both glasses to the table and sat down opposite Dallas.

Noticing the photograph on the table next to Dallas, Marcus referenced it with his chin and tipped his glass toward it. Dallas followed the lead and eyed the photograph. It was faceup and creased along one side.

"The boy yours?" asked Marcus.

Dallas was slugging back most of the water in his glass. Still, he managed a deep frown, the lines across his forehead deepening with hurt. He swallowed the water and cleared his throat.

"Of course," he said.

"Just wondering," said Marcus. He shrugged and took a sip of water.

"That question says more about what you think about Lou than it does me," admitted Dallas.

"Maybe," contemplated Marcus.

"His name is David."

"Who?"

Dallas frowned again. "The boy. My son. His name is David, after Lou's father."

Marcus drew the glass toward him for another sip. "Yeah?"

"His middle name is Battle."

Marcus stopped mid-drink. He glanced at the photo over the top of the glass. Setting it down, he reached out and dragged the photograph across the table, the glossy paper sliding like silk. He held it up to look at it again. He drew it closer then pushed it back, alternately widening his eyes and squinting.

"You blind?" asked Dallas.

Marcus was the one who frowned now, feigning offense. Lowering the photograph, he ignored the question and snorted. "Stupid name," he said, placing the photograph on the table.

"David?"

"Battle. Must have been your idea."

"What's your problem with me?" asked Dallas. "I don't remember you being so ornery, so disagreeable. I mean, you weren't all roses and cherries, but you weren't all thorns and pits neither."

Marcus tapped the photo with his finger. "My problem is this. You should have known better. One is a blessing. Two is a curse."

Dallas held his glass on the table with both hands, rubbing his thumbs up and down. His eyes were on the table, or somewhere beyond it.

"My problem," Marcus said, "is that you show up here unannounced, acting like nothing happened, and you want my help."

He ran his hand across the table, wiping a fine layer of dust with his fingers. The dust bloomed and dissipated.

"My problem," said Marcus, "is that you couldn't keep it in your pants. So you put your whole family at risk. You put Rudy and Norma at risk. Now you want to put me at risk."

Dallas's brows twitched and he lifted his gaze to meet Marcus's. His eyes were glossy. His frown having shifted from disappointment, or judgmental, to sadness, he opened his mouth to speak but didn't.

"What?" said Marcus. "Spit it out. You'd best start selling."

Dallas swallowed hard. "We didn't think we could have any more. It took so long to have the first. It was such a difficult birth that we thought we were good."

"Clearly you weren't."

His jaw tense, Dallas tightened his grip on the glass. "I didn't come here for a lecture."

"Then what did you come here for?" asked Marcus.

"We need you to get Lou and the baby to safety," said Dallas. "There's a place we know about. They take in families with multiple kids. They shelter them, keep out the guard."

"Why not one of those coyotes?" asked Marcus. "You know, the guys you pay to get you across the wall to wherever it is you want to be?"

"They're not trustworthy," said Dallas. "They turn you over to the guard or the vigilantes if they have a chance for more cash or drugs or whatever."

Marcus leaned back in his chair, the fabric cushion shifting uncomfortably underneath his weight. He rubbed the back of his neck with one hand. His skin was dry, leathery almost, and touching it reminded him of his age. What was he now? Sixty? He'd lost track. His thumb found a tight spot near the base of his skull, and he dug in to loosen the tension.

"Okay," said Marcus, "I'll bite. Let's say I leave the comforts of my home, as I've been known to do more than once in the past, and I manage to get to Baird. Then what? We caravan with a pregnant woman north to this… Valhalla?"

"She won't be pregnant when we get there," said Dallas. "She's almost due."

Marcus shook his head and snorted. "You're serious? You know there are vigilantes out there. It's not just the guard looking for pregnant women or families with more than one kid. That's just the first thing."

"I'm serious," offered Dallas. "It would be you, me, Lou, and the two kids. What's the second thing?"

"You left your woman to deliver the baby by herself?"

"You used to know Lou," said Dallas, a hint of a smile twitching at the corner of his mouth. "She's nobody's woman. And that's the first thing."

"True," said Marcus. "And the second?"

"She's got Rudy and Norma."

Both men sat there for a couple of minutes, letting the silence fill the space between them. They took sips of water, Dallas more hungrily than Marcus. He emptied his glass, tipping it almost upside down to inhale every last bit of it.

Marcus finished his too and then took both of them back to the counter to refill. He brought the refills back to the oak table and raised his glass toward Dallas, tilting his head with a question.

"This place you wanna go, you think it really exists? I've heard it's all myths and rumors made up to make people think they've got hope. Either that or it's a trap to draw out the families they can't find on their own. The guard doesn't just hunt babies here, they do it south of the wall too. Plus there are the tribes. It's a tough journey to the wall, and then once you cross it, it gets even tougher. I don't know my way north of the wall like I do south of it."

Dallas sat back in his seat and surveyed the kitchen. His gaze shifted from one side of the room to the other before settling again on Marcus. "You seem to hear a lot of things for being isolated out here," said Dallas, suspicion creeping into his voice. "Maybe you're not as much of a loner, afraid of hurting the people you supposedly love, as you claimed to be."

Marcus sniffed and wiped his nose with the back of his hand. He smiled. It was a genuine smile but was absent joy or humor. It was the smile of a man who understood that nobody knew who he was, what his motivations were, how he managed his lifestyle the best he could. He leaned forward on his elbows and laced his fingers together as if forming a church steeple, and shook his head.

"I never said I was isolated," he said. "I'm insulated. There's a difference. I keep a layer between the world and me. That's it, a layer. I'm not separate from everything, Dallas. I never said that. You know that. I explained myself again and again."

"Yeah, well," said Dallas, looking at the table as he spoke, "it sure seemed like isolated and separate to us. To Lou."

Marcus puffed out his cheeks and exhaled. He'd had this conversation before. Many times. It had been years, sure. But sitting here talking about his life choices and how they'd hurt others raked away the layers of insulation he'd worked to build between himself and anyone who meant anything to him.

"I'm not doing this. You came to me, Dallas. You wanna judge my life, find the door and walk out the way you came. I'm not that interested in a trip along the yellow brick road that leads to Oz anyhow. Been there, done that."

Dallas shifted in his seat and the chair creaked on the floor. Taking another sip of water, his face softened. "Sorry," he said. "You're right. I'm not here to open old wounds. I'm here to ask for your help. We need you, Marcus. Lou needs you."

"You said that."

"We know where the refuge is," said Dallas. "It's not a myth or a trap."

"How do you know that?"

"I just do."

Marcus studied Dallas. The dude believed what he was saying, even if he was wrong. After so many years, in so many places, Marcus could tell when someone was telling the truth and when he was lying. Maybe it was all the years alone. His senses were fine-tuned to better read people's expressions, their intonations, their body movements.

Hero

"Okay," said Marcus. "Where is it, then?"

"Hold up," said Dallas. "Before I tell you that, you in or out?"

Marcus picked up the glass, keeping his eyes locked on Dallas. The water was cool, but closer to room temperature than the first one. Swishing it around in his mouth, he took his time considering the question.

He didn't want to leave his home. He'd done it once for a woman he didn't know. A second time he did it for revenge. Neither of those had been good reasons at the time. The first was as selfless an act as man could offer. The second was as selfish as was possible.

This time was somewhere in the middle. It was selfless to help Lou and the children he'd never met. It was selfish to do it for himself, to peel back that insulation and do something that would make him feel a part of things again. He swallowed the water and exhaled.

"I'm in."

Chapter 3

APRIL 17, 2054, 1:00 AM
SCOURGE +21 YEARS, 7 MONTHS
ATLANTA, GEORGIA

Sally Miller pulled the hoodie over her head and tugged on the drawstrings. Sucking in as deep a breath as her lungs could hold, she centered herself. Slowly, through pursed lips, she exhaled.

"You ready?" she asked, her hand on the shoulder of the nameless woman next to her. The woman had a name, of course, but Sally didn't know it. She didn't want to know it. Plausible deniability.

The woman nodded and drew the newborn closer to her chest. The child was swaddled in black fabric, as was the woman. They needed to be as invisible as possible. This was, after all, the post-Scourge, mid-drought version of the underground railroad.

"We've got five blocks," she said. "Stay close to me. Do exactly what I tell you to do when I tell you to do it. The railroad works like this. I'm your first conductor. I'll take you to the second. The second takes you to the third. I don't know anything about your journey beyond my leg of it. Got it?"

The woman nodded again. Her eyes were wide, full of the anxiety of suspicion of someone on the run. Sally wished she could put black fabric over the woman's eyes. They were so wide, so white, they almost glowed in the relative darkness of the garage.

Sally held up two fingers. "It's just the two of you, right? I'm making sure. Just two?"

"Yes," said the woman, her voice trembling. "My husband is with our daughter. They're taking—"

Sally held her palm to the woman's face and shushed her. "I don't need to know. I don't want to know. All I need to know is that it's two of you and that you can follow my instructions exactly as I give them."

"Okay," said the woman. "I can do that. I can follow you."

Sally offered a flat smile and motioned with her head. "This way."

They maneuvered through the stacked boxes, old bicycles, and yard equipment toward a door at the side of the detached garage. The woman tripped over a pile of PVC piping, but Sally caught her.

Sally reached for the child. "I can carry the baby if you want."

The woman turned away from Sally, her white eyes turning black as they narrowed. She took a step back, almost tripping again before she steadied herself.

Sally waved her hands. "Never mind," she said, trying to reassure the woman. "It's fine. It's fine. You carry her."

"It's a boy," said the woman, the tension easing in her posture. "His name is—"

Sally put her hand on the woman's mouth. "I don't need to know. I don't want to know."

The woman appeared hurt at first, offended, that Sally wouldn't want to know the child's name. Then understanding washed across her worried face and she nodded.

"Let's go," said Sally. She checked her watch. "We're thirty-five seconds late. We've got to make that up. As soon as I open the door, you need to hustle."

Without saying anything else, Sally punched in the electronic code to the side garage door and it clicked. She tugged on the handle and opened the door wide enough to fit through. When the woman crossed the threshold, Sally shut the door behind them. It hummed and the lock clicked back into place.

They were in the heart of Atlanta, the seat of the government since the Scourge. Sally didn't remember the Scourge. Her mother and father had succumbed to violence in the immediate aftermath of the pneumonic plague. The plague killed two-thirds of the world's population. Violence killed much of what was left. She'd survived both.

Now she was smuggling women from the capital city to beyond the reach of the Population Guard, the elite branch of the military charged with policing the nation's unsustainable birthrate. Now she needed a drink. Her head pulsed at the temples. A stiff drink straight from the bottle was the prescription. She should have taken a dose before the mission. Sally flexed a trembling hand in and out and held it in a fist. Now was not a good time to take a break from the thing that fixed her, kept her steady and in control.

Sally hurried along an alley that ran behind a block of houses on the city's north side. Sensing the woman at her hip, she pressed forward at a pace between a fast walk and a jog. She resisted the urge to run, knowing that would draw attention to them. It was early morning, and the only people out this time of night were drunks, hookers, drunk hookers, drunks looking for hookers, and the Pop Guard.

They reached the end of the alley, and Sally held out her arm to stop the woman. Pressing her body against the side of a wooden fence, she peered around the corner toward a two-lane road that ran north and south. Four blocks to go.

"Let's go," Sally whispered.

They hugged the edge of the fence line that ran parallel to the road. The hard-packed dirt and low clumps of weeds crunched under their feet as they hurried north. So far, so good. A dog barked in the distance, surprising Sally. She didn't know dogs existed anymore. The drought had forced people to do things people hadn't previously done in order to survive.

They reached another intersection, where the fence line ended. Sally crouched down. Behind her, she felt the woman doing the same. The baby cooed, and Sally shot the woman a glare before eyeing the child.

"Keep it quiet," she said. "Three blocks to go."

The woman adjusted the black fabric over the baby's face, blousing it like a tent to give the child room to breathe.

Sally started to move but froze instead. In the distance she heard a sound that sent a chill along her spine. The hairs on her arms stood on end. She glanced back toward the source of the noise, then looked skyward.

She couldn't see the helicopter, but the thwack and thump of its rotors against the still, dry Georgia air were unmistakable. The expression on her face must have betrayed her concern. The woman touched her arm.

"What's wrong?"

Sally smiled weakly. "Nothing. But we need to move even faster now, and I've got to take an alternate route. Stay close."

She should have timed it better. Sally knew when the patrols would happen. They were like clockwork. Had she misjudged? This was a mistake. She'd correct it.

She stood and led the woman along an uneven sidewalk replete with cracks, lifted seams, and chunks of missing concrete.

The whir and beat of the helicopter grew louder. It was getting closer.

They hopped and danced as if avoiding land mines, moving swiftly and quietly toward another alley. This time, Sally didn't stop. She pivoted ninety degrees and bolted to the next block.

At that moment, as they dashed across the street toward the alley, a bright white light nearly blinded Sally. She didn't stop. The woman didn't stop. They hit the alley, rounding the corner as fast as they could go now. The worn rubber soles of Sally's shoes slid against the thin topcoat of loose dirt and gravel that coated everything in this town, but she maintained her balance and her momentum as she gathered speed.

The light followed them, searching for them, skimming across the alley and the houses on either side of the narrow passageway. The chopper was close enough now that the blades were deafening, and the wind whipping from their wash blew at them as they ran.

"*This is the Population Guard,*" blared a monotone voice over the whoosh of the wind. "*Under the authority of the New Government, we order you to stop running.*"

Sally glanced over her shoulder at the moment the light hit her face. Dust swirled in the downdraft from the rotors, particulate stinging her eyes before she could close them. Now she had trouble opening them. With her eyes watering and her vision blurred, she dodged a fence post and nearly pirouetted on her toes. Her hands trembled. The shakes. She had the freaking shakes.

Push through it, she told herself. *Push through it.*

The woman was with her, calling to Sally, shouting something under the din of the chopper and the aural chaos it conjured around them.

Ignoring the woman, because nothing she had to say was as important as getting away from the chopper, Sally turned left. There was only a block to go now. One block.

"*I repeat,*" came the almost mechanical warning from the chopper above, "*this is the Population Guard. You cannot escape us. If you don't stop running and lie flat on open ground, we will open fire.*"

Open fire? Seriously? In a residential neighborhood, these fascists would take aim from the sky to stop them?

She was less than a half block from the drop-off. She was breathing hard now, her muscles resisting her top speed. But she couldn't stop. Then she sensed the woman wasn't at her hip anymore. Sally considered not turning around, not losing her momentum, but she had to look. Getting that woman and her child to safety was her sole reason for running. There'd be no point if she failed her.

So Sally glanced sideways then over her shoulder. The woman wasn't behind her. She was at the corner where Sally had turned left. Hiding under the brick porte cochère that extended from the front of a home toward the street. The woman leaned against one of the pillars, her head hanging, the baby at her hip.

Sally grimaced. She cursed. But she ran back to get the woman and the child. The chopper was one hundred feet up. It was swinging back around to find her.

She reached the mother and grabbed the baby from her. "Now!" she yelled at the top of her lungs. Then she ran.

The woman gave chase, screaming behind her, keeping up this time. While Sally didn't want to do this, it was the only way. Enough runs on the underground railroad had taught her how to make things happen. More than anything, the threat of losing a child was the greatest motivator to the men and women who sought passage. Even if that threat was letting go of the child for a moment, relinquishing it to the hands of a benevolent conductor like Sally, it was enough to make a parent push past the point of exhaustion, fear, or resignation.

At the opposite end of the dead-end street was a house that was smaller than those around it. It almost looked like a garage in comparison to the more stately homes that lined the block. Standing in the doorway was the next conductor on the railroad. He was a tall, slender man dressed in black, who was waving at her frantically. Sally didn't recognize him. That was how it was supposed to be.

Evading the searchlight by finding a path along the edge of the street, she reached the man on the front stoop. She shoved the child at him in the moment before the mother reached them, panicked but alive with newfound purpose.

"Here," said Sally, "take it. I gotta go."

The conductor took the child and ushered the woman into the small house. Before the woman crossed the threshold, Sally yanked the black fabric from around the woman's head, bundled it into a ball, and cradled it against her chest.

"Get her a new one," she snapped at the conductor and bolted from the stoop.

It was the one and only time that address would be used as a station. Within seconds the new conductor, the woman, and her child wouldn't be there anymore. They'd be on the second leg of the journey, extending their tracks wherever they might lead. Sally would never know whether or not the woman reached her intended destination. It didn't matter. She'd done her job by delivering her to the station. Now she had to take care of herself.

The chopper was almost overhead. It was following her. There was no escaping it.

She cut across two yards and found herself in an alley. She sprinted along the length of the narrow passage until she found a wider street with more possibilities.

The spotlight from above illuminated everything around her. She couldn't see beyond the scope of the light. The wind whipped the hoodie from her head. It chilled the sweat that stuck her hair to her forehead and the sides of her face. Grit blasted her from all directions. The chopper was no more than fifty feet from the ground.

"Stay where you are," came the call from directly overhead. *"Do not move. This is an order from the Population Guard."*

Sally cursed again. Out of options, there was only one thing to do. She stood there, swaying, putting her face into the balled fabric at her chest. She nestled it there and spoke to it.

"You are smart to comply," said the voice. *"We are lowering a ladder. A team of guards will restrain you and take possession of your child. Do not resist."*

Sally didn't acknowledge the command. She tightened her hold on the bundle, protecting it from the whirlwind, soothing it against the noise.

A rope ladder dropped from the light, twisting and stretching against the wind until the weight of three Pop Guards steadied it. The helmeted men planted their feet on the ground.

One of them stood holding the ladder with one gloved hand. The other held an automatic rifle across his body armor. The second stood watch, holding his weapon level at Sally's head. The third was empty-handed and moved toward Sally with his arms extended.

With his palms up he motioned with his gloved fingers for her to hand the bundle to him. The wind whipped such that dust clouded the spotlight illuminating the guards, the ladder, and Sally.

She didn't comply at first. She took a step back, toward the edge of the light's reach. The guard with his rifle raised reacted, moving two steps closer, behind the unarmed guard's left shoulder.

"*Do not resist,*" boomed the loudspeaker above her head. "*We will use lethal force.*"

Sally buried her face in the fabric, waiting. Her timing had to be perfect. Her aim had to be spot on. Otherwise her time as a conductor, her time on Earth, was over.

The empty-handed guard motioned again and moved toward her, as did the one providing cover. They were a good twenty-five feet from the ladder and the third guard.

Wait. Wait. Wait. Now!

When the guard in front of her reached for the bundle, Sally withdrew outside the outer edge of the light and, in a fluid series of motions so effortless it must have seemed as if she'd rehearsed it, she tossed the bundle at the guard leveling the rifle.

He reacted by taking one hand from the weapon and the other from the trigger, trying to catch what he thought was a child. Sally dropped to one knee and pulled a .45-caliber Beretta from the concealed-carry pouch at the small of her back.

She punched two rounds into the legs of the empty-handed guard. He collapsed in pain, writhing, grasping at his shattered kneecaps.

The second he hit the ground, Sally unleashed a volley of rounds at the guard who now held a bundle of cloth against his chest. The first of the shots hit the armor plating at his chest and knocked him back a step. The second and third found his neck and jawline.

Without paying attention to what happened next, Sally stood, moved to her right, and spun. She emptied the magazine into the guard holding the ladder. His body went limp and tangled with the rope before he could return a single shot. By the time the men in the chopper knew what happened, she was gone, and the .45 was reloaded.

Sally darted into the nearest alley and found a large trash can. The chopper was higher in the air now, the searchlight dancing across the rooftops and empty streets. It was getting closer again. They wouldn't give her a chance to surrender this time. They'd kill her on sight.

Lifting the lid of the large can and bracing for the dank odor of rot that permeated its insides, Sally stepped into the can and crouched down while pulling the lid atop her.

The odor was almost overwhelming. She was sweating profusely. Beads of sweat dripped into her eyes, stinging them almost as much as the putrid stench inside the can stung her nostrils and throat.

Resisting the urge to puke, she swallowed hard and worked to slow her breathing. Her pulse thumped at her temples and her neck. Her heart pounded in her chest.

This was not the first time Sally had killed Pop Guards. She tried not to think about whether the men had families of their own: wives, children, homes. The Pop Guards were just doing their job. She knew that. But their job was to separate families, take children from their mothers. Their job was to control not only the population but the people themselves.

It was worth killing a guard or three to save the lives of a family truly in need. That was what she told herself as she listened to the beat of the helicopter's rotors grow louder and then fade into the warm Georgia night.

CHAPTER 4

APRIL 17, 2054, 6:45 AM
SCOURGE +21 YEARS, 7 MONTHS
NEW BOSTON, TEXAS

Warner leaned against the brick wall of a three-story building that was white on the bottom and red on the top. He struck a match and lit a hand-rolled cigarette that stuck to his dry, cracked lips. The match sizzled as it reached his fingertips. He let it burn for an instant before pinching it out, then drew the smoke into his lungs and let it peel from his nostrils into the early morning air.

The sun was rising, casting a fiery glow along the horizon, putting into shadow the buildings that dotted the small town. He took another drag and flicked the ash onto the dirt at his boots.

"Looks like everything's ablaze, don't it?" he asked Blessing. "Sky's all on fire, smoldering at the edges and ready to blow."

Blessing grunted. The man didn't say much. Didn't need to. His handiwork did the talking for him. When he did speak, it was all the more impactful.

"I love this time of day," said Warner, tipping the Duncanville Panthers ball cap back on his head. "So many possibilities are out there, ya know? The chance for so many good things lies ahead."

Blessing grunted again and ran the toe of his boot across the dirt in front of him. It scraped along and drew a divot in an arc, like a line nobody dared cross. He cleared his throat and folded his arms across his body.

"I always start my day all philosophical-like, ya know?" Warner's question was rhetorical. He knew Blessing knew that. "Then things happen during the day that bring me back down to Earth. This dry, mother-loving godforsaken Earth. A plague here, a drought there, tyrants all peppered betwixt and between."

Warner wiggled his fingers in the air as if sprinkling a dash of something onto something else before he took a long drag. He held the air in his lungs until the buzz of the tobacco made his head tingle. Then he exhaled. Another flick of the ash. Warner glanced over at Blessing then nudged him on the arm.

"I mean to say, that sunrise yonder, it has such promise," he said. "It makes me smile, but in a good way. Everything's on the way up. But by noon, it's all downhill. The sun drops, it gets dark, we go to work, and my smile's not so genuine anymore. The only hope I got by the time my head hits the pillow is that the sun's gonna rise the next day."

Blessing grunted. Then he chuckled. He lowered his left hand to his hip and rested it on a pistol he kept in a thigh holster. He tapped the side of the leather holster like he was playing a tune.

"What?" asked Warner, his eyes widening. He knew that chuckle and nudged the man again.

Blessing sniffed a wad of snot into his throat and then hawked a loogie into the dirt in front of his boots. It bubbled there on the arcing line for a second before Blessing turned to Warner and shook his head. "You're full of crap," he said. "You say the same thing every morning. I don't know who you're trying to convince. Me? Yourself? I don't know. I *do* know you're full of crap."

Warner eyed Blessing seriously for a beat, considering the marksman's assessment of his rambling. Without saying anything, he turned away from him and watched the sunrise turn from red to orange. Pinching the cigarette in his fingers, he took a final draw and flicked the butt out into the dirt. Dying wisps of smoke traced the butt's path to its resting place.

"You don't say much," he said, speaking as he exhaled, "but when you do, it's a humdinger."

The two men exchanged smiles. They laughed. And then they got down to business.

"You checked on 'em?" Warner asked Blessing, motioning toward the rows of barred windows that decorated all four sides of the building's facade on its second and third floors.

Blessing nodded and scratched the scruff on his chin.

"We did luck into this place," said Warner. "Perfect spot for keeping people where you want 'em until you don't want 'em there no more."

He pushed himself from his lean against the wall and took a couple of deliberate steps away from it. The sunrise was slipping from orange to yellow. The deep blue that framed it was fading. Another day was already on its way toward night.

Warner turned his back on the sun and eyed the building. The only entrance on the front side was a single door that sat under a crumbling wood awning that covered the six-by-six square of concrete serving as a stoop. It was five steps off the ground.

On the first floor, that brick painted white, were five regular-sized windows covered with bars. To say the paint was white was an overstatement. It had been white once. Now it was closer to yellow than white, maybe even gray. Bits of the underlying brick's true color pinked and clayed their way through the thinning, weatherworn paint job.

Warner stuffed his hands into his jeans pockets and surveyed the upper levels of the Bowie County Jail. They were red because there was no paint. The brick was a different color than that which showed through on the first floor, and it was different still from the burnt-colored bricks that wrapped the top of the rectangular building.

"Whoever built this thing lacked imagination," said Warner. "Four walls, three stories high, a door on each side, don't make much for architectural genius. But I like it. Makes it easy to keep an eye on, that's for sure.

"How many we got up there now?" asked Warner. "Six?"

Blessing nodded. He toed the dirt with his boot, mixing in the spit.

"Six pregnant women and six kids," said Warner. "I don't guess any of 'em are ready to pop. But that one we got a month ago? The one who speaks Spanish to her kid? She's getting close. Much bigger and the baby's gonna punch its way out straight through the belly button."

Blessing smirked. He rolled his shoulders forward and brought up his fists like a prizefighter. A couple of jabs and an uppercut later, both men were laughing.

"I ain't about having a baby birthed in my jail," said Warner. "Seeing as how we got six already, we could probably make a run. Don't you think?"

Blessing was shadowboxing his image on the wall of the former jail. His speed was impressive. Even in boots, the man was light on his feet. Warner wondered if Blessing had ever been in a street fight, then dismissed the notion. Of course he'd been in a street fight. Blessing had definitely killed men with his bare hands.

"Blessing," said Warner, "you think we could make a run?"

Blessing thrust a final jab and nodded.

"Let's get ready, then," said Warner. "The day's a-wastin'."

Blessing rubbed his chin, scratching the growth that ran along his jawline and down his neck. Without looking at Warner or saying anything, he plodded up the steps on the stoop and pushed his way inside the jail.

Warner followed. The heat draped over him like a heavy blanket as soon as he stepped inside. The jail, or what was left of it, didn't have power. The water, which leaked more than flowed, dripped from rusty pipes, making it both brown and undrinkable. The place made a third-world prison look like the Ritz. Although Warner hadn't been in either of those places, he'd seen pictures of both.

He gripped the metal handrail to a set of narrow stairs that led him straight to the second level. The chipped paint stuck to his sweating palms as he ascended the creaking stairs. Dust from Blessing's boots kicked in small puffs of brown at his face, and he closed his eyes until they reached the landing.

Blessing led Warner along a hallway that stretched from one side of the level to the next. All along the exterior wall to their left were cells encased in iron bars. Warner ran his fingers along the bars, clanking with each successive thump as he moved his way toward the end of the hallway.

Each of the cells was the same. Iron bunks hung from the walls; chains bolted into the brick held the beds mostly parallel to the concrete floors. Thin, life-stained mattresses covered the mesh frames of the bunks, no pillows or sheets. Opposite the bunks was a sink and toilet. Though neither were in working order, that didn't stop them from getting used.

The combination of heat, which was more suffocating on the second floor, and the stench of unwashed humans made Warner wrinkle his nose and take shallower breaths. Avoiding eye contact with the people inside the cells, he kept his watering eyes straight ahead until he reached Blessing at the last of them, where the hallway ended. Hanging on the wall was a series of hooks. Each of the hooks held pairs of iron cuffs. Blessing grabbed a pair by the chain connecting them and draped it over his shoulder. He motioned for Warner to do the same. Warner held the pair in his hands.

Blessing fished a large skeleton key from his pocket and, holding the bow between his fingers, slid the bit into the lock at the center of the barred door. The lock clicked, and the door creaked and whined when he pulled it open into the hallway.

Andrea Cruz stared back at them from the bottom bunk. Her eyes sunken, her hair matted with sweat, her skin pale, she was lying there with one foot on the floor. Her thin shirt was pulled up beneath her bosom, exposing her swollen belly.

Her child, Javier, was on the top bunk. He was shirtless and sitting cross-legged, facing the brick wall. His little fingers traced the maze of mortar between the red blocks. The boy seemed unaware the door was open and they had visitors.

"Hey there, Javi," Warner said with a wide smile. "How's it hanging?"

Andrea didn't move, but she scowled. Her voice was raspy, weaker than it was the last time Warner paid her a visit. "Don't talk to him. Don't say his name. Don't even look at him."

Javi looked at Warner, wide-eyed, his finger still touching the wall. There was hope in those eyes. It was something Warner wasn't used to seeing in the people with whom he came in contact. It surprised him, shook him from his game for a moment. He quickly recovered and winked at the boy, smiling from the corner of his mouth, before shifting his eyes to Andrea.

Warner stepped inside the cell, clanging the cuffs together. The ring bounced off the solid walls, echoing in the cell. When he reached the side of the bunk, he squatted, resting his butt on his boot heels. He lifted his chin toward the belly.

"You any closer to a name? I could make a few suggestions," he offered.

Andrea tugged at her shirt, lowering it over her belly as far as it would stretch. She scooted back onto her elbows and closer to the wall, angling herself away from Warner.

"Sarah's nice," he said. "Rachel's good. Both are solid names. Go way back."

Warner held the cuffs at his knees, rubbing the coarse iron with his calloused thumbs. He widened his eyes. "Ooh," he said and clapped the cuffs together. The sudden noise made Andrea jump. Her body shuddered and her scowl deepened. Her eyes flitted between Warner and Blessing, who stayed at the door. "I know the perfect name," he said. "You could call her Warner. It's a little masculine, I know, but sometimes people get into these, what do they call it?"

Warner grimaced as he searched for the word. Glancing over, he sought help from Blessing. The man shrugged and offered nothing. Then it hit him. "Unisex, that's it. They could be for boys or girls. Given these trying times, I'd think a strong name like Warner would benefit any hearty soul, be they boy or girl."

Andrea curled her legs closer to her body. She seemed to be as far away as she could get from Warner without leaving her bed.

"What do you think?" he asked. "You like Warner?"

No answer.

"Huh," he said, and stood. "All right. Think on it, then. Give it some real consideration though. None of this 'I'll think about it' then you summarily discard it for no good reason other than irrational bias."

Javier had adjusted his position on the top bunk. He was sitting with his back to the brick wall now, his legs straight out in front of him, his hands resting in his lap.

"Well now," said Warner, shifting his attention back to the boy, "this is helpful. I do appreciate you, Javi. I know your momma says I can't look at you, talk to you, or say your name, so let's just keep this here exchange our own little secret."

He winked again at the boy. Javier almost smiled, but he maintained an expressionless calm amidst this coming storm.

Warner took one of the cuffs and held it up. "I'm gonna take this bracelet and put it on your leg. It's gonna go on your ankle and you'll wear it for a bit. It's got a twin I'm gonna put—"

There was a flash of movement at the bottom edge of his peripheral vision, and the bed shifted in front of Warner in the instant before he felt a violent blow to his knee. The joint twisted awkwardly and he dropped to the floor, grunting in pain. The cuffs flew from his hands and clanged against the side of the bed before rattling onto the floor.

Before Warner could process what had happened, Andrea was on top of him, beating him with closed fists. The heels of her hands drummed his ribs and the side of his pelvis. Andrea screamed with her hoarse voice. It sounded like a cat wailing.

Warner tried kicking her off him, but didn't have the leverage. She'd knocked him onto his side, and one of his arms was trapped underneath him. The pain radiating from his knee was almost paralyzing. The beating only stopped when Blessing yanked the woman from atop him and held her standing in the center of the cell, writhing and spitting venom.

Warner caught his breath and gritted his teeth against the throb in his right knee. He painfully gathered himself and got back to his feet. Using the bed for balance, he leaned heavily on his left leg. His ball cap was on the floor. He gingerly bent down to grab it and set it back on his head. Standing again, Warner adjusted the hat and cleared his throat. Breathing in and out, his side ached from the short pummeling he'd taken from the surprisingly strong woman.

The dehydrated and malnourished woman was pregnant, likely on the verge of giving birth, yet she'd found a way to exact force on the man she blamed for her predicament. Though held mostly still within Blessing's grip, she looked to Warner like she might pounce again. Eyes wild, dry white clumps of spit collected at the edges of her lips; her chest heaved. The shirt stuck to her body, a thick sheen of sweat gluing it there.

"That wasn't very nice," Warner said to Andrea with his jaw clenched. "It wasn't smart neither. All you managed to do with your little spider monkey outburst was make me angry. That don't help nobody."

His voice was as even as it had been when he'd talked about baby names or putting the cuffs on Javier's ankle. It was the same tone as the one he'd employed when he'd first offered Andrea a hand near the wall a month earlier.

Warner found that the angrier he got, the more violent the content of the conversation, the more frightening he could be by keeping his cool. The softer he spoke, the more even-keeled he outwardly appeared, the more effectively he could make his audience wet themselves with fear. Affability, Warner was certain, was the most horrific thing on the planet if applied correctly to the right circumstances.

Andrea's reaction only proved to reinforce his hypothesis. The more he spoke, the calmer he kept himself, the smaller she became. Her defiance shrank into worry as she stood there. Her growling, feral demeanor was domesticated now. In fact, Warner thought she'd gone from alpha wolf to beaten pup in the span of a minute.

Sensing this, he stepped toward her, while at the same time reaching up to put a hand on Javi's knee. Warner didn't look at the boy as he did this. His gaze stayed square on Andrea.

"What you fail to understand, buttercup, is that you got no cards to play," he said. "You gambled, you lost. Your chips are gone and I hold the aces."

Andrea swallowed hard, her chest still rising and falling quickly. Her jaw clenched and flexed at the mandible. The woman winced when Blessing shifted his hold at her elbow.

Warner rubbed Javi's knee enough for Andrea to notice. He let go and patted the side of the bed. "I know what you're thinking. You're—"

"You have no idea what I'm thinking," Andrea spat. "You—"

"Ah, ah, ah," Warner said with a smile, wagging his finger. "Don't be rude now. Don't add insult to injury."

Warner shifted his weight again. The pain was dull but present, the throb enough to make standing on the leg uncomfortable. She hadn't broken or torn anything, he was pretty sure. Sprained probably, or twisted.

"And I do know what you're thinking, Andrea," he said. "You're thinking this here is my fault. Me and Blessing killed your guide, kidnapped you, held you hostage. This is our fault, you think. That's not the truth of the matter at all though."

Warner motioned for Blessing to let go of Andrea, which he did. The woman stood there, obviously unsure of what to do, so she did nothing other than cup her hands under her belly, cradling the life growing inside her.

"The truth of the matter is that you broke the law," said Warner, motioning to her baby bump. "You got knocked up."

Shrugging, he sat down on the bottom bunk. He patted the thin mattress next to him and winked at her, motioning to the mattress with his head. She took the hint and sat next to him. Warner leaned into her and spoke from the corner of his mouth, almost whispering.

"Now between you and me, I don't think it's a big deal," he confided. "One thing leads to another, you're knocking boots, then you got one in the oven. It's a natural thing. As natural as they come. But I don't make the rules, Andrea. I'm not the one who said having more than one child was illegal, am I? Tell me, did I make the law? Do I look like someone who makes laws?"

Blessing, who was standing at the open cell door again, chuckled and mumbled something under his breath.

Warner pointed at his marksman. "Even Blessing here knows I don't make the laws. But I'll tell you what I do make. I make things right. I put things back in order. If people are gonna break the law, I see fit that they reap what they sow."

Andrea's chin quivered as the corners of her mouth turned down into a frown that betrayed her worry. Tears pooled in her eyes, streaking down her gaunt cheeks.

"Look at me," said Warner, smiling. "I'm all full of metaphors today. Card games, buns in ovens, reaping and sowing. I must be inspired by you, Andrea. You must bring out the poet in me."

Andrea used the back of a hand to wipe the tears from her face. Reaching up, she touched her son's leg and held onto it, thumbing his calf affectionately. Javi leaned forward, peering at them upside down. The child clearly didn't understand the gravity of the situation.

"Roses are red," said Warner. "Violets are blue."

Andrea was crying now. Unable to contain her emotion, she verged on sobbing. Warner spoke louder so she could hear him over her whimpering.

"We've got a trip to take, and you're going to wear these cuffs without any further problems." Warner snapped his fingers and smirked. "Tarnation. That didn't rhyme. I guess it'll have to do."

Warner stood and limped a couple of steps to pick up the manacles he'd lost when Andrea had attacked him. Bending over, he picked them up and handed them to her. "Put these on your boy," he ordered, the kindness and humor gone from his voice. His tone was flat, commanding, absent compassion. "Do it now, or things get ugly. *Comprendre? Entiende?*"

Andrea nodded and took a deep breath. Taking the shackles from Warner, she stood and gently closed the first around her son's left ankle.

"*Esta bien*," she said to Javier. "It's okay, *mijo*."

The boy seemed unfazed by that cuff or the one she closed around his other leg. He wrapped his fingers around the chain that connected them and tugged on it. He flapped it up and down, smiling at the clanging noise it made.

"Now you're going to put a pair on yourself," said Warner. "If you don't do it, we'll have to do it for you. And that's not going to be pleasant."

Andrea reached for the cuffs hanging over Blessing's shoulder. He handed them to her and, one at a time, she did as Warner instructed.

"All right," Warner said cheerfully, "out of the cell. We've got places to go and people to see."

Andrea raised her arms and helped Javier from the top bunk. She led her son from the cell, brushing past Blessing and into the hallway.

She'd walked to the cell next to hers when Warner ordered her to stop.

Blessing plucked two more sets of iron cuffs from the wall at the end of the hall. Then he marched purposefully to Andrea.

"You're going to put these on your neighbor here," said Warner. "And the one next to her. And the one next to her. We got six of you in all. You're gonna be our proxy with these cuffs. Understand?"

Andrea glanced at the wall behind the men and back at them. Nodding her understanding, she took two sets of cuffs from Blessing, and the marksman moved past her to unlock the cell door.

The woman in the cell was standing at its center, holding her daughter's hand. The child was eight or nine years old, judging by her size. Both of them were towheads. Their pale skin and their blond, almost white hair made them appear ghostly. The woman was all baby, her body rail thin aside from the protrusion at her midsection.

Wearing the same frock since Warner and Blessing had found her trying to cross the wall, the woman was barefoot. The child wore molded plastic shoes that looked too big for her.

When Andrea entered the cell, the woman kept her attention on Warner. Her flat expression dripped with loathing. Warner was used to that. A pregnant woman hadn't looked at him adoringly in he couldn't remember how long.

Blessing stood next to him at the cell entrance, shoulder to shoulder. Stoic as always, the marksman raked his fingers along his neck. Warner noticed the stubble was flecked with more gray than he remembered. They were getting older, the two of them. Warner leaned on his good leg, trying hard not to put too much weight on his still-throbbing knee.

Javier squatted behind his mother as she leaned into the apparition of a woman. He played with the chain between the cuffs, sticking his finger in and out of the links, counting them silently.

Andrea cupped a hand at the woman's ear and whispered. Warner thought about reprimanding her, insisting that she speak aloud. He stopped himself, figuring that as long as they ultimately complied, it didn't matter how they did it.

Blessing moved his left hand to his hip and rested it on the thigh-holstered pistol. It was subtle, but Blessing made sure the women saw him do it. He strummed his fingers against the leather on the side of the holster.

Warner folded his arms across his chest and lifted his chin. Pulling his shoulders back, he cleared his throat. He too was sending a message.

The alabaster woman's eyes widened as Andrea spoke to her. She nodded and pursed her lips, visibly tightening her grip on her daughter's hand. The daughter seemed to float there in the middle of the cell. If it weren't for the shoes, Warner might have sworn she was hovering.

Andrea finished whispering, then knelt down and put the cuffs, one at a time, on the woman's ankles. She repeated the deliberate process on the child.

When she stood again, she turned to Warner, a sour look on her face. "And?"

Warner hesitated, mesmerized by the ease with which Andrea had completed the task. He wanted to ask what she'd said, what clandestine message delivered right in front of him had convinced the ghost and her offspring to comply. Instead he smiled and winked at her.

"And we move to the next cell."

When they were finished, and Andrea had delivered her whispered speech to each of the remaining women and their children before cuffing them, Warner led them down the narrow stairway, onto the first floor, and out the door into the dirt.

The sun was brighter than when he'd entered more than an hour earlier. The air was warmer too, though markedly cooler than the stale heat that permeated the inside of the old jail.

When he had all six women and their children outside, and

Blessing had locked the jail door behind them, Warner ordered the dirty dozen to line up against the wall. Blessing had a length of roped looped over his shoulder. He'd picked it up from the first floor while the women worked their way to the wall.

Andrea, clearly the new leader of the chain gang, protested. She stood on the bottom step of the stoop.

"We're not going to have you execute us like common criminals," she said, even as some of the women did as they were told. "We're not standing against that wall for you to kill us."

Warner pulled a cigarette and matchbox from his shirt pocket. He stuck the rolled paper between his lips and struck a match against the side of the box, touched it to the end of the paper, and let it burn to his fingertips before he snuffed it out.

Walking slowly to Andrea, he took the cigarette between his fingers and sucked in his cheeks, drawing a long slow drag. When he reached her, he exhaled and purposefully blew a stream of smoke at her face.

She fluttered her eyes and waved the smoke from in front of her as she coughed. The smoke hung there despite her efforts, and Warner moved to her at the bottom step. Blessing stood directly behind her.

Warner glared at her and said nothing for several seconds as he watched Andrea fight to maintain her resolve. Then he smiled broadly. It was a toothy grin, the kind reserved for photographs.

"Why would I go to the trouble of having you chain up all these fine women if I was just gonna shoot you? It woulda saved me and Blessing a whole heap of trouble if we'd just shot you in your cells. I mean, I like a hard day's work as much as the next fella, but I ain't about doing what's unnecessary. You know what they say, Blessing?"

Warner looked past Andrea at Blessing. Blessing shook his head.

"For the record," Warner said, the smile still darkening his face, "Blessing said he didn't know what they say. Can we stipulate that he said he didn't know, your honor?"

Hero

Andrea's brow furrowed with confusion for a moment. Warner took it to mean that the woman was truly beginning to wonder if he'd lost his mind, which was exactly what he wanted. He flicked ash at his feet and pointed at her with the cigarette as he spoke.

"I'll take that as a yes, buttercup," he said when she didn't respond. "What they say is that you gotta work smarter, not harder. I like to work smart. Blessing here likes to work smart."

Taking another pull on the cigarette, he studied her. He both admired her strength and feared it. A woman like her would be able to survive what he had in mind. She also might test him, make the task at hand more troublesome. He'd seen women like her before. He'd loved a woman like her before.

He blew out the smoke through his nostrils this time, turning his head slightly so as not to blow it in her face. Glancing down at Javier, who was staring back unblinkingly, Warner winked and flicked the half-finished cigarette to the ground.

"Take your place at the wall," he said flatly. "I've got instructions for you. I need your attention, all of your attention. Up against the building is the best place for it."

He nodded at the side of the building and stepped back to give Andrea room. She stood there for a beat before taking the last of the steps and moving to an empty spot along the wall of the building. Her chains rattled as she half-walked, half-shuffled to her spot amongst the five other women and their children.

Once she was still, and Javier held her hand, Warner crossed the dirt to stand in front of his dozen charges. Blessing stood next to him, his hand on his gun.

"All right, ladies," he said, "here's what's gonna happen. We've got a little road trip ahead of us. It starts here in a few minutes. We're gonna be walking till sundown. Then, when we get up tomorrow morning, we'll be walking till sundown again."

A couple of the women started crying. That led their children to cry, which started other children. Warner folded his arms and stood there patiently while the tears ebbed. Blessing grunted his disapproval of the delay.

"When you're rightly finished, we can set the ground rules," said Warner. "Are you finished?"

He scanned the women, pausing at each one of them as he surveyed the line from one end to the other. Then, with his hands behind his back like an officer inspecting his troops, Warner paced restlessly, studying the children. The youngest was probably Javier. He was the smallest of them.

"We're gonna walk together," said Warner. "Blessing and I are gonna carry rations for you. We've got canteens for you. You'll each get one to share with your young'un. When we pass a watering hole or a creek bed that ain't run dry, we'll stop so you can fill 'em up. We'll take breaks every couple of hours, give you a chance to rest."

One of the women, auburn haired with full freckled cheeks that almost hid her eyes from the puff of them, tentatively raised her hand. Her belly was barely showing beneath the loose floral-patterned cotton dress she wore. A boy, whose hair was more orange than auburn but who had just as many freckles as the woman, sat on the ground next to her. He was cross-legged with his elbows resting on the insides of his knees, and looked bored more than frightened.

Warner pointed at his mother. "Yes?"

"Can I ask a question?" said the woman in a sweet voice that betrayed her apprehension.

Warner waved his hand at her, signaling for her to speak. "Go on."

"What if we can't make it?"

"You'll make it," said Warner.

"But what if we can't?"

"You don't want that to happen," said Warner. "So let's just put that out of our minds."

The woman folded her arms across her chest, tucking her hands underneath her armpits. Lowering her head, she stared blankly at the ground in front of her.

"Any other questions?" asked Warner. "If not, we'd best get a move on. We got to get the rations, the canteens; then we can hit the road."

Blessing stepped toward the women, pulling the length of rope from his shoulder and unwinding it. With one end in his hand, he dragged the rest of it in the dirt toward the woman at the left end of the line at the building's facade. He crouched down and pulled the rope through a link in the chain between the first woman's legs. Then he drew it through the chain between her child's legs.

Andrea raised her hand and didn't wait for permission to ask her question, stepping forward from the building, commanding Warner's full attention. "Where are you taking us?"

Blessing kept working, pulling the rope through Javier's chain.

Warner smiled. "Well now," he said, tipping his cap toward Andrea, "if I told you that, it would spoil the surprise."

Chapter 5

APRIL 17, 2054, 10:45 AM
SCOURGE +21 YEARS, 7 MONTHS
CHATHAM, VIRGINIA

"Where did you get all of these weapons?" asked Dallas. He stood opposite Marcus at the kitchen counter. His palms were flat on the engineered stone. When he lifted them, the moisture from his hands left an afterimage before evaporating.

"This isn't that many weapons," said Marcus. "It's not like I used to have. It'll have to do."

Laid out on the counter between them were a half dozen handguns, three rifles, and the short-barreled shotgun with which Dallas was already well acquainted. Dallas's weapon, which Marcus had returned minutes earlier, was safely in his holster.

Next to the weapons were a pair of black backpacks. Both of them were worn, strained at the seams, and the synthetic fabric was faded to a color that more closely resembled gray with hints of red than black. There were a couple of jars of honey similar to the one on the kitchen table. A stack of waxy blocks was next to the jars.

Dallas wagged his fingers at the blocks and jars. "What's this about?"

Marcus checked a nine-millimeter magazine and slapped it into a Glock. "It's from my livestock."

"Livestock? You got cattle?"

Marcus picked up a jar and tested the seal on its top, twisting it clockwise as far as it would go. He repeated the process with the second jar. "No. Cows don't make honey. At least no cow I've ever seen."

"Then what?" asked Dallas. "Goats?"

Marcus laughed. It was a belly laugh, as if Dallas had been the first person in the history of the world to find Marcus's sense of humor.

When he'd stopped laughing, Marcus motioned toward the back door. After he'd taken a couple of steps and Dallas hadn't moved, he stopped and bent at his waist. With his hands he guided his guest to the exit. "Come with me."

The screen door creaked on its hinges, mirroring its twin on the front of the house, and slapped shut behind the men while they walked across the dirt of the backyard. Dirt kicked up from Marcus's boots, swirling around him like a dervish, like the dry earth was forming him into a man at that moment.

The men stopped when they'd reached a collection of pine boxes. A dull hum vibrated in the air around them.

"Bees?"

Marcus nodded. A lone explorer hovered in front of him. He didn't swat it away or move furiously to avoid it.

"Why?"

"Why not?" Marcus said. "They're incredible. Do you know how many different uses there are for honey? The list is endless. I wish I'd thought more about them back in the day."

A rogue sputtered toward Dallas and he ducked. "How'd you get into it?"

"A trade," said Marcus. "I had some venison when you could still find whitetail without too much of a problem. A woman a few miles from here knew about it. She was an apiarist. Had more than she needed. We swapped. She taught me the basics. It's made a huge difference."

"Huge difference?"

Marcus stuffed his hands into his pockets. He looked past the pine boxes toward the clusters of dead pines that stood sentry across his backyard. "Not just the food," he said, "the soap, the medicinal aspects of it. It's the keeping busy that I liked. I used to talk to my dead wife. I named my guns."

"I know," said Dallas. "Lou told me about it."

Marcus shifted his weight and attention toward Dallas and looked at the ground between their feet. A bee landed on his head. He didn't react to it. He exhaled loudly. "I'm sure she did. It wasn't healthy, you know? Watching movies all the time, naming guns after the characters, having full-on, deep-as-the-ocean conversations with my wife was a bad thing."

Dallas mimicked Marcus and buried his hands in his pockets.

"It kept me sane," Marcus said. "*If* I was sane, that is. But this, these guys…" Marcus turned toward the hives. The bee on his head zigged into the air and joined a half dozen others that zagged above one of the pine boxes. "They're living, breathing things. I can talk to them and listen to the collective buzz. It's like they're listening. Like they're talking back. Like that buzz has the answers buried in the transmission."

"You chose to be alone," said Dallas.

Marcus took his hands from his pockets and pulled back his shoulders. He folded his arms across his chest and lifted his chin. "I didn't choose it. Being alone chose me, Dallas. You seriously wanna go there? I don't think you wanna go there."

Dallas looked past Marcus toward the hives on the other side of him. He motioned with his chin. "You gonna open 'em up and let me see?"

Marcus stood there. He was stone.

Dallas tried again, breaking the uneasy, hum-filled silence. "I'd like to see."

"Nah," said Marcus. "The smoker's in the barn. So's my suit. We'd best get going, anyhow."

Marcus started back to the house, his boots scraping across the dirt and crunching the fine layer of packed earth. His shoulder bumped Dallas as he passed him. Marcus didn't apologize.

"What are you going to do with the bees when we leave?" Dallas called after him. "Won't they die?"

Without turning around or stopping, Marcus answered, "Maybe. They've managed to beat the odds so far."

Marcus wore a pack on his shoulders and held a rifle in each hand by the time Dallas shut the rear door behind him. The blocks of wax and the jars of honey were gone from the counter and from the kitchen table.

Dallas moved to the kitchen counter and rested his palms on its edge. "I shouldn't have said it."

"Nope," said Marcus. "You shouldn't have. I've seen a lot of dead horses since the Scourge. I never saw fit to beat one of them."

"I'm sorry."

Marcus slung one of the rifles and shrugged the pack higher on his back. With his free hand he tightened the strap that ran across his chest. Then he handed the other rifle to Dallas. "You're forgiven. Let's get going."

Within minutes they were on Business 29, the highway that ran north and south through what was once the town of Chatham. Now it was little more than a testament to abandonment, to the Scourge, the drought, and everything that had conspired to drive people away from it.

They walked south.

"It took me a half day to walk here from the train station," said Dallas. "It's a good twenty miles."

Marcus walked ahead of Dallas, not worrying about whether the man kept pace. He unshouldered the rifle and carried it in both hands. Marcus was wearing a cowboy hat now. It was black, a relic of the Cartel he'd kept as a souvenir.

"I don't have any money left for the train," said Dallas. "I used all of it to get here. Well, most of it. The rest got stolen."

"Stolen?"

"Bandits," said Dallas. "On the train."

A blackbird circled overhead, and Marcus craned his neck to watch it drift on the current. Its broad wings didn't flap; they hung extended, the feathers at their tips fluttering.

There weren't other birds in the sky. No murder of circling crow signaled decay. This was a solitary raven finding its way, searching for purchase somewhere.

He lowered the hat on his eyes and scratched the healthy scruff he'd allowed to grow on his face and neck. Most of it was gray. He didn't like that. It was a reminder of how old he'd gotten. But he liked shaving less, and he knew that getting old was better than the alternative.

"Tell me about this place we're headed," said Marcus.

"Baird?" said Dallas. "Same as it was. We're living in a different–"

Marcus frowned. "Not Baird. Valhalla. The magical fairy land where all good parents live happily ever after. Oz. Whatever it is."

"Norma knows about it," said Dallas.

"The place?"

"Yeah."

"How's that?"

"She worked with them," Dallas said.

"Who?"

"There's an underground railroad," said Dallas. "Not a real train. But—"

"I know what an underground railroad is," said Marcus. "They used it in the Civil War times to free slaves. They used it during World War II to smuggle Jews out of wherever the Nazis were. The

Ukrainians even had one during the war with Russia in the 2020s."

"If we can get to Atlanta, they can get us to the Harbor."

Marcus stopped in the middle of the road and waited for Dallas to pull alongside him. "That what it's called?" he asked. "The Harbor?"

"I don't know if that's the official name," said Dallas. "But it's what I've heard it called. It's what Norma called it. She helped smuggle out a bunch of women a couple of years ago."

Marcus tipped his hat back on his head and thumped Dallas on the arm with the back of his hand. "Then why am I doing this? If Norma can handle everything, you don't need me."

Dallas shook his head. "Norma can't handle it. The Pop Guard cut off the railroad south of the wall a year ago, south of Atlanta, really. We have to get to Atlanta."

"And from there?"

"I don't know," said Dallas. "I know we have to get to Atlanta. And given that Texas is still…Texas, there's no way we could do it alone."

"So we need to take a train, full of bandits, south to the wall," said Marcus. "Then we have to cross the wall and find our way through tribal territories back to Baird. Once we're in Baird, we head back north through said territories and cross the wall again. This time though, we've got a pregnant woman or a woman with two kids. Once we're north of the wall, we somehow avoid roaming Pop Guards, coyotes, and other ne'er-do-wells to Atlanta. And in Atlanta we meet up with an underground railroad the Pop Guard knows exists, and ride it, so to speak, to an undisclosed location called the Harbor."

Dallas scratched his head with his free hand and shrugged his pack higher onto his shoulders. The look on his face said he was running through the gauntlet Marcus verbalized a moment earlier. He nodded. "That about sums it up."

"Okay then," said Marcus. "I get why you need my help."

The men exchanged smiles and walked another few minutes

without saying anything to each other. The clop of their boots and the shuffle of their packs filled the space between them.

"We can't walk all the way to Texas," said Dallas. "Well, we could, but it's not safe."

"We're not walking all the way to Texas. We'll catch the train in Danville and take it as far south as we can."

"They've got stops now through Atlanta, Birmingham, New Orleans," said Dallas. "But it's not cheap. Plus, there are bandits."

"You said something about that. Even north of the wall?" asked Marcus. "I thought the government took care of that."

Dallas shook his head. "Nah. They look the other way. It's too much to police, I guess. As long as the trains run, it's like they don't care if the passengers get robbed. Part of me thinks the government is part of it."

"People just let it happen?"

Dallas shrugged. "What are they gonna do? Money's not worth what it was. Might as well let 'em take it."

"Money's still money." Marcus sighed. "Any other options?"

Dallas shook his head. "Not really. It'll take too long to get to the wall otherwise."

"We'll take it as far as we can. But I'm not giving anything to bandits."

"What does that mean?"

Marcus started walking again. "It means we'll kill whoever we have to kill to make sure we get to where we need to go without giving up anything. We're gonna need money south of the wall, and the bottom line is we gotta get to Lou. Whatever it takes. Right?"

Marcus could tell Dallas had a question hanging on his lips, but he dared not ask it. He also could tell Dallas didn't know whether he was being serious or not.

Truth was, Marcus didn't know either.

CHAPTER 6

APRIL 17, 2054, 11:15 AM
SCOURGE +21 YEARS, 7 MONTHS
BAIRD, TEXAS

Sweat bloomed on Lou's forehead and around her eyes. She swiped at it and took another look through the binoculars Rudy had handed her moments earlier.

"You have got to be kidding me," she said. "This is bad. Very bad."

Rudy nodded his agreement. "It's not good. I haven't seen them this far south in three or four months."

"You think someone tipped them off?"

"No telling."

Lou touched her belly. "I've been so careful. I don't think anybody knows."

"Maybe not."

Rudy took the binoculars and looked again, adjusting the focus. The crow's feet at the corners of his eyes deepened. His mouth drew up into the tight smile of someone squinting.

Lou looked in the same direction toward the hazy distance. A bead of sweat dripped into one eye, and she blinked away the sting. On the horizon, marching toward them on horseback, was a squad of nine Pop Guard soldiers. They were armed with automatic rifles and rode with purpose.

Without the binoculars they were warbling specks, indistinguishable as men on horseback. The sun was behind Lou, near its apogee in the cloudless sky. The heat of the day was building, the air still. As she watched the men approaching, it was stifling.

"They're coming this way," said Rudy.

"No doubt," said Lou. "And we don't have much time."

There's not enough time.

Rudy lowered the binoculars and sighed. They were sitting in a deer stand left over from the days before the drought. The stand wasn't for deer. It was a perch from which to see oncoming threats.

Their property was on the eastern edge of TP Lake, which sat south of Interstate 20. Highway 283 was to the west and ran north and south. The Pop Guard hadn't crossed the highway, as far as they could tell. They were on what used to be Bowen Road near the old FedEx Freight facility.

"Surprised they aren't in trucks," said Lou. "Don't they usually ride in trucks?"

Rudy shuffled toward the opening on the side of the stand. The aluminum snap-together frame was still solid, but the steel brackets that held it together were rusting. There were ladders on either side that also served as an A-frame support. His feet hit the rungs and he turned around to face Lou. "I heard they've been using horses lately. Element of surprise."

"Makes sense," said Lou. "Except you have to feed and water horses. There isn't a lot of either."

"We manage," said Rudy.

"Touché."

Lou slid on her bottom to the ladder on the opposite side. She didn't roll onto her stomach as had Rudy; she descended the ladder one foot, one rung at a time. With each step lower, she rested her back against the higher rung until her feet hit the dry earth. Her dress stuck to the small of her back. She hated dresses, but her jeans didn't fit.

It's too hot for April. Is it April?

Rudy was there to offer a hand. She took it and he pulled her from a lean to an upright position. She cradled her belly in both hands and exhaled.

"You gonna be able to stick to the plan?" he asked.

Lou smirked. "Asked the old man with the bad hips?"

"Touché again," said Rudy. "Norma's already moved David."

Lou nodded and started walking back toward the main cluster of buildings, farther away from the edge of the lake, or where the lake used to be. There was still water there, enough to call it a pond at least, and while it was too deep to cross on foot or horseback, it wasn't deep enough to keep the algae and murk at bay. Lou glanced across the lake and west.

Nine of them. All armed. All with horses.

Anybody approaching from the west had only one easy path to the heart of the property and the cluster of buildings. A road, as much dirt as chipped asphalt, cut around the southern edge of the lake, tracing its straight banks and the lone finger that jutted south. There were railroad tracks that ran north of the lake, but men on horseback wouldn't take that route. They wouldn't risk injuring their animals on the large track ballast that formed the bed between sleepers.

Had the men been smart or done any reconnaissance, they'd have split into two groups. One would have come west; the other would have ridden south from Interstate 20 on County Road 494 east of the property. The county road stopped north of the buildings, but provided a straight shot to the back side.

Lou hurried, waddling more than running, toward the largest of the four buildings on the property. It was what they called the main house and was where Rudy and Norma lived. It was a typical farmhouse, two stories with a wraparound porch and a crawlspace underneath a pier and beam foundation.

The three other buildings, which sat east of the main house and were positioned one north of the other, were Lou's house, a dry storage building where they kept their provisions, and an antenna-equipped barn that doubled as an emergency hideout. There were two horses of their own in that barn.

They were underfed and always fighting off disease. But Rudy was good with horses and, as he reminded Lou, they managed to keep the horses strong enough to ride.

She hoped the horses were ready for what was coming. This was no drill. It was not a test. It was a real emergency.

And there wasn't much time.

They'd planned for it. Even before she was late and worried and biting her nails to the quick, they'd planned. Living in rural Texas was an exercise in the defense of life and property.

Dallas, God bless him, was a problem solver. Where she was rash and swimming in sarcasm, he was calm and levelheaded. They were a good team. Like Rudy and Norma, they complemented each other, the perfect balance of strengths and weaknesses. The ideal mix of ideas and world views.

When she'd told him, choking back tears, that she was pregnant, he'd met the challenge as a problem to solve.

The baby was coming. There was no use worrying about it, he'd told her. Something about serenity and change and acceptance. She'd only half-listened, her mind drifting to the dark side, the what-ifs, and the could-bes.

Lord, grant me the strength…

Dallas insisted they'd meet the challenge. Instead of letting fear paralyze them, they should act. They'd survived the Scourge, the Cartel, the Dwellers, the Llano River Clan, and being friends with Marcus Battle. They'd survive this. So would their baby.

Lou moved through the main house, setting in motion the things they'd readied but hoped never to use. She pictured Rudy doing the same in dry storage as she stepped out the back door. She used the pine railing to descend the porch and walked diagonally across the dirt to her house.

As much as she focused on the tasks at hand, and how little time she had to complete them, her mind drifted to her husband. It had been a week since he'd left.

Had he made it to Virginia? Had he found Marcus? Would Marcus help? Of course Marcus would help. Wouldn't he?

Dallas hadn't wanted to leave. His plan didn't call for that. Lou had insisted. If they were going to stay together as a family and find that safe place, that refuge they'd heard about in whispers, they'd need help.

They couldn't travel the yellow brick road to Oz without Dorothy.

Now she wished she hadn't sent her husband north of the wall and all the way to Virginia. She wished she could click her heels and he'd be home, beside her, helping her keep their family together.

Lou moved through the narrow hallway of her modest home. Using the wall for balance, she found her way to her bedroom. In the closet, behind the hanging clothes, were two backpacks. One was large; one was small. She grabbed both, heaving one over a shoulder and carrying the other by its strap. The weight of the pack on her shoulder played with her equilibrium, but she managed to wind her way back through the house to David's bedroom.

There's no way this works.

She reached inside the door, turned the lock in the handle, and closed it. Lou tugged the handle on the outside, trying it, testing it. It didn't budge. She headed out to the meeting place in the barn.

David and Norma were there waiting. The horses were saddled. They were restless.

Norma met Lou as soon as she entered the space, taking the smaller backpack from Lou's hand. A weak smile flickered across her face. "You okay?" she asked. "You look terrible."

"Thanks," said Lou. She pulled her shoulders back to stretch. "I can always count on your candor."

Norma's smile broadened, then evaporated. "I've gotta go. You stay here unless and until you hear the alarm."

Lou nodded, and Norma walked over to David. The boy was sitting on a wooden stool in front of the smaller of the two horses. It nickered at him. He seemed oblivious to the danger at hand. Either that or he was consciously avoiding it.

"David," said Norma, "let me put this on your back, okay?"

The boy nodded. As Norma approached, he extended his arms out so he could slide the straps over them, then gripped the straps and shrugged the pack onto his back.

"I hope this works," said Lou.

"You and me both," said Norma.

Chapter 7

APRIL 17, 2054, 11:40 AM
SCOURGE +21 YEARS, 7 MONTHS
BAIRD, TEXAS

Rudy sat in a chair on the front porch. Norma was next to him, knitting. They exchanged glances as the men on horses stopped in their yard and the leader dismounted.

"We should have primed the booby traps," Norma said under her breath. "Damn the consequences."

"Too late now," said Rudy.

They'd decided not to set the traps because killing or maiming one group of soldiers would only beget a larger one. Violence was their last option.

"Howdy," said the soldier. "I'm Sergeant Bowden. I'm with the Population Guard."

"I'm Rudy. This is my wife, Norma."

Rudy looked past the sergeant to his men. Two of them had their rifles pulled to their shoulders, the barrels aimed at the porch.

Bowden took the glove off his right hand, plucking at the fingers one at a time until the heavy suede came free. He held it in his still-gloved left hand and approached the steps. "Can I come up?"

Rudy nodded, glancing again at the armed horsemen. His face

brightened and he motioned for the sergeant to join him on the porch. "Of course. What can we do for you? We don't see much of you around here."

Bowden, a tall, thick man with a strong jaw and smallish ears, climbed the steps one at a time, his boots thumping on the pine slats. The man looked and moved like a pre-Scourge Greco-Roman wrestler. Rudy remembered watching wrestling during the Olympics. He missed the Olympics.

The sergeant extended his hand, and Rudy took it without standing. They shook. The man's grip was viselike. The fingers were muscular. Rudy didn't know fingers had muscles like that.

"Ma'am," said Bowden, briefly turning his attention to Norma.

She faked a smile but kept knitting. Knit one, purl two.

"Is there a reason you've got those soldiers aiming their rifles at us?" asked Rudy, his voice still pleasant enough. "You're on my land. If I didn't know better, I'd think you were being hostile. You're not being hostile, are you, Sergeant Bowden?"

The sergeant took off his other glove and tucked both of them in the wide width of his belt. He scratched his temple, his eyes narrowing. "Do I have a reason to be hostile?"

Rudy laughed. "I'm an old man sitting on my porch. I've got bad hips and occasional gout in my big toe. My wife suffers from arthritis in her fingers. Knitting isn't the fun it once was, but it passes the time. That's all we're doing, Sergeant. We're passing time."

Bowden stiffened, studying both of them. He glanced at the front door, then at Norma and her hands, then Rudy in his chair.

"You can lower the weapons," he said without looking back at his men. "For now."

Bowden pivoted, his boot heels grinding on the pine, stepping deliberately past Norma toward the corner of the porch. He leaned on the railing, looking along the southern face of the house and toward the three buildings to the east. He drummed his fingers on the railing, glanced back at his men, then spun on his heels and stalked back toward Rudy and Norma.

Rudy's mouth was dry, his heart pounding in his chest. The blood thumped at his temples. He hoped the sergeant couldn't see the throbbing blood vessels betraying his nerves. He reached over and put his hand on Norma's arm, feeling the flex of her muscles as she knitted. He rubbed a sweaty thumb on her soft, crepe-textured skin.

"What are those three buildings over there?" asked Bowden.

"They came with the place," said Rudy. "We use one for dry storage, one's a barn, one's a guesthouse."

"We don't ever have guests," said Norma. "Present company excluded."

"Mind if we take a look around?"

Rudy chuckled. He stopped rubbing Norma's arm but kept his hand there. "Do we have a choice?"

"Not really," said Bowden.

"Then go ahead," said Rudy. "You need me to show you the place?"

"No, thanks."

Bowden faced his men and made several motions with his hands. The men dismounted and made their way toward the house. Two of them stayed in the yard, their weapons aimed at the ground, but their attention squarely on Rudy and Norma.

The air was still, almost suffocating now. A wind chime at the edge of the porch trilled softly, moving infinitesimally despite the lack of breeze.

The other six marched up onto the porch and followed Bowden into the house. From their seats outside, Rudy and Norma could hear the men's heavy boots and their lack of care. Pots clanged; heavy furniture scraped against the floor with protesting squeals; doors opened and slammed shut.

As heavy steps clomped up the stairs to the second floor, the front door opened again and Bowden stepped onto the porch. His hands were behind his back.

"Find what you're looking for?" asked Rudy.

"Now see," said Bowden, rubbing the back of his neck, "what's interesting to me is that neither of you asked why we were here. Neither of you thought it was odd that my team, who looks for multi-children families, made a point to travel all the way out here to your sprawling estate."

"We were being polite," said Rudy.

"Where's the child?"

Rudy frowned. A chill ran along his spine and pimpled his skin. He resisted the magnetic urge to look at his wife. Instead he played dumb and worked hard not to let the sudden explosion of nerves spark in his voice. "What child?" he asked as dispassionately as possible.

The chime clanged once, a melodic ding accentuating the question like the signal of a correct answer on a television game show half a century earlier.

Bowden pulled his hands from behind his back. In one of them was a wooden toy, a little horse on wheels. He held it out in front of him, inches from Rudy's face, and shook it.

Rudy's eyes fell to the toy. He'd helped Lou make it for David. She'd carved the crude shapes with a knife and then whittled it to a recognizable Trojan pony. He'd fitted the axles and hammered the wheels into place. It had been a Christmas gift. Rudy remembered the joy radiating on David's face when he'd seen it under what passed for a tree in the living room.

There wasn't much joy in this world. It was difficult for children to be children. Lou knew that as well or better than anyone, forced to become a fierce survivalist at such a young age. She wanted something better for her son.

"Let's make him a toy," she'd said to Dallas. He'd suggested the horse, and Lou had gotten to work. She was so proud of it.

In the hand of Sergeant Bowden, it was anything but a gift. It was everything but a toy. It was an instrument, a harbinger of the violence to come.

Rudy reached into the small of his back and withdrew his pistol. As he leveled it, he slid his hand to the trigger and pulled. A loud blast cracked across the open space of their land like thunder, and Bowden dropped the horse. It rattled against the wood decking.

The sergeant staggered back, clutching his gut. He'd hardly had time to find the source of the blooming dark red expanse on his uniform when a second shot hit him center mass. An expression that combined both confusion and anger washed across his suddenly pale face. He dropped to a knee, managing only a squeak before he fell face forward onto the porch. His body slapped against the wood, the percussion vibrating in the soles of Rudy's boots.

Norma was on her feet and moving toward the front of the deck like a stalker, a gun in her hand. It was up; it was aimed. A trio of shots from the pistol sounded like firecrackers. Another pop, one with more volume and bass, came from Rudy's right. Shards of pine exploded from the bannister to his left, spraying Norma with debris. It barely missed her.

Although all of this happened within seconds—parts of seconds, milliseconds—the world slowed around Rudy. He focused and spun around, his back to the house. One of the guards left in the yard was on the ground on his back, his legs twitching, his blood leaching onto the dry, cracked earth and staining it wine colored. The second had his rifle up, smoke curling from the end of the barrel. Norma returned fire. Neither hit the man. Rudy shifted his aim and fired another two rounds. The man's body jerked awkwardly. He pivoted, the rifle now raised at Rudy. Norma fired a shot that ended him.

Rudy called out to her, above the echo of the gunfire, "You okay?"

Norma nodded. While there was worry etched into her expression, Rudy recognized something else too. Resolve. Beneath the fear there was strength, the strength of a woman who'd stood in the middle of the street with a radio at her hip, ready to face an oncoming horde of marauders. There was the resilience of a kidnapping victim who never gave up hope or lost faith. Rudy wanted to grab her, hold her, promise her they would get through this. There wasn't time.

"Stick to the plan," he said. "I'll catch up."

Norma nodded and blew him a kiss. Eyes wide, jaw set, she bolted. When she reached the edge of the porch closest to the barn, Norma swiped at the aluminum wind chime hanging from a loop screwed into the fascia. The cacophony of chimes cut through the still air like the proverbial bull pushing its way through a china shop. As if the gunfire wasn't alarm enough, the chimes would tell Lou what to do next.

A loud bang snapped Rudy's attention to the man in the doorway. He spun in time to see one of the guards at the threshold, the screen door swinging back toward him. He stood there, a look of confusion on his pinched face. Rudy fired another shot. And another. Two quick pops and twin holes dotted the guard's brow.

He didn't move at all at first. Then the life drained from his eyes. He collapsed into a heap in the doorway as though someone had magically yanked his skeleton from his body. His rifle clattered to the deck.

Rudy dropped to the deck, reached for the rifle, and dragged it across the wood.

Heavy footsteps pounded toward him. Angry voices. Calls for vengeance.

Rudy shouldered the weapon. The house was dark from here. Vague shapes shifted inside. Flashes of light. Gunfire. Something hard smacked him in the side as he applied pressure to the trigger.

The rifle punched against him with the shot. Another punch hit his bicep.

The thick ache of blunt force gave way to searing heat and pain. He was hit. At least twice. Adrenaline surging, Rudy fired again. Again.

Cries of pain. Grunts. Cursing. More shots. More flashes. Another solid hit to his arm.

Rudy dropped the rifle. The bodies in the doorway, which now numbered four, made it tough for him to see inside the house. There were two more guards, if he remembered correctly. If he could count. The pain sizzled in his body. It pulsated, clouding his thoughts.

Rudy tried lifting his right arm but couldn't. He tightened his left hand into a fist and flexed his wrist. His left was fine. He picked up his pistol and aimed it at the dark opening to his house. He had to buy Norma more time. Lou and her children had to escape.

He extended the gun. It rattled in his trembling hand. He stepped forward, ignoring the tug of agony at his side and in his right arm. Another step and he realized his right leg, near the hip, was heavy, like someone had dipped it in lead.

He managed to climb over the lifeless, still-warm bodies in the doorway and steady himself in the foyer. Sweat drained into his eyes, swamped his armpits, and painted the back of his neck. A chill ran down his spine and he shuddered. He moved past the stairs and deeper into the house.

"I'm coming for you!" he shouted into his house. Upstairs he heard skittering. At least one of the men was on the second floor.

"All your buddies are dead!" he called. "We've got you outnumbered now. We're thinning the population the old-fashioned way."

His voice hung in the air. The house was otherwise unnaturally quiet. Rudy stood against the wall that led toward the rear of the house, using it to stay upright. So much pain radiated through his body he couldn't tell where the actual injuries were. He gritted his teeth.

A creak from the other room, maybe the parlor, caught his attention, and he held his breath. It was a loose floorboard he was suddenly glad he never fixed. The entry to the parlor was to his left, a wide open doorway framed by chipped but elegant crown molding.

The parlor was on the other side of the wall against which Rudy leaned. He thought about firing through the wall into the parlor. The walls were plaster. It would eat the small pistol round. Rudy pressed his back against the wall, its cool texture chilling his sweat-drenched shirt.

If he knew where they were, they knew where he was. Somebody would have to make a move.

Rudy clenched his teeth, tightening his jaw against the tsunami-like waves of pain that threatened to drown him in agony. His adrenaline could only do so much to stem the tide.

He took a deep breath through his flared nostrils and sank to the floor. The bend of his knees and waist forced tears from his eyes, and he suppressed the urge to scream.

He steadied himself on the floor, twisting onto his side, extending the pistol toward the parlor opening. His finger was sweaty on the trigger.

"Where are you?" he called out, his voice more of a croak than he'd expected. The position of his body and the weakness flooding him were taking their toll. "I'm coming for you. Better you end this now."

Another creak from the parlor. Another. The second was decidedly closer to the hallway. The man was taking the bait.

Rudy stayed low, willing himself as flat as he could keep himself while on his side with his left arm extended. His arm trembled with exhaustion, and the gun was heavy. It was so heavy. Each beat of his heart sent rivers of mind-altering pain through his core and outward to his fingers and toes.

His vision blurred. Another creak. He blinked. Tried to focus. Another creak. He narrowed his gaze like a man without his reading glasses staring at fine print. He held his aim. His unsteady hand. The blood pooling beneath him. It was warm, sticky, slippery. He couldn't focus.

Another creak and a blurry figure stepped into the hall. Then focus. Clarity.

The man had his rifle aimed chest high. He didn't see Rudy on the floor until it was too late. He tried shifting his aim, lowering it, but a succession of rounds peppered him. One after the other, in a seemingly random pattern, shattered his knees, punctured his gut, made less of a man of him.

The man managed a single pull of the trigger, aiming at the ceiling as he collapsed. Plaster showered Rudy as he rolled onto his stomach. With the back of his pistol hand, he wiped the sweat from his eyes, clearing his vision. The target was rolling on the floor, his legs splayed oddly, his hands trembling. Odd gurgling noises, like a baby blowing raspberries, came from his mouth.

Pushing aside the debilitating pulses of nausea that racked his gut, Rudy managed to push himself to one knee. He looked down at his arm, his body; his clothing was drenched in his own blood. The fabric stuck to his body. He couldn't see the tears in the shirt to know where he'd been shot. There was too much blood.

As he pushed himself to his feet, he slipped in it, but caught himself. A lightning bolt of electric pain sparked across his midsection. Rudy was light-headed, the edges of his vision sparkling with light. His focus was intermittent, mouth dry, breathing uneven.

Rudy shuffled, dragging one foot, toward the stairs. At the same instant he reached the bannister, a guard appeared at the top, his rifle drawn. Rudy didn't have enough time to raise his weapon before the guard opened fire.

Chapter 8

APRIL 17, 2054, 11:50 AM
SCOURGE +21 YEARS, 7 MONTHS
BAIRD, TEXAS

Lou was on the horse, David in front of her in the saddle, her hand gripping the leather reins when Norma burst into the barn. The echo of the wind chimes danced louder in the still air with the door open.

Ghostly white, Norma moved past a wooden bench loaded with electronics. Wires stretched from the table, up the wall, and to the roof's antenna. She was breathless and waving the gun in her right hand. "We've got to go," she said. "Now."

Lou searched the open door expectantly then locked eyes with Norma. "What about—?"

"Now," Norma growled, grabbing the saddle horn of the other horse. She planted a foot in one stirrup, pushed, and swung her other leg over the saddle. "We are out of time."

Lou kicked her heels into the horse's ribs and clicked her tongue against her teeth. She tugged on the reins, directing the horse toward the opening. It jerked its head and responded.

The horse was already jogging when it left the barn. The acrid odor of spent gunpowder fouled the air. Norma was behind them at first, but pulled alongside as they turn right and headed north toward the southeastern edge of TP Lake.

Lou had one hand on the reins, the other around David. She pulled him into her belly, reminding him to hold onto the horn with both hands. She glanced back at the main house. There was no sign of anybody or anything. It was quiet. Too quiet.

"Where's Rudy?"

Norma shook her head. She kicked the horse and leaned in, urging it north, past the lake. Lou's full attention was on Norma. The woman was stone, but there was something in her eyes that answered Lou without words.

They rode north, the cracked edges of the lake to their left. The brown water at its center was still and unmoving. Lifeless.

Lou's chest tightened. The breeze from their movement stung her eyes.

"Stop the horse!"

Lou didn't understand at first. It took a beat.

Norma yelled again, "Stop the horse!"

Lou's attention shifted past Norma and toward the railroad tracks that ran east to west on the north side of the lake between their position and the highway.

Standing end to end, like an army measuring its opponent before charging, were six mounted Pop Guard soldiers. They *had* been smart.

"Turn around," Norma told her. "We can't go this way."

"We can't outrun them," Lou said. "Those horses are bigger and stronger. You can see it from here. They'll overrun us."

"So what do you suggest?" Norma snapped.

"We fight," said Lou.

Norma's eyes widened. "You're a lunatic."

"I sent Dallas to get the lunatic," Lou said. "I'm just a hopeless optimist."

Somehow, in the midst of this, Lou drew the faintest flicker of a smile from Norma. No sooner had it flashed than it was gone.

"You have a child," said Norma. "You can't fight. We need to run."

Norma was right. Fighting was stupid. If she didn't have David, if she wasn't pregnant, Lou would unleash her fury on these intruders. Then again, if she didn't have David, if she wasn't pregnant, the intruders never would have come.

"Okay," said Lou. "Let's go."

The women turned their horses and spurred them back toward the main house. The horses jogged at first then galloped. David held tight to the horn, his body bouncing in the saddle, his back rubbing against Lou's belly. She held him around his chest with one hand and guided the horse with the other.

"We're going to be okay, buddy," she said. "I got you."

He put one small hand on hers and squeezed. His chest was rising and falling, his heart racing.

The horses were coming now, the men atop them shadows in the sunlight and clouds of dust that bloomed underneath them, billowing outward and upward like smoke from a fire.

Lou and Norma cut their horses wide around the back side of the outbuildings and then west past the barn toward the main house. Norma rode ahead, urging her horse to take the lead. That was when Lou saw the first of the bodies.

Lou wasn't squeamish; she'd killed before. But it had been some time since she'd been so close to a dead body. And David hadn't seen one.

She spoke in his ear again, her face bumping against him as the horse slowed. "Cover your eyes, baby."

"Why?" he asked, but did it anyway without an answer. His hand left hers and he put it over his eyes.

As they rounded the corner of the house, two bodies emerged, both of them flat on the ground as if planted there. Limbs twisted, ghastly expressions hardened on their faces, they were without question dead. A crack of gunfire drew her attention toward Norma and then to the steps leading from the yard to the porch.

Norma pulled her animal to a stop. Lou did the same. A lump thickened in her throat. She couldn't swallow. She couldn't breathe. Rudy was standing there. He was bloodied and so badly wounded. The right side of his body seemed to hang on him, like a marionette, and his stance was such that he wasn't upright of his own volition.

The man behind him, the one with a gun pointed at his head, held the strings. The Pop Guard jabbed the weapon into Rudy's temple. Rudy didn't seem to notice. Lou couldn't be sure he was even conscious.

"Toss your weapons," the guard spat. "Do it. Or I kill him right here, right now."

Norma complied, tossing her handgun to the dirt. She raised her hands above her head.

"You too," the guard said to Lou. "Do it."

"I don't have a gun," said Lou. "I've got my son."

The guard stared at her, measuring her, his eyes darting nervously across her, David, the horse. He nodded.

"Get off the horses," he said. "Now."

Lou sat in her saddle, not moving. "Stay on the horse, David," she whispered.

Norma dismounted. The sound of the coming horses rumbled in the distance. It was thunder on the horizon.

"Get down," said the man.

"Can I get some help?" Lou asked. "I'm pregnant. You know I'm pregnant. That's why—"

The man motioned to Norma with the pistol then aimed it at Lou. "Help her get down."

Norma started to move.

"Stop," said the guard. His voice was tremulous. His nerves raw. "Don't move."

Norma shrugged, keeping her calm. Somehow she stayed calm. "You told me—"

"Slow. Move slow."

The rumble of the coming horde was loud now. They couldn't be too far.

Norma reached Lou. They were maybe fifteen yards from the man, from Rudy. Lou reached out with one hand to Norma, keeping the other free.

"Careful now," said the man, stepping to the side of Rudy, exposing himself for just long enough. "No funny—"

The knife slid from her sleeve with a wrist flick. The Damascus steel was warm in her hand, the flat handle as comfortable as an old glove. It was in her fingers for a split second.

As she dismounted, Lou forcefully whipped the throwing knife underhanded. It spun end over end, whipping the short distance with force, its revolutions blindingly fast. Before the man even saw it coming, it was in his chest.

Then Rudy came alive and shoved an elbow backward, driving the knife past its hilt. The guard gasped and stumbled back. Rudy dropped to his knees and collapsed, the surge of violence enough to drain him.

Norma rushed to the porch. She took the gun from the dying guard's hand and stood over him. She said something Lou couldn't hear and fired a single shot. Then she dropped to the ground to check her husband.

Lou hurried to the body closest to her, took the rifle and an extra magazine, and clambered back to the horse. Instead of climbing into the saddle, she reached out for David.

"Can I open my eyes?" asked David.

"Not yet," said Lou. He sank into her arms and she set him down. She took the larger of the saddlebags and carried it on her hip to the nearest of the much larger horses. It was an Appaloosa. Mottled and sleek, it was a beautiful horse. And it was fast.

She slid the rifle snug in its scabbard and attached the pack at the side. Lou still had a pack on her back.

Hero

The horde of men was coming. They were at the edge of the lake now, making a straight line for the house. They'd be here in less than three minutes. They would overrun Rudy and Norma. Yet if she stayed, she and Norma could take out six.

It was stupid. It was rash. It was a horrible thing for a mother to do. But Lou couldn't abandon the two people who'd stood by her when so many others had left.

Lou clenched her jaw. She wasn't going to let them down. They wouldn't leave her. She couldn't leave them.

Chapter 9

APRIL 17, 2054, NOON
SCOURGE +21 YEARS, 7 MONTHS
BAIRD, TEXAS

Rudy was cold, his body weak. He'd lost so much blood.

"Talk to me," Norma said, taking his hand. "Rudolfo Gallardo, stay with me. We're going to be okay."

Rudy opened his eyes and squeezed her hand.

Lou marched toward them.

"What are you doing?" asked Norma. "You need to go. Take David. Get away."

"I can't do that," said Lou. She extended a rifle toward Norma. "Get up. I figure we've got three minutes."

Norma stared at her and scowled. This girl *was* a lunatic. Norma cursed at her, at the predicament, and gently laid her husband's head on the ground. She pulled off her jacket, balled it up, and tucked it under his head.

Standing, she took the rifle. "Why three minutes?"

"The guard's cavalry is almost here," said Lou. "I'm not leaving, so you'd better help me."

Norma cursed again and leapt onto the porch. "Help me with him."

They set down their weapons and picked up Rudy's heavy, limp body. Together they half carried, half dragged him over the bodies and into the hallway.

"That's as far as we're getting him," said Norma. "I got your boy."

She picked David up with her free arm and settled the boy on her hip. Lou handed Norma the rifle and they clambered up the stairs to the second floor. From high ground, they had a better shot at picking off the guards.

Norma ran into one bedroom and Lou went to the other. Norma set David on the floor. Then she moved to the bed and yanked the thin mattress from it.

"Get under this," she said. "It'll keep you safe."

"Can I open my eyes?" David asked.

Norma hadn't noticed until now that they were shut. She smiled at him and put a hand on his head, tousling his hair. "Yes, sweet boy," she said, "you can open them. But you might want to cover your ears. It's going to get loud."

David hid behind the mattress, burrowing himself underneath it. Norma hustled to the window and unlatched it. She pulled it up and knelt, resting the barrel on the wooden sill.

The sun was almost directly overhead. There were virtually no shadows outside. The air was warm and dry, and the dust tickled her nose.

Lou, she hoped, was in the corner bedroom with windows on the north- and west-facing sides of the house. She'd be the first line of defense.

David's feet stuck out from beneath the mattress. His tiny little feet. Norma thought they were so cute.

"Your mother is a moron," she muttered under her breath. "The two of you should be long gone. She's risking everything by—"

The first reports of gunfire broke the relative silence. Norma whirled to her right, keeping her eye to the rifle's sights. Nothing yet. She scanned back toward the deer stand. No movement. Another volley of gunfire crackled through the midday stillness. It was return fire.

It was a gunfight now. And Norma was blind. Plus, she was useless.

She got up from the floor and called out to David as she rushed past him, "Stay there, sweet boy," and bounded along the hallway, pinballing herself off the walls until she gathered herself and launched into the corner bedroom.

Lou was beside the window, hiding. The rifle was pointed straight up toward the ceiling. Rounds zipped through the air, puncturing the walls on either side of the door. Norma dropped to the floor. She banged into a dresser, the mirror atop it wobbling and falling to the floor, shattering next to her. A jagged shard cut across her leg, drawing blood. She crawled to Lou, staying low.

"You should have gone," she said, wincing. "What good are you dead? If you're dead and Marcus gets here, he'll kill you."

Lou rolled her eyes. Then her expression hardened, her gaze dancing around the room.

"Where's David?" she yelled over the gunfire.

"Safe in the other room," she said.

The return fire paused, and Norma reached beside her, picking up a large piece of the mirror. She lifted it up above the windowsill and angled it toward Lou.

"What do you see?" Norma asked.

"Four are down," said Lou. "One of them might be alive, but he's not going anywhere."

"There were six," said Norma. "Weren't there six?"

Lou nodded and pulled a knife from her hip. The two of them exchanged glances and bolted for the hallway back toward the front bedroom.

They were at the top of the stairs, feet from the front bedroom, when one of the guards appeared halfway up the steps. His rifle was already at his shoulder. He managed a single shot that exploded into the wall next to Lou's head. He wasn't fast enough to pull the trigger a second time.

While Norma brushed past her, almost bowling into her, Lou sidearmed the knife, zinging it into the meat of the man's thigh. It shocked him off-balance and he fell backwards, tumbling down the stairs. The wounded man's head hit the wall at an odd angle. His neck cracked with an unnerving sound as the second soldier appeared at the bottom of the steps.

Norma had the drop on him. The moment he appeared at the bottom step, she fired. The first shot missed him. A quick second pull grazed his shoulder, giving Lou enough time to draw another knife and whip it at the man. It hit him in the clavicle and he dropped his weapon.

While he grasped at the knife, trying to pull it free, Norma took aim. One shot ended the man's struggles, and the house was silent again.

Norma lowered her weapon, but kept it pointed at the men at the bottom of the stairs. Her finger was on the trigger, ready to fire again at the slightest movement.

Before she descended the stairs, she glanced behind her. Lou was in the front bedroom, crouched into a squat and holding David in her arms. His eyes were open.

Step by step Norma moved down the stairs. Her hands were sweating, greasy on the rifle, as she swept the weapon back and forth.

Adrenaline surged through her body. It was keeping her from collapsing, from sinking to the floor in a heap and wallowing in her pain.

Reaching the bottom of the steps, she poked the rifle's barrel at each of the two men. Their bodies gave against the push but didn't otherwise move. Using one hand to balance herself, she pressed her fingers against the plaster wall that ran along the left side of the steps, and stepped over the bodies.

In the hall near the door where she'd left him, her husband lay motionless. Norma swallowed hard, glanced through the front door, checking for threats that weren't there, and laid down the rifle. She lowered herself to her knees and crawled the short distance to Rudy.

Awkwardly, she repositioned herself to sit with his head in her lap. She pulled him onto her, cradling him. Stroking his matted hair from his forehead, she suppressed the urge to cry. It hurt. In her chest, her throat, the backs of her eyes. The ache was building, pushing like too much water against a weakened dam.

A lifetime raced through her mind. Postcards one after the other, like flipping through an album of them.

She saw Rudy. A young man, strong and handsome. There was a spark between them. It was invisible, ethereal, and unmistakable. She saw fishing on piers, at docks, banks of lakes and ponds. Him threading the needle through the bait for her, but refusing to help her pull in her catch. She'd need to be self-reliant one day, and any wife of his should be confident enough to know she could do anything. Anything but hook a worm.

Courtship at the last drive-in theater, the heat between them and the fog on the windows of a car that barely ran. A small wedding and no honeymoon. But they had the beginnings of a good life together.

There was the Scourge that left them alone but self-reliant. Then came men who took her, held her against her will, forced her to draw every ounce of strength from her core.

She never doubted her husband would come for her, and he had. He'd brought with him a hardened man who'd helped to give them a second chance at life.

That man, Marcus Battle, was also their undoing. Violence followed him. Or more likely, he courted it. Like people who couldn't exist without drama, Marcus was a ghost without death around him.

He'd settled with them here in Baird. He, Lou, and the two virtually mute women who'd left without notice long ago made a home for a short time.

She stroked Rudy's face absently as she thought about those days.

Hero

They were good. At least, they were as good as one could dream in this wasteland.

Then she'd told Marcus to leave, and he had. Then they'd found a bigger piece of land outside town, one better suited for the drought.

Lou fell in love; she married Dallas; they had a child. Those were the days better than the dream. Rudy and Norma were like grandparents. They *were* grandparents.

A wave of nausea washed through Norma's body. She rubbed her fingers against the coarse texture of Rudy's beard. Her jaw clenched and Norma held the tears at bay. The knot in her throat was sore. It hurt. She swallowed past it and thought about what was coming.

Now Marcus was coming. The violence, as if sensing his approach, had returned ahead of him. It was a harbinger of Marcus's reemergence in their lives, and it had cost Rudy his. It had cost Norma. What was worse was that this was only the beginning. More violence was on the horizon.

Norma wanted to scream. She wanted to vomit. She wanted to blame God, and the Scourge, and the drought, and the Llano River Clan, and Marcus. It was irrational.

The damned Pop Guard and the junta that proclaimed itself the government was at fault. Norma knew that. But she needed someone tangible to blame as she traced her husband's lips and the lines that framed his cheeks.

His skin was cold to the touch. His lips were changing color.

"I love you," she told him. "You are my hero, Rudolfo. My rock. My companion. My reason for being."

A noise behind Norma startled her. She jerked around to see Lou standing in the hall, David in front of her, her hands over his eyes.

Tears streamed down Lou's face, leaving clean streaks through the sheen of dirt and dust. Her olive skin, usually radiant and softly glowing, was dull. Her bright, intelligent eyes were reddened and puffy. The confident way in which she carried her thin, muscular frame was turned inward, making her appear smaller.

"Is he…?" Lou let the question hang in the air between them.

Norma stared at her for a beat, locking eyes with her, giving her the answer without saying it. It was too hard to say it.

Lou's chin trembled. Her voice warbled with abject sadness. "He died saving me," she said. "Saving us. If it weren't for—"

Norma held up a hand, stopping her from saying any more. "Don't say that. Rudy loves—loved—you. He would do anything for you."

David whimpered. He pressed his hands against his mother's over his eyes. His little chest heaved up and down. Lou hadn't covered his eyes and ears.

"Let him see," said Norma.

Lou drew away her hand, her son holding onto it and keeping his eyes shut. Norma extended a hand to him.

Tears were coming now. Norma couldn't hold them back any longer. "Come here, sweet boy," she said. "Come say goodbye to Rudy."

As the boy moved toward him, Rudy's eyes opened. His chest rose as he took in a deep, rattling gasp of air. A pained groan filled the house as he exhaled.

"Rudy?" Norma's voice was a squeak. "Rudy?"

He gasped again and tried speaking. His lips moved, but nothing came out.

"Hurry," said Lou, "let's get him onto the bed. He's going to need help."

Norma sat frozen for a moment, not processing that her husband was alive. Her mind had already drifted to burying him. She'd put him next to their dog Fifty.

She thought he'd like that. That old dog was faithful to him to the last.

The dog that had been as good a companion as any human, maybe better, had lived a long, good life, which was more than Norma could say for a lot of animals post-Scourge.

Lou shook her from the reverie. "Norma, c'mon now. If his pulse was weak enough you thought he was dead, he's damn near it now. We gotta help him. I can't do it on my own."

Norma moved out from under her husband's body. Together, and with difficulty, the two women managed to half carry, half drag Rudy to the master bedroom. Then they'd collapsed with him onto the bed.

Now his feet were elevated. His head was on a pillow. His shirt was off and Norma was cleaning him to find the source of the blood, the holes and gashes threatening to drain the last ounces of life from his wounded body.

Norma sat on the edge of the bed next to her husband. Exhaustion began to take hold. She wasn't sure she could stand if she tried and wondered if she looked as tired as Lou did. The poor girl had one hand at the small of her back and the other cupped under her belly. It was awkward looking, but Norma imagined being nine months pregnant in this environment was always awkward. She felt for the poor girl, for the life growing inside her.

"David asleep?" asked Norma.

"I think so," said Lou, motioning with her head toward the parlor across the house. "He's tired."

"We all are."

"I'm so sorry," said Lou.

Norma swallowed, putting her hand on her husband's leg next to her. It was under the blanket, but she could feel the muscle of his thigh above his knee. "Sorry about what?"

Lou shifted from one foot to the other, from one side of the door frame to the other. Both hands were underneath her belly now, caressing it. The girl looked at the floor. "Everything. The pregnancy. Sending Dallas to get Marcus. Today. Everything."

"You didn't think you could have another baby," said Norma. "It's not your fault. And sending Dallas to get help was the right thing to do."

Lou looked up from the floor. "Was it?"

Norma tilted her head to one side. Inhaling through her nose and drawing in a deep breath, she considered the question. She concluded an honest answer was the best.

She eyed her husband's chest and torso. There were three bullet wounds, not counting the nick at his neck that seemed to bleed more than the penetrating wounds on his side, in his hip, and on his arm.

"I'm not sure Marcus would have been my first choice," she said. "Blood follows that man everywhere, Lou. You know that. We all know that. That's why he left. It's why he didn't come back. I so much as told him not to come back."

Blood preceded him too. It was everywhere. Norma listened to her husband's breathing. It sounded odd, like air through a straw.

"I think he's got a sucking chest wound," said Norma. "He might have a punctured lung."

Norma scanned the first aid supplies she'd spread out on the bed next to her husband. There was a plastic card amidst the gear that explained how to shape a splint. Norma found a petroleum jelly packet and squeezed it onto the edges of the card. Then she wiped away the excess blood at the wound in Rudy's chest and pressed the card against it.

Norma watched as Rudy inhaled. It pulled the card tight against his chest, creating a vacuum so he could breathe. When he exhaled, the card lifted and blood oozed through the jelly.

"I don't think there's anything else I can do for that," she said. "He seems to be breathing okay right now. I can't risk trying to pull out a bullet or anything else."

Lou stood behind her now, hovering. "Is there anything I can do?"

Norma shook her head. "I've got to treat these wounds, stop the bleeding. Maybe you could get him some water? A cold cloth?"

Lou nodded and left the room. Norma could hear her shuffling in the kitchen.

The wound in his side appeared to be a clean shot, through and through. She carefully rolled him onto his side and poured iodine over the entry and exit wounds.

Rudy groaned and coughed, his face contorting in pain. Sweat drenched his forehead and cheeks, matting his hair to his head.

Norma shushed him and told him to stay calm. She checked both wounds, wiping them clean again. The exit wound on his back was wider and more ragged than the entry wound.

She slathered gauze with Neosporin and stuck it on both sides, using surgical tape to affix the gauze. They looked like weirdly shaped patches above his love handles.

Although Rudy still hadn't said a word, he was conscious and tolerating the pain. That was good.

"Can you move your fingers and toes?" she asked, taking his hand.

He squeezed. It was weak, the grip not enough to open a mason jar of preserves, but it was there. She looked at his feet. His ankles shifted.

She moved to his thigh. There was no exit wound. The bullet was lodged in his leg. For now, she'd have to leave it there. Like the chest wound, Norma saw no advantage in trying to remove the bullet. She wasn't trained to do it. Basic first aid was about as far as she'd advanced.

Lou came back with a large glass of water and a damp rag. She handed Norma the rag first. Norma folded it in half and placed it gently on Rudy's forehead. He opened his eyes and closed them again.

"I need you to take a sip of water, Rudy," she said. "And swallow some pills."

She ripped open a package with her teeth and shook a pair of white tablets into her hand. Lou handed her the glass. Together they managed to lift Rudy's head enough for him to take the pills and swallow two sips of water.

"They're pain pills," Norma said. "I don't know if they're any good, but it can't hurt. Says they were made in Atlanta three years ago."

"Where'd you get a kit from Atlanta?" asked Lou.

Norma shrugged. "I guess Rudy bartered for it."

Both women turned their attention to the patient. He was propped up on pillows. His eyes were half open, his skin pale. Sweat had dried and bloomed again.

"You're a mess," said Norma. "But you're my mess."

Rudy opened his lips and said something below a whisper. Norma couldn't hear it, so she moved closer to him. She turned her head and put her ear next to his mouth.

"I love you," he said.

Tears welled in Norma's eyes. A tremor shook her chest, but she held it at bay. She had to be strong right now. The time for tears was later, when he was out of the woods.

With her hands on both sides of his face, Norma lowered her lips to his and kissed him gently.

Norma glanced back at Lou.

Aside from the lack of an Astros ball cap, Norma thought Lou looked like the young girl she'd met so many years ago. It was hard to believe so much time had passed, so many things had happened in that time. Time was different since the Scourge, even more so since the drought took root. While the days were long and dragged, weeks and months flew past, and years dissolved into a collection of fleeting moments like powder into water.

"Marcus is old now," she said. "Like Rudy."

"What do you mean?"

Norma pulled her shoulders back, lifted her chin. "Rudy did what he could today. Ten years ago and this happened? He'd be dragging the bodies to a hole in the ground. Age takes things from people. Marcus is no different, Lou."

Norma watched the gears turn in Lou's head. The girl—she still thought of her as a girl even if she was in her thirties now—was easy to read. Anger. Fear. Joy. Lou wore every emotion as if it were a T-shirt with the words stenciled on it.

"I wouldn't have sent for Marcus," Norma said with a shrug. "I'm being honest. But what's done is done. And you need to go now. Take David and get out of here."

"I'm not leaving you and Rudy alone," said Lou. "I can wait until Dallas gets back with Marcus."

Norma moved her hand from her husband's face and put it on the mattress beside her. She pushed herself to her feet. Her knees ached; her shoulders were sore. She rubbed her neck with the back of her hand. Tendrils of her gray hair twisted and strained against her touch, pricking as if pulled.

"I've worked too hard for too many years not to give you this chance," Norma said. "I never planned on you needing it, but you do. The time is now."

"I know you've worked hard," said Lou. "I know opportunities on the railroad don't happen for everyone. But I can wait for my husband, for Marcus."

Norma sighed. "I'm going to keep it real here, Lou. We don't know if they're getting back. For all we know, Dallas didn't make it. Or he did and couldn't find Marcus. Or Marcus wouldn't come. Or they don't make it back. Or—"

Lou pulled back her shoulders and crossed her arms over her chest. Her expression hardened defensively and she shook her head. "I get your point. I get it. I get it."

Norma bit her lower lip. "Sorry, I shouldn't be so negative. Let's say they're on their way. They can help me once they get here."

"You just said—"

Norma stepped closer to Lou and put a hand on her shoulder. Lou tensed for a moment, then relaxed.

"I know what I said," Norma said, her voice maternal. "I was wrong to say it. You have to get out of here. For all we know another group of soldiers is on its way already. And if not, it will be soon. We don't have any idea how long you have. If you're here when they come back…"

Lou's eyes drifted past Norma's shoulder. Like she was staring through some portal into the past, her face twitched and her eyes welled with tears as she appeared to relive the events of the day. Then she blinked and looked directly at Norma. "How do you think they found us? We're out here in Baird. Actually, we're not even *in* Baird. I don't get it. I've been so careful."

Norma shook her head. "Probably one of the neighbors. You know they walk by on the highway. They wander the north side of the lake looking for water. All it takes is one person with a scope or binoculars. A mother might turn in her daughter for the bounty they offer now."

"We should have run when we saw them coming," said Lou. "We shouldn't have waited."

"It was too dangerous at that point," said Norma.

Lou nodded at Rudy. "No more dangerous than what happened. We should have fought from the beginning. We could have picked them off as they rode up. Rudy wouldn't be fighting for his life."

"That was never the plan," said Norma. "You know that. Rudy thought it was best to try to avoid any violence. There was always a chance they'd move along."

Norma lifted her other hand to Lou's shoulder and pulled her into her. Sliding her hands to Lou's back, she held the girl tightly against her. Between them, the bump shifted and moved. Norma relished the sensation of the baby kicking.

"You need to go," she whispered, her voice thick with emotion. "Let's go get David."

Lou tightened her grip on Norma, and her body shuddered as she cried. Beneath her hands, Norma felt the girl's back rising and falling with her sobs, and she fought to maintain her composure. She had to be strong despite what the day had wrought.

When we woke up this morning, this wasn't the plan, she thought, stroking the back of Lou's head. In the bed behind her, she'd awoken next to her husband, his warm body touching hers. Even after all these years, they still slept with their legs intertwined, faces toward one another.

He'd told her, his rank morning breath as intoxicating and familiar as it was foul and off-putting, he loved her, running his thick and calloused fingers along the side of her face.

"You need to trim your nails," she'd said. "They could cut glass."

He'd snorted a laugh. "That could come in handy. We're always looking for good tools."

Norma had scooted closer to him and buried her head in his chest, inhaling him. She loved his smell. It was home.

"You're a tool," she'd replied. His long nails raked softly across her back. She'd flexed like a cat, relishing the moment. "A good tool," she'd purred.

Norma swallowed against the thought and pushed it from her mind. Now wasn't the time to wallow. There was plenty of time to feel sorry for herself. Rudy needed her now. Pulling away from Lou, she steeled herself and forced a smile.

"You know where to go?" she asked, searching Lou's face, taking in its complexities. She wanted to remember it.

Lou nodded. "I've got the directions you gave me."

"You'll take back roads. And you've got Rudy's coat to hide that bump?"

Lou wiped her nose with the back of her hand. "Yeah," she said. "I do."

"I'll send Marcus and Dallas for you. They can meet you there."

"Okay."

"But at a certain point," Norma cautioned, "you're going to have to go on your own."

"I know."

"You have the location? The contact?"

"Yes."

Norma pursed her lips and eyed the baby bump. She put her hands on the round top of it. "What will you do if—"

"I'll be fine."

"But—"

"I'll be fine," Lou cut in. "It's not like I haven't done it before. And it's not like Dallas was a whole heck of a lot of help last time."

Norma laughed. "Or Rudy."

"Men," said Lou.

"They're all little boys when you get down to it," said Norma.

"Don't I know it. Some of them even name their weapons."

Norma stepped back, appraising the girl in front of her. Lou was a woman, a strong woman who, in earlier times, would have fought for the right to vote. She would have marched for equality while at the same time eschewing safe spaces or overbearing political correctness. She would have demanded that everyone get a fair shake. A woman of color, she would have had a powerful voice. People would have listened. Norma was convinced that, in another time, Lou would have done great things beyond the scope of her own life.

Now she was running for her life and those of her children. She was a knife-wielding woman born of the apocalypse and its unrelenting landscape. Norma was at once proud of her and deeply, profoundly sad for her.

"I love you," said Norma. "So does Rudy."

"I know," said Lou. "I love you too. Now let's stop with the crying and stuff. I've got to go get my knives."

"I can help you."

"No, thanks," said Lou. "I'll enjoy this. I know that's sick. But you know…"

Norma blinked. "I do."

"Could you get David ready?"

"Of course," said Norma. "I'd do anything for you."

Chapter 10

APRIL 17, 2054, 12:05 PM
SCOURGE +21 YEARS, 7 MONTHS
ATLANTA, GEORGIA

Sally Miller's head was pounding and her tongue was thick in her mouth. She opened her eyes, squinting against the crust that had formed in the corners and the bright daylight shining through the windows in her efficiency apartment. The fuzzy image of a large bottle on the coffee table reminded her why she felt the way she did.

Untangling herself from her sheets and wiping the crud from her lids, she rolled into a sitting position on the edge of the Murphy bed that dominated the small room. Sally shut her eyes, trying to stop the spinning that made her want to puke, and sat there for a good long minute before she tried to stand.

The room tilted when she finally put her feet on the floor and stood up. She had to quit drinking. Had to. The occasional morning like this was turning into too many of them. And now they'd become afternoons like this.

She lustily eyed the bottle before turning around to lift the bed into the recessed portion of the wall. The springs and hinges creaked as she collapsed the legs and closed the door that hid the bed. This was not ideal, but it was what she could afford, what the railroad provided.

The underground railroad. How did she end up involved in this? Was it benevolence or masochism? Maybe a little bit of both. Sally couldn't stand the idea of women being told what to do or not do with their bodies. More than that, though, Sally didn't allow herself to be happy. Never had. There was too much unhappiness, sadness, and pain in this post-Scourge/mid-drought world that there was something deep within her that truly believed any sense of peace was unfair to everyone else suffering. Like a monk prone to self-flagellation and vowed to a life of silent, selfless poverty, Sally was dedicated to the proposition that she should wallow.

With the bitter aftertaste of last night's liquor in her mouth, she slinked over to the sofa, the only piece of furniture in the place other than the coffee table, and sat on the edge of its misshapen foam cushions. Running one hand through her hair, combing it with her fingers, she used the other to pick up the bottle.

She cursed. It was empty. How much did she drink before passing out? The memory was as hazy as her vision, but her recollection of the near disaster and the men she'd killed was as clear as the empty glass liquor bottle. It was too close a call.

Sighing, and trying not to focus on the throbbing at her temples, Sally set the bottle back on the table and sat back on the sofa, sinking into the shapeless cushions that provided absolutely no comfort.

This was her life, and it was becoming increasingly unbearable. She understood why there was a saying about good deeds being punished, though the exact phrasing escaped her.

She laid her head back on the sofa and stared at the ceiling. A slow-spinning fan rotated above her, the pull chain swinging as the housing rattled against the popcorn ceiling.

To stop the unnatural spinning in her head, she tried focusing on a single fan blade, following it as it orbited the round off-white housing. That didn't help. It actually made it worse.

Hero

Sally choked down a thin rise of bile and dropped her chin to her chest. She was almost out again, the sour sting of the bile sitting in her throat as she teetered in the thin vale between consciousness and sleep, when a pounding at the door woke her up.

The pulse at her temples matched the impatient thump at her door as she wobbled toward it. It was different from the night before. This wasn't a headache from jonesing for a drink, from playing the game with half a deck. This was a headache from having called that jones and upping the ante. Using the back of the sofa to get her feet under herself, Sally reached the door and stood on her tiptoes to stick an eye to the peephole.

The fish-eye image of a man she didn't recognize fidgeted outside her apartment. He was scratching one arm and nervously checked over one shoulder then the next. He was about to knock again when Sally leaned into the door and spoke. She had to clear her throat twice when the first attempt came out like a croak and not a voice.

"Who is it?"

The man at the door looked straight at her through the peephole. His long, thin nose warped into a beak in the fish-eye lens of the hole.

"You can fool some of the people all of the time," he said in a hushed voice, "all of the people some of the time, but you can't fool all of the people all of the time."

Sally stepped back from the door and cursed under her breath. This dude was from the railroad. He was a porter, someone whose job it was to give the conductors assignments. She wasn't even sober yet, and they were back wanting more. They always wanted more. Exhaling to control the frustration building inside her, she stepped back to the door.

The man was up against the peephole now, speaking into it. "You can fool some—"

"A house divided cannot stand," Sally said, cutting him off.

"Four score and seven years ago," he replied.

Sally unlatched the four heavy deadbolts on her apartment and punched the electronic keypad on the wall next to the door. A mechanical whir preceded a series of clicks.

Pulling open the door a crack, Sally eyed the man without the distortion of the peephole. "Who are you?"

The man was wringing his hands. He glanced over each shoulder, leaning back. "Aren't you going to let me in?" he asked. "We shouldn't speak out here."

"Give me a name."

"We aren't supposed to—"

"Any name is fine," she said, arching an eyebrow to provide a clue. "Should I call you Lincoln?"

The man's eyes widened with understanding. He nodded vigorously. "Yes," he said. "I'm Lincoln."

"I'm Mary Todd," Sally replied. She widened the door and let the man inside, closed the door behind him, reset the locks, and stood at the entry, watching him take inventory of her small home.

She sensed his judgment. "What?"

The empty bottle was still on the table. There was another on the stove in the kitchen. At least they were a matching pair.

Lincoln shook his head nervously. "Nothing. Nothing at all. Should I sit down?"

Sally motioned toward the sofa. "Knock yourself out," she said and followed him there, sitting down after he sank onto one of the cushions.

The two sat there in silence for a moment. Lincoln scratched the back of his arm and adjusted himself on the sofa repeatedly, either unable to find a comfortable position or unable to find comfort within his own skin.

"Virgin?" Sally asked.

Lincoln tensed. He frowned and his brow furrowed. "I don't think that's any of your business," he said and not-so-subtly glanced at the empty bottle on the coffee table, "Mary Todd."

Sally raked her finger across her aching scalp and rolled her eyes. "That's not what I meant, Mis-ter Pres-i-dent," she said, affecting the accent from a famous actress who'd starred in films a hundred years ago. Although Sally couldn't remember the blonde woman's name, she'd seen pictures of her.

"I meant is this your first job for the railroad," she elaborated. "You're a new porter. You seem unsure of yourself."

Lincoln's tight expression relaxed. His cheeks flushed and he looked into his lap, shaking his head. His knee was bouncing up and down now. "I'm sorry," he said. "I thought…I didn't…"

Sally reached over and touched his knee. "It's not a problem. Just chill. We're safe here."

Lincoln chuckled. "I don't think it's safe anywhere, is it?"

The new guy hadn't admitted to her that this was his first job, but all of the signs were there. Paranoia, internal struggle, twitchiness. All of those things, plus he still had life in his eyes, the sweet softness of innocence.

Cynicism was the biggest thing recognizable on the faces and in the voices of the seasoned conductors and porters, Sally believed. She might pass them on the street, never having seen them before, and she'd know they were like her. It was in the hardened expressions, the way one walked with an awareness of the potential dangers big and small, the overwhelming sadness etched into the creases on their faces, the hunch of their shoulders.

"I guess nowhere's safe," she admitted. "But this is as safe as it's going to get for you now that you're in the game."

He skipped a response and went straight to the business at hand. "There's a new job for you," he said, having buried the lead. "I have the details. The time, place, pass phrase. I memorized it."

Sally stood up. There had to be another bottle somewhere. No way she'd finished the emergency stash. Moving around the sofa, she walked toward the front door and then sidestepped to the apartment's only closet.

Opening the door, she pulled out a footstool. Its feet scraped across the floor.

"Don't you want me to—" Lincoln, the eager beaver, started to say before she held up an angry index finger and shook it at him.

She climbed the stool and stood on her tiptoes, cursed her short stature, and reached onto the shelf above the hanging rack. Fishing around behind boxes and blankets, her expression brightened when she grabbed ahold of a long, thin glass bottle neck.

Sally dragged it free, wiggling it from the shelf, and held it up by the neck like a fisherman hoisting the day's big catch. It was a bottle of Tito's vodka. Her salivary glands flooded her mouth with the anticipation of a drink, almost tasting the sweet sting of it.

She'd heard rumors that after the Scourge, when the fabled Cartel ran Texas, getting a bottle of Tito's north of the wall was damn near impossible. Texans had hoarded the sweet corn taste to themselves.

Sally put the stool back into the closet, closed the door, and slinked back toward the sofa with renewed vigor. Without saying anything, she sat down and, with a twist of her hand, uncapped the bottle. It was room temperature, but she didn't have the patience to wait for it to chill in the freezer. Vodka was vodka. Warm, cold, tepid, its proof didn't change with the temperature.

Holding up the bottle to Lincoln, she raised her eyebrows and shook it as an offering.

Lincoln shook his head. "I don't drink."

She shook the bottle again. "Yeah, you do."

His expression soured. "No, I—"

Sally shoved the bottle at his chest. "You do. I don't trust people who don't drink."

Lincoln frowned but lifted the bottle and took a tentative swig. He swallowed and coughed. His eyes watered.

"Take another," said Sally. "The second swallow always goes down easier."

The newbie did as instructed. This time, his pull on the bottle was longer. His cheeks swelled and then shrank as he gulped down what he'd temporarily held there.

Sally motioned with her hand. "Gimme. I don't trust someone who drinks too much."

Lincoln coughed again. It started as a laugh but morphed. "Who *do* you trust?"

"Exactly," she said, and gulped down the vodka like it was ice water. Four, five, six healthy pulls later, she wiped her mouth with the back of her hand and set the bottle on the table.

Leaning back on the sofa, she glanced toward her guest and pulled one leg up under her. Sally studied him again. The anxiety had thawed.

"All right," she said. "Tell me why you're here."

"I already—"

She waved him off. "No. Not what your job is. Why are you part of this now? What sucked you onto the tracks?"

"I didn't think we were supposed to share personal information," he said. "They told me to keep it very—"

Sally glanced at the bottle and cleared her throat before shifting her attention back to Lincoln. "I don't know your real name; you don't know mine. Since they sent you here, they'll be moving me to another apartment after this next job. The least you can do, sweetie, is give me a little something."

The lights in her apartment flickered overhead. There was a hum as they fought the surge of power coursing through her building. Lincoln searched the room as if he'd find his answer in the strobing lights.

"It does that," she said. "Never mind it. Tell me your story."

"What's yours?"

Sally cocked her head to one side. "Nunya," she said. "I don't know you, Lincoln. You don't get to ask."

"I don't know you," he said. "You're asking."

"It's my house. And it's my vodka that gave you the gumption to pry. You don't get to pry."

They sat there, studying each other, measuring, gauging, judging.

Sally sighed. "I'm a masochist. That's as much as you get."

"My sister," he said. "Pop Guard showed up one day and found the basement, the false floor. Took the baby. Then they—" Lincoln's eyes welled, and his jaw tightened. He reached for the bottle and took a long healthy draw.

"They did what they do," said Sally. "I can fill in the rest."

Lincoln tipped the bottle toward Sally and she took it. Her drink was as long as his. She almost couldn't taste the liquor anymore. The inside of her cheeks, her tongue, her throat were going numb. Numb was good.

When he told her the job, the place and time, and gave her the pass code, she nodded silently and took in the information. It absorbed into her system like the vodka.

"Aren't you gonna write it down? Take notes?"

Sally chuckled and shook her head. A few minutes later, she ushered him out of the apartment, closed the door behind him, turned to appraise the apartment that soon wouldn't be her home anymore, and sank to the floor. In three years of working for the railroad, she'd lived in sixteen apartments in various parts of the city.

This one was her favorite. She liked its simplicity. Its walls were bare, its floors solid wood, and the bed was firm.

As the alcohol consumed her, Sally sobbed. Her body shuddered, her chin trembled, and she didn't understand the sudden burst of emotion. Then she did. It was her own story, her own past that had her chest heaving, her breaths coming almost too quickly for her to control them.

She didn't fight it. Sally allowed the pain to steep. That was best. It was always best to let the pain tear her down and build her anew, strengthen her resolve.

Sally got to her feet and struggled toward the sofa. She collapsed onto it facedown, praying for sleep to take hold.

Hero

In a few hours she'd be sober and out on the streets again. In the darkness of night, it was her job to be the light for someone else.

CHAPTER 11

APRIL 17, 2054, 4:45 PM
SCOURGE +21 YEARS, 7 MONTHS
NEW BOSTON, TEXAS

The cuffs at Andrea Cruz's ankles felt like they were slicing into her skin. They weren't, but they'd rubbed her legs so raw each step was an exercise in pain.

She clenched her jaw and drew slow, measured breaths in through her nose. Her son's hand in hers, she walked as deliberately as possible. There was no way Andrea was going to let Javier see her as anything other than a pillar of strength and determination.

The pungent odor of sweat and grime wafted past her, and she felt a presence at her side. It took everything in her not to look. She didn't have to. Andrea knew who was there.

"How we doing?" asked Warner. "I worry about you. Carrying all that weight so low. You know they say if you carry low, it's a boy."

Andrea tried holding her breath. Keeping her eyes forward, she tightened her grip on Javi's tiny hand.

"It's an old wives' tale, sure enough," said Warner. "But you're glowing too. That's another sign of a boy. I heard tell that if a woman is having a girl, the baby steals her beauty. Gives her bad skin and such. That ain't the case with you. Maybe some of these other women. Not you, Andrea."

They were walking south. The sun was to their right as it sank in the pale blue north Texas sky. After they'd passed a prison unit on Texas Highway 98, they'd stopped and rested. It wasn't long enough. All the break served to do was tighten the muscles in her legs and lower back that she'd already taxed.

"Then again," said Warner, "you've been ornery. Moody. Grumpy even. That, they say, is a girl's doing."

Warner hadn't stopped talking the entirety of the trip. He'd moved from woman to woman, offering his wisdom about anything and everything. This was his second attempt to engage Andrea.

"Then again," he said as if playing his own devil's advocate, "you've been through it. I mean to say, Andrea, you got every right to be testy."

He stressed the consonants, lingered on the vowels. It accentuated his twang and made listening to him all the more unbearable. Andrea tried to focus on the metal rubbing against the popped blisters at her ankles. It was more palatable than Warner's incendiary diatribe.

He sidled up closer to her, his stench drawing a line of bile up her throat. She swallowed it and winced. His voice was a whisper, a secret between the two of them.

"See, here's the thing," he said. "Things ain't gonna get better. You're just gonna get testier when you find out what I got planned."

She didn't bite. He wanted her to bite. He was baiting her. Dangling a hook.

Warner put his hand to his chest, half turning his body toward her and almost walking backward to keep his gaze on her. "See, I'm a businessman. That's what I do. I see a need, I fill it. Pure and simple. People need babies. Well, not all people. You don't need babies. You got one. Javier's a fine young man. Strapping even."

It took everything in her not to punch him in the throat, to cut out his tongue for having said her son's name aloud. He didn't deserve the privilege. Andrea kept walking. Her ankles must be bleeding now. Something warm and wet was squishing underneath her foot inside her shoe.

"You've had your allotment," he said. "But some people, good people, can't have babies. More precisely, they can't have *a* baby." He held up his index finger. "One baby. Not a single baby, let alone two or three."

Andrea cupped her free hand under her belly. The life inside her kicked. A soft thump to remind her of what was coming, that any day now those kicks would be against the air. Those perfect feet, soft and pink, new to the world beyond that inside her womb. It made her want to puke. She wasn't ready. Not like this.

"I'm just seizing an opportunity here, Andrea." Warner raised his hands and made air quotes with his index and middle fingers. "See, the *government*, as they like to call themselves, and their *Pop Guard*"— more air quotes—"use the drought as an excuse for their *one family, one child* dictate."

Warner spoke with his hands. His cadence sped up. He was into this. Excited by it. He was telling his story to someone who had to listen to him. She was, in every sense, a captive audience.

"The Scourge killed off more than enough folks to compensate for our lack of food and water now," he said. "Sheesh, what was it? Two-thirds of the world gone?" Warner snapped his fingers. "Like that. Two of every three people, vanished."

Andrea had been a child when the Scourge took her father and her older sister. Her mother lived for four years. She'd gotten a job with the Cartel to provide shelter and protection for the two of them. One day she hadn't come home from work. It was an entire week before Andrea left the house, waiting for her mother to return.

Bad things happened then. Flashes of those things still haunted her, gave her nightmares, made her fiercely protective of her own child. The boy didn't have a father. Neither of the children did. It made her two parents in one. It gave her resolve. She would do anything to stay together, to prevent Javier from living a life as she had. She would do anything to rescue the unplanned life growing within her. Pain bred strength. As much as she'd endured, Andrea was made of steel.

"So," said Warner, snapping her from the brief reverie, "there's plenty of food and water. Even if there ain't much. The real thing is power." Warner shook his finger didactically and winked. "Power. That's what it's about. The *government* saw what happened to every other group that tried to control things after the Scourge. They were outnumbered or spread too thin and lost control. These folks, the ones on the throne now, they ain't about to let that happen."

Andrea uncapped the canteen strapped across her body and took a sip of the warm, metallic-tasting water. She offered some to Javier with the warning to drink slowly.

"They want your children so their power can grow," he said. "There's no real shortage. It ain't like that as far as I can tell. Yeah, things are tough, sure. But limiting births like they did in China back in the last century? They ain't gotta do that."

Andrea took the canteen from Javier and recapped it. She slung its strap over her head and adjusted it at her side.

"They take your kids to indoctrinate them," said Warner. "That the right word? Indoctrinate?" He repeated the word, trying different inflections, testing it. "Indoctrinate? I got it, Blessing?"

Blessing, who was up ahead with the front of the line, glanced back and nodded.

"Yeah," said Warner. "They want to make your kids think like them. As they grow, their numbers grow. Their power grows. They control everyone and everything. It's smart, if you think about it."

Andrea thought about the man who'd fathered Javier. Although his name escaped her, his brutality didn't. That was impossible to forget. For the longest time, she'd thought him the most barbaric, heartless human on the Earth. He placed second behind the man next to her.

"Sure, the government don't mess with some of the tribes that run scot-free around the cities," said Warner. "But those people, those savages, ain't about to take on a government yet. For now, they're happier than pigs in—"

"I get it," said Andrea, giving in to the temptation to shut him up.

She couldn't take it anymore. His droning on and on, pontificating about his plans like the evil villain from some twentieth-century spy thriller she'd once seen projected on the wall of a bar in Abilene.

Her voice was sharp, exasperated. "You're a businessman," she said. "This is business. It's not personal. You're going to sell us to the government. The government will take my children. They'll put me to work or worse. You'll get your cash or your booze, or however they pay you, and then you'll prey on someone else. I know how it works."

She expected him to tell her she was right, that she was too smart for her own good, and that it was best to keep her thoughts to herself. Thinking aloud wasn't good for anyone, she expected him to tell her.

Warner didn't do any of those things. Instead, he whistled. It was a long sweet whistle that somehow was melodically condescending. The sustained, shifting pitch of it told her, without Warner having to say a word, that she was wrong.

Am I? How could I be wrong?

That was what the vigilantes did. That was what she'd heard. If they caught you, they sold you to the Pop Guard.

"Hey, Blessing," Warner said playfully. "Buddy, come back here."

Blessing stopped in place. He stood there on the pitted asphalt of the two-lane state highway and waited for the line to pass, for Warner, Andrea, and Javier to catch up to him. When they did, Blessing took steps to keep pace. Turning toward Warner as they walked, he raised an eyebrow.

Warner aimed a thumb at Andrea and chuckled. "You know what our little friend said? It's good. You're gonna laugh."

Blessing lowered the eyebrow. His expression flattened and he turned his attention toward the road ahead. He couldn't have looked more disinterested if he'd lain down and closed his eyes.

Oblivious, Warner grinned, the smile stretching across his face, his black eyes glinting with humor. "She thinks we're selling her to the government, to the Pop Guard," he said. "That's cute, ain't it?"

Blessing marched forward. His expression unchanged, like he hadn't registered what Warner said, he shifted his attention to Andrea. They locked eyes until it was uncomfortable and she looked away.

"Nothing cute about it," said Blessing. His voice was monotone, robotic almost. But it carried weight, electricity. "Your sense of humor is lacking."

That only made Warner's grin broaden. The man beamed. He took off his hat and ran his fingers through his hair. Then he put the cap back on his head and adjusted it until the brim was just so at his forehead. "You don't say nothing for hours or days on end. When you do, you're a critic. Figures. Reminds me of that old joke about the monk."

Blessing rolled his eyes. Andrea figured he had heard the joke before, but was playing along.

The joke was a cruelty, she understood. It was meant to delay telling her what his intentions truly were. If he wasn't selling her to the government, what was he doing? Where was he marching all of these women and their children?

"This man decides to join a monastery," Warner said. "He's had it with the world. His family died in the Scourge, and he can't take fending for himself anymore. So he climbs up this mountain and reaches the top."

A tug on the chain between Andrea's feet interrupted her stride. She hitched, but the slack returned and she moved forward a step at a time. Her mind raced about where it was they were going.

Dallas? It isn't Dallas, is it? Please don't be Dallas.

"When he gets to the top, he meets the head monk. The monk

tells him he can join the order, but he's got to take a vow of silence. He can only say two words every five years when he goes before the council of monks."

There was a tug against Andrea's ankles. The cuffs dug into the front of her legs. She tried looking back, but the tug of the woman in front of her prevented it. Andrea kept shuffling.

"After five years, the man goes before the council," says Warner, as if he's got a rapt audience. "They ask him if he has anything to say. He does. He tells them, 'Bed hard.' That's all he says and he goes back to praying or whatever."

A sharp pain dug into Andrea's shins. She tottered forward at the tug, stopping her momentum. A shrill cry came from the back of the line. Warner ignored it and kept walking, talking.

"After another five years, same thing. He gets to the council. He says, 'Food bad.'"

The line stopped. None of the women or their children were moving now. Blessing's attention had shifted from Warner to whatever was happening at the end of the chain. He craned his neck to focus. The cry had become a moan.

"The man goes back another five years later," Warner said, finishing his joke with the relish of a man who couldn't wait to share the punch line, raising his voice to be heard over the pained wail of a woman in agony. "It's been fifteen years now, and he's said four words. The council asks him to speak. He tells them, 'I quit.' The head monk laughs at him and says, 'I ain't surprised. You been complaining since you got here.'"

Warner snorted a laugh. His Adam's apple slid up and down along his throat. Andrea wanted to slam her palm into it. She was close enough. She could do it. Catch him off guard and inflict a little pain on this sadist who trafficked people's lives.

She let her anger give way to worry and managed to maneuver her body enough to see the commotion behind her. The moan had given way to heavy breathing and grunts.

Hero

It was a familiar pattern of sounds now. While Warner ignored it, Blessing made his way toward the end of the chain. Andrea recognized what was happening.

The woman was in labor. She was about to give birth right here on Texas Highway 98, a few miles south of a prison, and north of whatever hell awaited them.

Chapter 12

APRIL 17, 2054, 10:45 PM
SCOURGE +21 YEARS, 7 MONTHS
GREENSBORO, NORTH CAROLINA

Marcus rubbed his eyes and tilted his hat back on his head. He yawned and leaned his head against the window, vibrating from the train's coarse movement on the tracks. The vibration was in his bones.

"Can't sleep?" asked Dallas.

"Nope," Marcus replied.

Dallas was fidgeting, twiddling his thumbs, staring out the window. It was dark outside. His reflection looked back at him in the dim light of the train car.

Marcus had paid for a private cabin on the train. It wasn't much more than the cheap seats, and it gave them more privacy.

Dallas warned it made them more of a target for the bandits, should they pick this train to rob. He hoped that because it was a late train, they might skip it. Bandits had to sleep too.

Marcus told Dallas it was better to have the privacy. They could have their weapons out and would be ready for whatever came their way.

The train reached a curve in the tracks. The wheels screeched as they leaned into the rails, and Marcus felt his body shifting with the momentum.

"I wish you'd brought Lou with you," said Marcus. "Would have saved us a lot of trouble."

Dallas frowned. "What do you mean?"

"We're going south to go north again," said Marcus. "It's a huge waste of time. You could have brought her and the kid with you. Then we could have made a much shorter trip to wherever it is this Garden of Eden's supposedly—"

"We couldn't do that," said Dallas. He leaned forward in his seat, planting his elbows on his knees and using his hands to accentuate his words. "No way we could do that."

"Why not?"

"Too dangerous," said Dallas. "The two of us, David, by ourselves? No way we could get to the rendezvous point without help. Did you see the scanners they were using when we boarded the train?"

Marcus had seen them. Every child held their hand up to a scanner when they boarded. He'd seen the scanner buzz one kid, and the family was pulled from the boarding queue. The mother had protested and tried to run. She didn't get far.

"I saw it," said Marcus. "Biochips, right?"

Dallas nodded. "Yep. When you have a kid, the hospital or doctor embeds a chip in the back of the baby's hand. The parents get a chip too, and the chips all match."

"What if they don't have the baby at a hospital?"

"You go find somewhere to get it done," said Dallas.

"And if you don't?"

"If you don't have one or if it doesn't match, they take the kid. That's how they know if you have more than one kid. That's what stops families from splitting to escape. If they find a pregnant woman with a chip, they know she's had a kid. And she can't take the chip out. Leaves a nasty scar on the back of the hand."

"Can't you fake it?" asked Marcus. "Isn't there a black market?"

Despite him and Marcus being the only two in the compartment, Dallas looked around with paranoid, wide eyes and lowered his voice. "The government's always changing the chips," he said. "People try. They always get caught. Always."

Marcus frowned in a way that expressed understanding. He nodded slowly.

"See?" asked Dallas. "There was no way she could come. David neither."

"Then you should have sent me a letter," said Marcus. "Would have cost me half as much for the train, and it's a lot easier to move around as a loner. Would've saved you money too. Plus you wouldn't have left your very pregnant wife alone. Still can't believe that, Dallas."

Dallas looked away from Marcus. "No such thing as very pregnant. And you wouldn't have answered the letter."

Marcus nodded. "You're probably right."

"About pregnancy or you ignoring the letter?"

"Both," said Marcus. "Still, this seems like a stupid way to go about it. There had to be an easier way."

Dallas sniffed and wiped his nose with the back of his hand. "Maybe. But we're pretty desperate. We ran through a thousand different plans before settling on this one. Believe me, I didn't want to do this."

The train rumbled around another curve. Marcus felt the inertia tug at his body. He pressed his hands flat on the seat to keep himself in place. There was a knock on the door to their cabin.

"Who is it?" Marcus asked. His hand moved to the Mossberg shotgun on the seat next to him. His eyes were on the solid sliding door that separated their cabin from the train's narrow corridor.

"Porter," said the voice on the other side of the door. "Would you like anything to eat or drink?"

Marcus turned to Dallas and lowered his voice. "They have food?"

Dallas shrugged.

Marcus raised his voice. "No, thanks. We're good."

"Okay then," said the porter.

Releasing his grip on the shotgun, Marcus motioned to it. "I'm surprised they let us bring these on the train no questions asked. Back in the day, there was no way you'd get a weapon on a train."

"I don't think they care," said Dallas. "Like I said, I kinda think the government likes the violence. Plus, we're paying customers, so…"

"Doesn't make a lot of sense," said Marcus. "Then again, nothing does anymore. Nothing has made sense for a long time."

The two sat in silence for a few minutes, the jostle of the train filling the space between them. It was loud. Occasionally a tree branch would scrape the window as the train rushed by it. The high-pitched sound made Dallas jump every time.

Marcus reached for his shotgun, slid it over, and laid it on his lap. The butt was against the exterior wall of the train, the barrel aimed at the door.

"Thank you," said Dallas.

"For what?"

"Doing this."

Marcus chuckled. "I haven't done anything yet."

"You know what I mean."

"Yeah," said Marcus, "I do. You're welcome."

Laughter from the cabin adjacent to them filtered into their space. It was mixed company. At least one woman and a couple of men, Marcus thought. There were three distinct voices, laughs. Maybe more.

"Can I ask you something?" asked Dallas.

"Can I stop you?"

"Why did you ignore us?"

"Ignore you?"

"Why did you leave?" said Dallas. "Then stop writing, stop

responding? It hurt Lou, you know."

Marcus sank in his seat. He adjusted the plant of his boots on the cabin's floor. He took a deep breath through his nostrils and exhaled through a frown. "This again?"

"You never really answered me," said Dallas. "Well, you did. But you didn't."

Another burst of laughter came from the cabin next to them. There were two women. Marcus could distinctly hear four voices. It was louder this time, the kind of laughter that came from drinking alcohol. Now he'd never get any sleep.

The train jerked to one side. Then it corrected and shimmied to the other.

"I'm no good, Dallas," said Marcus. "That's the beginning and end of it. I'm no good to myself, no good to anyone else."

"Need help with that cross?"

"What?"

"You're being a martyr," said Dallas. "I'm not asking to hear your self-loathing, woe-is-me crap, Marcus. I want to know the truth."

Dallas's tone surprised Marcus. The kid sounded like a man.

"All right," said Marcus. "Truth, then."

"Yep."

"I left because I wasn't wanted anymore. That's not self-loathing. I'm not playing the martyr. It's the honest truth."

"Who didn't want you?"

Marcus chuckled wryly. "Who *did*?"

Dallas's expression flattened.

"Seriously," said Marcus, "I was a liability. I don't remember if you were there or not, but after the last big blowup in Baird, when that army of losers came looking for me and killed good people, some things were said. Those things were right."

"About you bringing as much death as you stop?"

"Yeah, that."

"You can't help that you're a magnet for that stuff," said Dallas.

"If I remember, you never started anything. You just finished it. Lou told me about what you did for that woman."

"Which woman?"

Dallas raised an eyebrow. "Lola? The one who came to your house in Rising Star. You helped her find her kid. That's what started the whole Mad Max thing, right?"

A smile threatened to form at the corner of his mouth. Marcus hadn't heard that nickname in years.

Mad Max.

A reference to his resilience and penchant for over-the-top violence to survive whatever he faced. Of all the movies he'd watched in the early years after the Scourge, *Road Warrior* hadn't been one of them. The humor of it gave way to the memory of what ultimately befell Lola and Sawyer and Penny.

A pain as acute as that when he'd seen their bodies in the yard, on the floor, in the bed, tightened in his chest. It surpassed the deaths of his wife and son in the early days of the Scourge. Not because he loved them more, but because he'd failed to protect his charges a second time.

His mind flashed to the burial plots behind his house outside Rising Star, Texas. Marcus looked at his hands and balled them into fists, remembering the cold, hard feel of the chisel in his hands as he carved the epitaphs on their graves.

A prayer he'd long since pushed to the darkest parts of his memory clawed its way forward, and he whispered it, the words hanging on his lips. It was like he'd never forgotten them or, better yet, tried to forget them.

"As far as the east is from the west," he said, "so far has he removed our transgressions from us."

Dallas looked confused. "What?"

Marcus looked up without lifting his chin. "Nothing. It's something I used to say before killing a man. Sometimes I'd say it after."

Dallas looked at Marcus's hands, then back at Marcus. The train jostled him and he extended an arm to brace himself.

"There was a farmer," said Marcus. "Before I went to Atlanta, he gave a truck to me. Told me I didn't have to thank him for it."

"I think I remember this," said Dallas.

"He told me that if I took the truck, that meant I would be taking my violence with me. He said it was more than an even trade."

"Yeah," said Dallas, nodding, "I do remember this."

"Lou tried defending me. She told the farmer that I'd kept Baird safe for more than a year. She was sassy when she said it."

"Sounds like Lou."

Both men chuckled.

"The farmer was defiant," Marcus went on, his eyes in some distant place now. "He said I'd nearly gotten everyone in town killed that day, and the week before that, and the month before that. He said my being sheriff had only brought him a never-ending rot in his gut. He said he'd give me ten trucks if it meant I'd never come back."

Dallas scratched his chin. "That didn't mean you couldn't write, stay in touch, let Lou know how you were doing."

Marcus chuckled, his gaze still absent. "Rudy defended me, sort of. Norma stopped him. I remember looking at her. Her eyes told me she loved me like a brother, but she didn't want me around anymore."

"Yeah, but—"

Marcus blinked back to the moment. "It was better I keep my distance. Once I got settled in Virginia, it was better. Lou knew I was alive. I was okay. That was enough."

"It really wasn't," said Dallas. "You hurt her."

"Better than getting her killed."

Dallas frowned and was about to speak when the pop of gunfire and a scream from the room next door stopped him cold. The hair on Marcus's neck stood on end when another pop cut short a second screaming plea for mercy.

"Bandits," said Dallas, his eyes wide.

Marcus stood, Mossberg in hand. He motioned for Dallas to grab his weapon. Dallas picked it up, shouldered it, and looked to Marcus for direction.

The Mossberg in Marcus's hand was a unique weapon. It was a short-barreled shotgun with a pistol "bird's-head" grip. Technically, the Shockwave model was a pistol-grip weapon with a fourteen-inch barrel. From muzzle to grip it was less than twenty-seven inches, which meant it wasn't really a shotgun, but it walked like a duck, it talked like one, and its quack was loud as hell.

Marcus's left hand was under the pump-action barrel, between the grip and the nylon strap. He racked it, snicked off the gun's safety, and motioned for Dallas to open the door.

The world slowed as Marcus stepped into the narrow hallway. Two men were to his right, both wearing bandanas over their faces. They held pistols aimed into the cabin in front of them. They didn't see him. They didn't hear him.

Marcus unloaded the first of the nine one-and-three-quarter-inch mini-shells into the man closest to him. The buckshot hit the man in the side and he grunted in pain. Dropping his weapon, he reached for the peppering of wounds.

Marcus pumped again and pulled the trigger. A second blast hit the man's face and he toppled back into his partner.

With the Mossberg raised above his shoulder and in front of him, Marcus took two deliberate steps forward. Pump. Boom. Pump. Boom. The sound was deafening in the narrow confines of the train corridor.

The blasts dropped the second man. Both were on the floor writhing in pain.

Dallas was in the hall behind him now. Marcus pumped again. Five shots left.

"Deal with them," he said of the men in the hallway. He didn't wait for Dallas to respond.

Two more steps and he was at the open doorway at the moment a third bandit peeked his head out from the cabin. Marcus lifted the Shockwave and pulled the trigger. The mini-shell left major wounds on the man's face and neck. He dropped to his knees, his cries deafening in the small space.

Pump. Four shots left.

Marcus stepped over the men and into the room. He lifted a boot and drove the heel into the man on his knees, hitting him squarely in the jaw. It knocked him unconscious and he dropped to the cabin floor with a whack. The train shimmied on the tracks, knocking Marcus off balance. He caught himself against a wall and scanned the room for more threats. There were none. He pried the pistol from the bandit's cold hand and tucked it in his waistband behind his belt buckle.

It was a Glock. Not sexy, but reliable, and unlikely to jam.

Slumped in the corner, still in his seat, was an older man, his chin on his chest. There was a hole in the center of his forehead and a Rorschach of blood on the wall behind him. A matching wound was at the center of his chest.

A woman was next to him, holding his hand, her alabaster skin almost translucent with shock. Mascara stained her cheeks, making her look like a crying clown. Marcus didn't know women still wore makeup.

Across from them was another couple. The man had money in his trembling hands. A faint yellow puddle was at his feet. A broad dark spot painted his pants at the crotch. An unconscious woman was at his side, leaning awkwardly in the corner of her seat at the window.

Marcus aimed the Mossberg at her. "She okay?"

The man nodded. "F-f-f-fainted."

Marcus wondered how people so ill-equipped for violence had made it this long. Hadn't they seen death? Hadn't they killed?

The money in the man's hands was folded neatly in a thick stack. Marcus wondered why money was still a thing. He would have figured digital currency would have long ago replaced otherwise worthless cotton paper. Why did money have any value at all now?

Somehow these people, worthless as money should have been in a post-apocalyptic world, were still alive. At the moment, they had Marcus to thank for that. He considered emptying the Mossberg to put them out of their misery.

"There are more," the woman said tentatively, her voice warbling with emotion.

Marcus spun to her and lowered the weapon. Behind him Dallas put a bullet into one of the men on the floor. The woman jumped, her body shaking uncontrollably now.

"More what?" Marcus asked.

The man answered. "Robbers." He rested the money on his knee and plucked at his crotch. His sour face flushed and he looked at the floor in front of him. The woman next to him was still out, her body jostling with the train's movement on the tracks.

"Where?" asked Marcus.

The man hooked a thumb behind him. "Back there."

"How many?"

The man held up three fingers.

Marcus nodded. He stepped back into the hall. Dallas stood over two dead men. They locked eyes and Marcus motioned with his fingers toward the front of the train car.

"Are we doing this?" asked Dallas.

"What do you think?"

Marcus started moving. Heads peeked out from cabins and disappeared back inside. Doors slammed shut.

Marcus bumped against the walls with his shoulders. "They should put locks on these things," he said. "Would cut down on the crime."

He reached the end of the car. The cabin door was open. Inside were large canvas bags. They were on the floor, on the seats, open and empty. Marcus recognized them as the kinds of bags that held weapons and ammunition. This was where the bandits had waited until starting their assault. Instead of attacking a moving train, as Dallas had suggested might happen, these bad guys had bought tickets.

"We could wait here," said Dallas, joining him at the doorway. "Ambush them when they come back."

Marcus considered it. Not a bad idea. It would contain the violence to come. But what havoc would these bandits wreak if they waited, if they allowed them to go compartment to compartment and person to person? They'd already killed one man in cold blood.

He shook his head. "We can't wait for them." He stepped to the door at the front of the car and pressed his face to the window that looked into the car in front of them.

That car didn't have cabins. It had a narrower center aisle and rows of seats on either side. There were six across, three on each side of the aisle. No bandits. There was blood on the floor. It leached from underneath one of the rows to the left.

Marcus clenched his jaw. He heaved open the heavy metal door and stepped onto the platform between the two cars. A wind, colder than he expected, swirled around him and cut through him.

The night air was dry, the sky above cloudless. Stars twinkled against the black. A waxing gibbous moon glowed white. Marcus adjusted the black hat on his head. A shiver ran along his spine and he tugged open the door in front of him.

Dallas shut the door behind him, and heads turned. Eyes widened. Chins trembled. Hands went into the air.

"Where did they go?" asked Marcus, knowing the answer.

Several hands pointed toward the next car. Whimpers grew into sobs to his left. Marcus moved forward, one slow step at a time, his body turned to the side to accommodate the narrow aisle.

"How many?" Marcus asked. "Three?"

Heads nodded. More cries. Marcus stepped over the spreading pool of blood in the aisle and looked to his left.

A young woman was slumped into the empty middle seat, her

hands still clutching her bag. The man at the window tugged at his hair, threatening to pull it out by the roots. His red eyes darted around the room until they found Marcus.

"She wouldn't give it to them," he said. "There's nothing in it. It's empty. But she wouldn't give it to them."

Marcus's voice was like a low growl. He sounded almost feral. "We'll get them. All of them."

He moved faster now. Dallas was behind him, walking backward. The men were back to back, keeping watch for each other as they approached the front of the car.

Marcus stopped at the window and peered through it. The next car was identical to this one. The bandits were there. Three of them. They worked the rows one at a time. All three were armed. One had a handgun; two had rifles or shotguns. With their backs turned, and the grime on the windows, Marcus couldn't tell for sure. He paused to pull more shotgun shells from his coat pocket and feed them into the bottom of the Mossberg.

He slung open the first door and stepped back into the chill. The wind swirled around him, and he put a free hand on the top of his hat. He pulled it down on his brow, above his eyes, and glanced back at Dallas.

"As soon as I open this door, they're gonna turn around and fire," he said above the whoosh of the wind and the deafening rumble of the steel wheels on the tracks. "I'm gonna drop to a knee and fire. I need you to stand here, firing the second that door swings open."

Dallas nodded. He steadied himself against a railing and drew the rifle to his shoulder.

Marcus knelt down and laid the Mossberg on the lip in front of the door. He pulled the pistol from his waistband and checked the magazine.

"Ready?" he called out to Dallas.

"Ready."

Marcus pulled back the door. Dallas fired his rifle, a percussive blast popping above Marcus's head. Then a second shot. A third. A fourth.

Pistol already leveled in his right hand, Marcus raised his left to the grip and fired. The Glock 19 popped and he pulled the trigger again.

The onslaught sounded like firecrackers. Multiple rounds drilled into the bandits before they knew what hit them. Two of them dropped immediately, tumbling awkwardly over one another into the aisle. The third was hit twice but kept his balance. He returned fire, slamming two rounds into the rear wall of the train car before Dallas finished him.

The echo of gunfire evaporated into the car. It gave way to heavy breathing, sighs and prayers of relief, emotional whimpers. Ahead of him was what was left of the bandits. Two of them didn't move, either unconscious or dead. The third was conscious. His moan was a low hum, barely audible above the other noises and mechanical pulse of the train.

Marcus motioned toward the bodies with his chin. "Keep an eye on them for a second."

"What—" Dallas started to question.

"Just do it."

Marcus squeezed past Dallas and marched back to the previous cabin until he reached the frightened, pale man next to the dead woman slumped in her seat. He put his hand on the man's shoulder, looped it under his arm, and lifted him into the aisle. Then he placed the Glock into the man's hand.

"You ever fired one of these?"

The man's face was drawn long with shock. He nodded. His teeth chattered.

"I'm sorry about her," Marcus said. "Wife?"

Tears welled in the man's eyes and spilled onto his cheeks. He didn't speak.

"Come with me."

Marcus tugged him along the aisle to the next car and to the dying bandit on the aisle floor. They stopped there and stood over the man. Dallas inched out of their way.

The man glanced at the bloody criminal on the floor and back at Marcus, the gun hanging loosely in his hand at his side.

"Do it," said Marcus.

"Do…what?"

"Finish him," said Marcus. "Eye for an eye."

"I don't understand."

"They killed your wife," said Marcus.

The man waved the gun across the heap of bodies in front of him. For a moment it appeared as though he might pull the trigger. He didn't. He lifted his head and locked eyes with Battle.

"Nothing's going to bring her back," he said. "Nothing I do, nothing you do. Nothing. She's gone. For nothing."

The man lowered the Glock, then offered it to Marcus. He lowered his head, turned, and started walking back to his seat, to his dead wife.

Marcus took the gun and started to put it back into his waistband, but stopped short. Extending his arm, he took aim at the gurgling man on the floor and pulled the trigger twice.

It silenced the car. It silenced the bandit. But the dead woman's husband spoke.

Voice cracking, he called out to Marcus, "Why did you do that?"

Marcus put the Glock into his waistband behind his belt buckle and stomped toward his own car. Dallas followed. As they passed the dead woman's husband on their way to the back of the car, Marcus shot the man a steely glare.

"He had it coming," said Marcus.

He gripped the handle on the car door and slid it open, stepping onto the platform. The wind whistled through the gap between the cars. Cold air filled his lungs when he inhaled.

Marcus bent down and picked up his Mossberg from where he'd

left it on the lip beyond the entry. Moving with speed and against the whipping wind, he led Dallas to the second car. His gaze was straight ahead, intentionally avoiding the dead woman in her seat. As he passed her row, he muttered a prayer and kept moving.

When they'd entered the third car, Marcus made his way past the bandits' cabin and to the one next to his. The survivors were huddled next to one another, consoling and commiserating.

Marcus stood in the open doorway. A strong whiff of urine stung his nostrils. "Why'd they pick you?"

"What?" asked the man with the money still in his hand.

"This cabin," Marcus said. "They skipped a bunch of others. Why you first, before they hit the cars with open seating?"

"I went to the ladies'," said the woman. "They waited for me outside the door and forced me back here."

Marcus nodded. "They're dead," he said to the cabin. "Every one of them."

He backed away from the opening and took the few steps back to his cabin. He sank into his seat, resting the Mossberg in his lap. The Glock's pistol grip dug into his belly at his navel. He ignored it.

Dallas sat across from him. "Dumb luck."

"What was dumb luck?"

"The woman going to take a piss," he said. "She holds it a little longer and they're all alive."

Marcus laid his head back, tipped his hat forward over his eyes, and sighed. Maybe now he could sleep. Chances of anyone else trying to rob the train between here and the next stop were less than nothing, as far as he was concerned.

"Could be," said Marcus. "A lot of things in life are dumb luck if you look at it through that lens. But if that woman doesn't go to the bathroom, we don't hear the bandits. They run amok in the other cars. More people die. Ten? Twenty? Half the train?"

"Still dumb luck," said Dallas. "Bad luck for the people next to us. Good luck for the others."

"Or it's not luck at all," Marcus countered.

"What's that supposed to mean?"

Marcus opened his eyes and tipped back the brim of his hat. He shrugged. "My dad used to say that if you aren't doing what you're not supposed to be doing, things that aren't supposed to happen won't happen."

"That doesn't make any sense."

"Sure it does," said Marcus. "Don't put yourself in bad spots."

"I get what it means, I'm saying it doesn't apply here. These people weren't doing anything bad. They were sitting on a train heading south. They paid for their tickets. They were minding their own business. None of them deserved what happened. It was just bad luck."

Marcus sat up and withdrew the gun from his waistband. He set it on the seat next to him and rubbed his eyes with his thumb and index finger. "That's assuming you believe in luck," he said. "In my experience, luck has very little to do with anything."

"Predetermination and all that?"

Marcus snorted a laugh.

"What's funny?"

"Nothing's funny," said Marcus. "I never expected to hear those words come out of your mouth is all."

Dallas folded his arms across his chest and crossed his feet at the ankles. "I'm not stupid," he said. "I can read."

Marcus took off his hat, setting it atop the Glock next to him. He raked his fingers through the thinning hair on his head. He needed a shower. "I'm not saying you're stupid. Lou wouldn't have you if you were a moron. I just didn't expect such a philosophical conversation. I expected to be asleep by now."

"You started it."

Marcus rubbed his chin. The scruff was like fine sandpaper on his fingertips. Dallas was a man, but he was a child. Lou mothered this one. No doubt.

He sighed. "Look, Dallas, I'm not attacking you. I'm only trying to express my view of the world. That's it. Doesn't mean you're wrong or stupid or need someone to change your diaper and fix your boo-boos. None of that."

"Then what's your point?"

"The longer we talk, the more points I need to make."

Dallas's expression tightened. His frown deepened. "You're going to lecture me, then."

"I don't have the energy or the inclination to lecture you."

"Then *what?*"

"One," said Marcus, "I'm putting this to bed. Whatever residual anger you have about me going my own way and not communicating with you—"

Dallas uncrossed his legs. "With Lou."

"With Lou," said Marcus, "you need to get over it. I'm here now. I'm helping. Against my better judgment, I'm doing what you asked me to do. So enough. Okay?"

"What's two?"

"My original thesis," said Marcus. "It's that there's no such thing as luck. What's going to happen is going to happen. You can either put yourself in a position to be there when it does, or you don't. I'm saying these people put themselves on the train. That woman put herself in the bathroom. The bandits picked this trip. So did we. It all converged."

Marcus held his hands out in front of him and laced his fingers together, sliding them in and out for effect. He held them there until Dallas spoke.

"Sounds like luck to me."

Marcus chuckled. "You believe what you want to believe. I'm not trying to convert you, I'm only making conversation, sharing my thoughts on the cosmos."

The train squealed, the car shimmying on the tracks. Thinking they were done talking, Marcus lay back and closed his eyes.

"That's saying we have no control over our own fate," said Dallas. "I thought you were a religious man. I thought you prayed. Why would you pray if you think everything is already determined?"

Marcus opened one eye.

"If you've got no choice in anything you do, if it's all on a map—"

Marcus lifted his finger to his lips. "Shhh," he said. "You're doing what you're not supposed to be doing. That means something that's not supposed to happen is going to happen."

"What do you mean?"

Marcus opened his other eye. "I'm going to shoot you and go back to Chatham."

Dallas opened his mouth to say something but thought better of it.

Marcus shut his eyes and leaned his head against the cold window glass. No sooner had he begun to drift off than the train's whistle blew and the train lurched.

They were at their first stop. Four more to go before they hit the wall.

Chapter 13

APRIL 17, 2054, 11:55 PM
SCOURGE +21 YEARS, 7 MONTHS
EAST OF RISING STAR, TEXAS

Lou couldn't be sure this was the place. She'd never seen it in person. But she was pretty sure this was it. There were the burned remnants of three large buildings on the property, connected by a semicircle drive. And there was a treehouse in an old oak that, despite the drought, was still alive.

Most of the other trees on the property were dead, as far as Lou could tell. The fence that separated the large piece of land from the highway that ran across its face was in disrepair. Everything was dead or in disrepair along Highway 36 heading east.

She'd stopped at two other places first before dismissing them. This one, though, down to the overwhelming sense of sadness that hung heavy in the air, matched the images she'd seared into her memory from countless detailed stories about her friend's time here.

She couldn't see everything. It was midnight. Her flashlight only offered so much definition of her surroundings. She cranked it again, turning the handle counterclockwise, and the LED bulbs brightened.

"Who lived here?" asked David.

"Marcus," Lou replied.

They were in the treehouse. Although it wasn't an easy climb for a pregnant woman, it gave them a modicum of shelter. The flashlight served as a nightlight for David.

"Marcus Battle?"

"Yes," said Lou.

Their horse was tied off at the base of the tree. It was restless. Lou hoped it would calm down and rest. It had been a long ride here.

"Tell me more about him," said David.

"About who?"

They were flat on their backs, a blanket underneath them and another on top. David was nuzzled up against her. The child couldn't have gotten closer had he tried.

"Marcus."

The flashlight dimmed and Lou stared up at the ceiling of the treehouse. Through the slats, gaps in the wood, rot, starlight twinkled high above. She recognized some of the constellations as the same she'd watch move across the night sky in Baird.

There was Ursa Major, the Big Bear. Leo the Lion.

Lou ignored her son's question and pointed through the widest of the spaces in the roof. Her finger traced the object, like she was painting the sky. "See the lion?" she asked.

Lou hadn't planned on coming here. It was a last minute decision when she'd left Baird. The easiest path was a straight shot along Interstate 20. She couldn't risk that. Even covering her bump, a woman traveling alone with a young child was a target.

So she took the long way, less traveled farm-to-market roads, county roads that jogged south and east and sometimes a little of both. It was dusk, the sky on fire with a brilliant sunset to the right when she hit Cottonwood. Old rusting signs told her she could head south farther than she'd planned and, at Cross Plains, turn east again. That would take her to Rising Star.

Rising Star. She'd only ever heard of the place because of Marcus

Battle. He'd spoken about the town both affectionately and with disgust.

"I see the lion," said David. "I don't see the bear."

Lou took his hand with both of hers. She extended his index finger and guided it across the sky.

"I see it!" said David. "I see it there."

Lou let go of his hand. She turned toward him and kissed his head. The boy's head stunk. It was a mix of sweat and oil. But she loved it. She loved him.

Lou never considered having kids until she was pregnant with David. The thought of being a mother was terrifying enough. The idea of raising a child in this apocalyptic world made it an even worse prospect.

When David came kicking and screaming into the world, her perspective changed. It wasn't that she was any less concerned about her son's future. She was, and perhaps more so. Rather, it was the love that swelled in her chest. It was overwhelming, nearly suffocating.

There were no words, even for a woman as well-read as Lou, that could describe the all-consuming sense of responsibility and wholeness that came from being a parent. It was like someone flipped a switch, turned on the power, and the world exploded in lights and colors never before visible.

She slid her hand up under the layers of fabric covering her belly and spread her fingers on the taut skin that stretched across her midsection. She didn't know yet what she was having. Boy or girl, it didn't matter. She already loved this second child.

It was stupid to have another child. Yet she was anxious to give birth, to expand her family with Dallas.

Dallas was a great dad. He was the fun one, the playmate. Lou was the disciplinarian and the teacher. David would learn two things in his life, if nothing else: how to read and how to throw knives.

"Whose fort was this, Momma?"

"What do you mean?"

"Who built it? Who played here?"

"I don't know," said Lou.

"Marcus?"

"Yes," said Lou. "He built it. He told me he built it."

"Who played here?"

"His children."

David yawned. "Who were his children?"

Lou clenched her jaw. "I don't know."

"How many children did Marcus have?"

Lou exhaled through pursed lips. "I don't know."

She knew. First there was Wes. He was Marcus's biological child, the only one he'd had with his wife, Sylvia. Then there were the children he raised as his own. Sawyer, Lola's boy, whom Marcus had rescued from the Cartel, and Penny, an orphan he'd essentially adopted at the Red River.

All three children were long dead. The women were too.

Lou didn't count herself among the children to whom Marcus had given his love, his protection. She was, though. He'd stepped into her father's long shadow after his death. He'd made her laugh. He'd taught her life was worth living. He'd taught her about sacrifice and faith.

"Can we ask him?"

"Who?"

"Marcus."

"Sure," she said. "Now, get some sleep. It'll be a long day tomorrow."

"Is he coming here?"

"Marcus? No. We'll meet up with him. Now go to sleep."

Lou put her lips to her son's head and kissed him again. She kept her eyes on the starry sky and listened to David's breathing. When it slowed, and she knew he was asleep, Lou carefully slid away from him and managed to climb down the ladder to the hard ground.

Breathless, she walked a few steps before cranking the flashlight to life. The light brightened and she held it out in front of her. Lou took a deep breath and swept the light back and forth, illuminating a path across the cracked earth between the treehouse and circular drive.

Once there, she swung the flashlight to the left. The beam was dimming, casting barely enough light for her to see the black pile of debris. She lowered it and cranked it again, took a few steps forward, and got a better look at the mess.

The char was odorless now. It had been more than a decade since Marcus had burned it. He'd told her about that day. It haunted him. His nightmares. His daydreams. It was always there ghosting him, following him, stalking him.

Lou stepped to the edge of the pyre. It seemed to go on forever. She pivoted on her heels and took steps toward the main house, her boots crunching against the ashy dirt. There wasn't anything but a foundation there now. That and some scattered, unrecognizable infrastructure.

She stepped up onto the concrete and aimed the flashlight past the house to what would have been the backyard. The light dimmed and she cranked again, checking to make sure the noise hadn't awoken David.

While Lou didn't want him waking up alone, scared, she also didn't want him to see where she was going. He'd have too many questions she wouldn't want to answer.

The beam brightened and Lou high-stepped her way across the expanse of concrete until she reached the rear of the slab. Her grip tightened on the flashlight and she angled it down to the jagged edges of rough plumbing.

In her mind, the black surrounding her dissolved into light and she floated into the air. Beneath her, Marcus stood at the kitchen sink, shoulder to shoulder with Sylvia. She washed while he dried. They bumped hips playfully and he nuzzled her.

Wes was sitting at the kitchen table, eating a plateful of cookies, getting more of them in his lap and on the floor than in his mouth. His cheeks and fingertips were stained with chocolate.

This was a happy place. Until it wasn't. The light dimmed. The room was dipped in shades of gray.

Now Lou saw Marcus alone. He absently cut vegetables, staring through the window into the backyard. He asked questions aloud and answered them. It was like he was having a conversation with someone who wasn't there. He plucked a piece of radish from the cutting board and popped it into his mouth like candy, chewing while he cut.

Lou turned again, and the warm glow returned to the room in her mind. Marcus was at the island, standing across from Lola. She was tired, frightened. But there was something in the way she looked at him, the way he looked back, that told Lou there was an undeniable and unspoken connection between the two of them. It was as though Lou sensed they knew they could be each other's salvation.

Then the images evaporated into the dark, and Lou was standing there alone again at the edge of the slab. A shudder ran through her body and she shivered involuntarily.

She cranked the flashlight again, the beam brightened in front of her, and she aimed it into the yard. In front of her was a tangle of dead vegetation in a raised bed of dirt. Lou remembered what Marcus told her about his property, and stepped off the slab. With the light guiding her, Lou marched to her right toward the back corner of the yard. As she approached the edge of the cleared land, she lowered the beam to scan the ground in front of her feet.

At first she didn't see them; then, under a thin layer of dirt and debris, she found what it was she sought. Crouching down and resting her butt on her heels, she held the flashlight in one hand while swiping at the dirt with the other. Under her fingers, she traced the rough edges of chiseled stone.

Lou leaned onto her knees, set down the light, and swiped at the dirt with both hands. Hurriedly, as if on the verge of uncovering long-buried treasure, she swept away the dirt from one stone, then two.

When she'd finished minutes later, there were five stones in front of her. Sweating now, Lou backhanded a fine sheen of perspiration from her forehead.

For a moment, she knelt silently, listening for any sounds from the treehouse, but heard none. David was asleep.

Lou eyed the dark. The shadowy outline of the large oak and its treehouse loomed beyond the slab and the driveway. The sky, a lighter shade of black, framed the thick tangle of branches and the angular edges of the pine boards that held her son.

She found the flashlight on the ground next to her and picked it up. A few counterclockwise cranks later, she had the beam aimed at the rocks. Each of them was crudely inscribed with a name and a date. Although the carvings were barely legible, Lou already knew what they said, so it was easier for her to decipher.

Sylvia. Wesson. Lola. Sawyer. Penny.

These were their graves. This was the spot where Marcus told Lou he'd buried his loved ones, where he'd spent painful hours digging the holes, filling them, finding the stones, chiseling them, and praying before them.

A thick knot swelled in her throat as she rubbed her hands across the stones. Her memory flitted to her parents' deaths.

Her mother died first, taken by the Scourge. She and her father had burned her body in a pyre in their backyard in Austin. Years, and miles, later, her father died protecting her.

She'd avenged his death, killing the men who'd taken her dad from her. So much of her life, she thought, was about death.

As she knelt in the dirt, in the dark, she understood how Marcus's had been that way too. They were decades apart in age. He'd had a life before the Scourge; she really hadn't. But the two of them were kindred spirits. Both suffered. Both survived. Both exacted punishment. Both lived with the pain, the nightmares, that came from all of it.

Lou's chin quivered. She clenched her jaw, repressing the urge to cry. She couldn't, however, stop the tears. They blurred her vision until she closed her eyes, pressing the tears down her cheeks.

No wonder he'd burned this place. No wonder he'd wanted to leave and never come back.

Sobbing such that it was difficult to breathe, Lou understood Marcus better than she ever had. She felt closer to him, yet she had never felt so far away. She held her belly, cradling her unborn child.

Calming herself, swiping the tears from her cheeks and thumbing them from her eyes, Lou caught her breath and exhaled deeply. Then she clasped her hands in front of her.

"Two things," she said to the assembled tombs. "Just two. That's all. And I'm not crazy for talking to you. This is more for me than it is for you. I don't know…maybe I'm crazy. Maybe I've lost it. It could be the hormones. I read that hormones are crazy when a woman is pregnant."

Lou snorted a chuckle and sniffed back the snot dripping from her nose. "What am I telling you? You know, right? You had kids."

The light in her hand dimmed. She didn't bother to crank it.

"I'm not a religious person. I don't know if this counts as a prayer. I'm not really talking to God or whatever, so I don't think it's a prayer. It's more of a confession."

Lou tilted her head back and laughed. "Sheesh. I'm freaking losing it. I'm not making any sense."

The stones on the ground stared back at her blankly. Lou rubbed her fingers across the one with Sylvia's name carved into it. She traced the first letter with her index finger.

"Back to the two things. The first one is a thank-you. Thank you for making Marcus the man he is. Without him, I wouldn't be here. I'm mean, I'm a badass in my own right. My father made sure of that."

Lou smiled, thinking of her father. He'd taught her everything she knew about survival. He knew there'd be a day when she was alone and had prepared her for that as best he could.

"And Marcus," she said, tracing the *Y* in Sylvia's name, "he can be an ass. I'm sure you know that. The guy has some serious psychological problems. I know I'm preaching to the choir on that one."

Another chuckle. "Is that even a saying anymore? Where did that come from? Preaching? Me?"

The conversation was easy now. The words came easy. The audience was captive if not captivated.

"Anyhow, thank you. Your sacrifices sent him to me. And he saved me. Even though you didn't know me or choose to die. I know that's weird. But I'm grateful."

A warm breeze rustled through the brittle branches of dead trees beyond the graves. Lou felt it on her cheeks, drying the tears that clung there.

"Second thing," she said, swallowing past the knot threatening to return in her throat, "is that I'm sorry. As grateful as I am, I'm also sorry."

She brushed dirt from Lola's headstone. Her thumb ran along the jagged grooves that made up the first *L* in her name.

"I know you want the best for him. You want him to find peace, to live the rest of his days as happy as a man like him can be. I do too. But I'm being…I've been…selfish."

Lou half expected one of the women to talk back to her, to say something. She paused, waiting for it. Then she sighed and bit her lower lip.

"I need him again, so I'm pulling him back into the fray, into the nasty world he's wanted to avoid. I wanted to give you a heads-up about that. And tell you, since he loved all of you so much, that I'm thankful and sorry. I'm both. And I'm glad I met you."

Lou wiped her hands on her chest and then ran her fingers through her hair. Puffing her cheeks, she held the air in her lungs as long as she could before blowing it out.

She pushed herself onto her toes and then stood awkwardly. A stitch in her side caught her by surprise as she stretched, and she winced. The baby was lower. It was getting into position. Before long, she'd be delivering the kid on her own.

"I don't know why I did this," she said to the graves. "I don't know why I came here, why I was compelled to talk to you. I'm not even sure what I said, really, and I'm pretty sure it didn't make sense."

Lou swept the flashlight across the graves one more time. She knew exactly why she came here. She knew exactly what she'd said, as inarticulate as it might have sounded.

She was seeking forgiveness. And she sought it from herself as much, or more, than she did from the ghosts of Marcus Battle's past.

Rudy was badly hurt; Norma was alone; her children were in danger; her husband was on a fool's mission. She was putting everything on the shoulders of an old man who'd wanted to spend his final years alone and in peace.

Lou started toward the treehouse. She took two steps when a sharp cramp doubled her over. She clutched herself underneath her belly and suppressed a groan. The sharp pain intensified, swelled. She held her breath and gritted her teeth.

The cramp dulled and the pain ebbed. Lou exhaled and stood up.

"You've got to be kidding me," she said. "Now?"

Chapter 14

APRIL 18, 2054, 1:07 AM
SCOURGE +21 YEARS, 7 MONTHS
ATLANTA, GEORGIA

"You're late," said the gruff voice on the other side of the wall.

Sally sat against the hard wooden back of her seat. It was dark inside the confessional. It smelled like sawdust and varnish. She pressed her sweaty palms flat against the bench, leaned toward the partition, and whispered, "No, I'm not."

"Seven minutes," said the voice.

"Forgive me, Father, for I have sinned," she said with more than a hint of sarcasm.

"Not funny."

"Sorry," said Sally. She wasn't. The tone made it obvious. "I got here as fast as I could. It's not easy moving around at night. You know that."

"I do," said the voice. "The longer you do this, the harder it gets."

Sally turned enough to see the shadow of the man on the other side of the confessional. He had long hair that shaded his features, though a strong Roman nose extended outward at a sharp forty-five-degree angle.

From the sound of his voice, he was middle-aged, and he smoked. Sally could hear it in the gravelly voice and smell the stale pungency of it in the booth. She'd never met him, had no idea who he was other than that he was important enough to be doling out her next assignment.

He cleared his throat. "Last night was a close call."

Sally didn't say anything. She wasn't sure what to say.

"Too close," said the voice.

Through the opaque screen wall that separated them, Sally saw the man brush his hair away from his face. He put a cigarette in his mouth and lit it. The sound of the paper burning snapped in the quiet of the booth. The tobacco sizzled. The man exhaled and the strong odor of smoke filtered into her side of the confessional.

"No," said Sally.

"No, it wasn't too close?" he asked.

"No. I don't mind if you smoke. Thanks for asking."

"Oh." The man chuckled. "Sorry about that. It's a bad habit, I know. I should quit. Yet there are so many other things that are more likely to kill me, I figure a vice like smoking isn't so bad."

"Whatever," said Sally. "You do you."

"Plus, the smoke masks the smell of alcohol that flooded the booth when you entered."

Sally flushed. Did she really reek?

She'd brushed her teeth, put on deodorant, thought about showering.

"What's the point of this?" barked Sally. The tone was more acerbic than she'd intended, but she didn't walk it back.

The man took another drag. The end of the cigarette glowed red and faded. "We're moving you," he said, a stream of smoke pouring from his nostrils as he spoke.

"I figured as much. You sent the porter to my apartment. When that happens, I move. I know the drill."

"You misunderstand. We're moving you out of Atlanta."

A wave of nausea washed over her. Her stomach sank. "What? Why? When?"

"I'll take those questions one at a time," he said smoothly. He flicked the cigarette with his thumb and took another pull. After he exhaled, he shifted in his seat and leaned toward the partition. "First, the what. We are moving you from Atlanta to another location. You're needed elsewhere."

"Where?"

"Let me explain the why next," he said, his tone even and unflinching.

Sally thought the more agitated she became, the calmer his voice was. It was like he was a parent coping with an upset child.

"We are moving you because you've done what you can do here. You've been at this for a long time. It's taken its toll. That's obvious to all of us."

"All of us? Who is all of us?"

He ignored the question. "When you're not on the job, you're drinking heavily. You're reclusive. When you are on the job, your work is more…frenetic…than it needs to be."

"Frenetic?"

Every answer drew another question. Sally curled her hands into fists, her fingernails dragging along the wooden bench.

"Last night you almost lost your passenger. You almost got caught, you compromised a safe house, and you killed Pop Guards."

All of it was true. She couldn't deny it. Things happened. It was a dangerous business. People *almost* got caught all of the time. Safe houses were compromised. That was why they moved them constantly. And guards, as regrettable as it might be for their cause, got killed. It was them or her. Simple as that. Them. Or. Her. Still, she didn't have a response. The shock was taking hold.

Moving her? From Atlanta? Taking her from her home?

"As for the when," he said flatly, as if relaying a recipe for unleavened bread, "it'll be a couple of days. Maybe more. You'll be in a holding pattern until then."

Sally was stunned into silence. She brought her hands to her temples and rubbed them. Her eyes burned from the smoke. Her throat was dry. The world was spinning around her. This was like a hangover but worse.

Okay, she thought through the haze, *maybe not worse.*

But it was bad.

"As for 'all of us,'" he continued, "you know the railroad is multilayered. We have cells that run autonomously. One may not know what the other is doing. Names are withheld; plans are secret; routes change. There are—"

"I know all of this," said Sally. "What's your point?"

"Despite the independence of cells, there is a hierarchy. The railroad has leadership. The leaders all know what the cells are doing. So we're aware of everything that rolls along the tracks, so to speak."

Sally always assumed this. The railroad couldn't run as efficiently as it did, save as many women and children as it did, if there wasn't someone at the top coordinating it all or, at the very least, staying abreast of it.

"All of the leaders know about you, Sally."

Sally. He said it. He said her name. That couldn't be good. The urge to puke rose in her dry throat. The smell of the varnish, the sawdust, and the cigarette smoke made her head swim. She tasted the sour sting of bile on her tongue and gagged. She swallowed, sending the acid back down her throat.

"We all know you're an asset," he said. "We know how many families you've kept together and how many guards you've had to kill to make that happen. We know how many sleepless nights you've had and how many bottles of liquor you keep under things in your apartment."

"How many?" asked Sally.

"What?"

"How many? You said you know how many families, guards,

sleepless nights, bottles of liquor, whatever. So how many is it?"

"I understand you're upset—"

"You don't understand me," she said through her teeth. "Don't begin to tell me what you think you know about me or what I've had to do."

He shifted in his seat, the dark shape of his body moving against the screened wall. He appeared to tuck his hair behind his ears. "Fair enough. I won't do that. What I will do, though, is tell you what you have to do now."

Sally pressed her face to the screened wall. "*Have* to do? You're telling me I have no choice?"

"You don't. You have to do what comes next."

"Or what?"

"Or we provide your name to the Pop Guard," he said. "They find you. They execute you. Or worse."

That was not the answer she expected. Truth was, she hadn't expected any of this; not the in-home visit from a virgin porter, the summons to a church confessional, the suffocating cigarette smoke, the ex-communication from the railroad, and certainly not the do-or-die ultimatum.

"We can't have you on the street anymore, Sally. You're a liability. If you can't see that, then we have to see it for you. If you can't leave the city under our plan, you'll leave it under somebody else's."

The defiance was gone, now came the bargaining. She had to change his mind, find a happy medium with which they could both live.

"Look," she said, "I know last night was rough. I walked us into a bad situation. That's a one-off. Think of all the good I've done, all the lives I've saved."

The man put another cigarette between his lips. He lifted a lighter and flicked on the flame. Tendrils of smoke drifted from his lips and the end of the burning paper.

"I can stop drinking," she said, the words spilling from her before she'd thought them through. "Well, I can cut back. Seriously, this is a good wake-up call. This is what I needed."

The end of the cigarette burned red. It glowed, almost strobing as the man sucked at its opposite end. A long pull on the stick and then streams of smoke plumed from his nostrils.

Sally used her hands to emphasize her understanding of the situation. This was a warning, that's all. "I get it," she said. "This is the wake-up call I needed. I've been taking too many risks. I should have timed last night's run a little better. The helicopters always run the same schedule. The Pop Guard is so predictable."

She chuckled nervously and folded her arms over her chest. She scratched her forearm with nails she should have trimmed. A stray hangnail raked uncomfortably across her skin. The man on the other side of the wall took another drag. He flicked the ashes onto the floor and held the cigarette pinched like a blunt between his thumb and index finger.

"I get it," she said. "Message sent."

The two sat quietly for long moments. Sally stretched her jaw and wiped her mouth, ridding it of the dry white spittle in the corners. When he finally spoke, his voice was barely above a whisper. She had to lean in to hear him.

"It's not a message," he said. "It's not a warning. The decision is made."

Sally wanted to explode. She couldn't sit or stand or grit her teeth or scream.

"I don't like doing this," he said, "but it's best for all of us. Do this last thing for us and you'll live a good life. It won't be this life. And it won't be in Atlanta."

She was cornered. Stuck in a box. The literal box had a door. She could get up and walk out. The figurative one was locked. It was filling with water and she was chained to the floor.

Bargaining, which was momentarily the edge of mania, gave way to resignation.

"Fine," she said. "What is it?" Maybe they'd send her to Loretto, Kentucky. She'd heard rumors that there were black-market distilleries opening there.

"We've got a woman coming from south of the wall. An old friend down there tipped us off. They're heading to Atlanta. When they get here, you're going to take them to the Harbor."

"The Harbor?" she asked. "That's real?"

The man dropped his cigarette, stomped his shoe on it, and ground it into the floor of the confessional. The sound echoed in the small space. "Of course it's real. Where do you think we've been sending families all this time?"

"I never thought of it," Sally said. "I never thought of what happened after they'd left me. I focused on the next one coming up the line."

"Huh," said the man. There was a long pause, then, "That's interesting."

"Where is it? The Harbor?"

"You know I can't tell you that. This will work like everything else. You'll get information as you need it."

"They're coming from Texas?" she asked. "Will they make it?"

"I have assurances they'll make it. If they don't, we'll find another task for you. The timing is right with this one. It'll be a few days before they're here. You need some time to sober up."

"I'm sober."

"Please," he said, tucking his hair behind his ear. "I can smell the liquor in here. Why do you think I keep lighting up? I'm trying to dull my senses so I don't get high from the proximity."

Sally sniffed the air. Then she blew hot air onto her palm and sniffed it, wincing at the sour stink on her skin. "What happens to me?"

"Now or later?"

"Both."

"Now you go to the address on this piece of paper," he said.

"You'll stay there under supervision and await further instructions."

The man stuck a small rolled-up piece of paper, similar to the cigarettes he'd been smoking, into a slit in the partitioned wall. She took it and held it in her fist.

"Look at it," he said. "Memorize it."

Sally did as instructed. Squinting in the dim light, she eyed the address. It wasn't far from here.

"Got it?" he asked.

"Yes."

"Now swallow it."

"What?"

"Swallow it."

Sally pinched the piece of paper and set it on her tongue. Saliva flooded her mouth and she broke up the paper with her tongue and teeth. She swallowed. "Okay."

"Then you're good with what to do now?"

"Yes," she said. "And later?"

"TBD."

"What does that mean?"

"It means it's to be determined," he said. "You'll be taken care of regardless. Wait here for five minutes. Then get up, leave the church, and go straight to the address on the paper you swallowed."

The man stood in the booth, slid open the door, and was gone. Outside the confessional, she could hear his heavy footsteps echoing on the marble floor of the cathedral.

Her shoulders drooped and she slumped into the corner, resting her head on the hard, solid wood. Sally fought the urge to cry. Instead, she reminded herself how miserable she'd been.

This could be good, she thought. *It's a fresh start in a new place. New people, new experiences. Less death.*

She laughed at herself. Less death. There was no such thing in this world, regardless of where she lived. Sally was convinced of that. Death was everywhere. Even when it wasn't staring you in the face, it was hiding in the shadows and lurking around the corners.

It didn't really matter whether she was in Atlanta or the Harbor. Life was life, plain and simple. For a moment, she considered turning herself in to the Pop Guard. What was the difference? If life was so awful, and death was everywhere, mocking every move, why not end it all?

No. She had one more mission and she wasn't about to let her lasting legacy be that she bailed. After all the good she'd done, after what it had cost her, she'd be stupid to give up now.

Better to do what they were asking of her and then make that decision. Go out a hero. Then choose the next path. Take matters into her own hands again.

Sally figured she'd waited long enough and got up. She slid open the confessional door, and a rush of cooler air filled the cramped space. She stepped out into the cathedral and moved toward the aisle, which separated the two rows of wooden pews.

At the rear of the building, in a loft of sorts and open to the acoustically favorable space, was a huge pipe organ. Its console was fixed at the center, its metal pipes lining the walls on either side of it. Cobwebs draped the various-sized pipes, and dust danced in the light from above. Sally wondered what it sounded like, if it even worked anymore. It didn't look like it.

The altar at the front of the cathedral was bathed in white light that shone onto the pulpit. A single floral stained-glass window was set into the wall beneath the steep arch that ran the length of the building's high ceilings.

She stared at the blue light filtering through the stained glass despite the late hour, and studied the intricacies of its design. Sally wasn't much for church, wasn't Catholic, and hadn't ever visited what was once Cathedral of Christ the King.

While it was still a church, it was as much a refuge for the growing homeless population and a place to escape the outside world.

She glanced at her feet and noticed the floor, chipped and

unpolished, looked like a runway. Chevrons, all aimed toward the pulpit, decorated the length of the aisle. The pews were empty except for one man leaning on an elbow. Sally wasn't sure if he was asleep or awake. Her eyes fell back to the chevrons, the arrows, pointing her toward the light at the front of the cavernous house.

Sally stuffed her hands into her pockets and marched toward the exit, every footstep echoing. Using her shoulder to open the heavy door, she pushed her way back out into the night and onto Peachtree Street.

The distant flutter of a helicopter thumped above her. She looked up, beyond the surrounding buildings, and toward the cloudless sky. She stepped to the crack-laden sidewalk that ran along Peachtree and turned left. Her holding cell, her detox bed, was waiting for her.

Chapter 15

APRIL 18, 2054, 1:30 AM
SCOURGE +21 YEARS, 7 MONTHS
NEW BOSTON, TEXAS

"She's crowning! It's close."

"It's been close for five hours," Warner snapped.

It was more like nine hours since the woman had gone into labor in the middle of the dusty highway. They'd spent too much water on her, wasted too much time. Nine hours. They could be another twenty miles closer to their destination.

But no, they were stuck here in the middle of nowhere, and Warner was helping deliver a baby. Firelight cast a warm orange glow across them. It crackled off to the side of the road where the other women and children rested.

Blessing had built it with flint and tinder. Dead branches, cured from lack of water and the hot Texas sun, made for perfect kindling.

"He's facedown," said another voice. "That's good."

The expectant mother, leaning in the dirt on her elbows and doing her best to push, tried lifting her head. Bathed in sweat, her hair matted to her face, she whimpered. "Is it a boy?" she asked.

Andrea, at the woman's head, answered, "We don't know yet."

Blessing had removed Andrea's chains so she could help with the delivery. That, and Andrea had insisted. The only way to get her to shut up was to let her help.

Warner was between the woman's legs, a sour look on his face. "Push," he told her. "C'mon, lady."

Andrea glared at him. "Help her," she said, the firelight dancing on her face. "The faster she does this, the faster you get back on schedule."

Warner rolled his eyes. "Push," he said as sweetly as he could muster. "You can do it."

The woman grunted, her legs trembling. More of the baby's pink head, covered in dark hair, inched outward. The scene was primal: firelight, live birth, an audience.

He spun his John Deere ball cap backwards and put his hands on the woman's knees and pushed them back. "C'mon," he said. "Almost there."

The woman grunted, moaned. The moan turned into a scream. The children, gathered together in a circle at the side of the road, were crying now. None of them understood what was happening. Their mothers were trying to keep them occupied. But young kids couldn't play poker, and the deck of cards Blessing had loaned them only did so much to keep them occupied when they weren't napping or snacking on dwindling rations.

Warner gagged. It wasn't so much because of the sights and smells of childbirth, though those didn't help. It was because of the memories they brought back to him. They were memories he'd pushed deep into the recesses of his mind. The memories that haunted him at night.

He wasn't special. He knew that. Everyone in this world had demons.

Some rose above them, used them as motivation to do good. Warner wasn't one of them. He wasn't a hero.

Warner embraced the demons, invited them in, and partied with them. They were an excuse to lash out, to succumb to man's basest instincts. They spoke to him, told him how best to survive in a world where most laws were guidelines as much as anything.

Warner clenched his jaw against the waft of odor threatening to overwhelm him. He'd heard once somewhere that smells were the strongest sense of memory. Whoever had told him that was right.

Before he was a black-market hustler, a human trafficker, Warner had been a dryland cotton farmer. He'd worked the fields as long as he could remember. It was what his father had done, and his father before that. They had a thousand acres east of the Pecos River in the Permian Basin.

They were north of Crockett County and west of the Rolling Plains. It was Heaven on Earth. Amongst the jack rigs and grain sorghum, their cotton season ran from mid-April to December. From planting to harvest, they could produce as much as three hundred pounds of lint per seeded acre.

When he wasn't working the farm, he was playing football or baseball and staying out late with his first and last girlfriend. Her dad was a mechanic and owned a shop in town.

Both had plans to go to A&M, major in food science and technology, and raise a brood on one of their family farms. They were juniors in high school when the plague took his mother and two brothers and both of her parents. She was orphaned and an only child.

So she moved in with Warner and his dad. They slept in separate bedrooms, mostly, and spent their days working the farm with Warner's dad. Then his dad dropped dead from a heart attack and they were alone. They were twenty years old.

Between what she'd learned from her mechanic father and what they both knew about farming, they managed to keep things running. Given that it was semi-desert there, they didn't feel the drought as fast as other parts of the country.

They were far enough off the beaten path that the Cartel left them alone. A couple of times, Warner had to defend their home from stray patrols. But he was smart and crafty and good with a gun. Nobody took anything from them without Warner and his girl giving it to them of their own free will. Even without consistent power, they managed.

They married at sunset on her twenty-first birthday. They were already husband and wife, for all intents and purposes, but Warner wanted to make a proper woman of her. So they exchanged vows, he gave her his mother's wedding ring, and they tied the knot.

At twenty-two, she was pregnant. He was ecstatic. The apocalypse seemed manageable with the love of his life at his side and a child on the way.

Warner pampered her. Despite her protests, he demanded she stay off her feet as much as possible as the pregnancy progressed. She reluctantly complied.

"It ain't long," he told her, his dark eyes locked with hers, "and you'll be the one doting. So you might as well enjoy it while you can."

"You're changing the diapers," she'd said, "and you're washing them too. Especially if it's a boy."

"That's fine. I'll change 'em and wash 'em. But you're getting up in the middle of the night. I need my beauty sleep."

Those were the salad days. Warner was happy. The bigger she got, the wider his smile.

And then, in the thirty-eighth week, the smile disappeared. She woke him before dawn. She was crying. There was blood everywhere.

Warner did his best. He tried. And for a moment he was the father of a baby boy. Then he wasn't. He wasn't a husband anymore either.

He was alone, in a soiled bed, the bodies of his wife and child in his arms. For a full day Warner didn't move. He couldn't. He wouldn't.

Something snapped inside him. When he finally rose, cleaned himself of the blood in which this new Warner had been baptized, and buried his family, he knew what he had to do.

No longer would the world take from him. He would take from it. He would be the aggressor, the alpha male, the man who refused to push down the demons. He would seek their counsel, allow his quiet rage to fuel his existence.

If he couldn't have a family, why should others? Especially those who broke the law? Why should they get to cheat the system and death when he hadn't? They shouldn't. He'd make sure of it.

When he met Blessing outside Abilene, the two had joined in purpose. They complemented each other. Neither had a soul worth saving anymore. These years later, Warner still didn't know what had driven Blessing to their rogue existence. The man had never offered it up, and Warner never asked. But the man was a kindred spirit. Warner saw it in Blessing's eyes, in the way he carried himself, heard it in his voice when he spoke.

"Help her," said Andrea, snapping him into focus. "She needs your help."

The woman, her skin cold and sweaty, screamed in pain. The baby's head was out now. Its shoulders were almost there. The fire crackled and popped behind him. Waves of dim heat washed over him, carried in the soft breeze he didn't even know was there.

The scent of burning wood in his nostrils, Warner leaned in, using his shoulders to keep the woman's legs apart. He reached down and took the child by the shoulders. It was warm, hot almost, its skin slippery and smooth. The body was like a bird's, strong but delicate.

He pulled. She pushed. He pulled. She pushed. And the child came free.

Warner slid his hand around the umbilical cord and loosened it from around the child's waist as he flipped the baby over onto its back. He stuck a finger in the child's mouth, clearing it, and cradled it.

He patted its back, tugging on the cord, and the baby coughed its first cry. The body trembled against him.

"Is it okay?" cried the mother, trying to see between her legs. Her chest heaved. "Is it breathing okay?"

Warner nodded. He put his hand on the back of the child's head and, for an instant, felt human. His chest tightened. Before he allowed the emotion to swell, he lifted the baby and handed it to the mother.

"It's a girl," Andrea said to the mother and then to everyone, "It's a girl!"

The tired crowd of mothers offered a smattering of weak applause and halfhearted congratulations.

Blessing crossed the road and offered Warner a knife. "Cut the cord."

Warner took the knife and opened it, his wet hands slipping on its handle. He reached down and pressed the blade against the cord, folding the fleshy casing in half before sawing it apart. "You can close your legs," he said to the mother. "I'll give you a few minutes. Then we need to get going."

Warner stood and motioned to Andrea. He pointed at the chain gang and waved her back to the group.

Andrea scowled at him. The fire cast shadows on her face that deepened the lines in her forehead and along the sides of her mouth. The new mother's body was propped up, resting in her lap.

"You're kidding me," she said. "It's the middle of the night."

"Your job is done. Get back there with your kid. Get something to drink, to eat. We leave in thirty minutes."

Andrea gently removed herself from the woman and stood. Fists balled, venom in her voice, she charged toward Warner. Blessing stepped between them and held out a hand to stop her.

Andrea stood on her tiptoes to yell at Warner over Blessing's shoulder. "She can't leave in thirty minutes! She just gave birth!"

Unfazed, Warner wiped his hands on his shirt and pulled off his ball cap. With his shirtsleeve, he wiped his forehead clean of sweat. Then he spun the ball cap and put it back on his head. He spent a few extra seconds getting the John Deere logo centered.

"How's that look?" he asked Blessing.

Blessing glanced at the hat and shrugged.

Andrea's face reddened and her glare blazed. "Did you hear me? She can't travel."

"Then she stays here," said Warner. "It's the child that matters, not the mother."

Andrea exploded toward Warner. Blessing held her back. She fought against him, but the sharpshooter stood silent and strong, like the wall that separated Texas from the rest of the world.

"Get her back with the others," said Warner. "I'm gonna help the little lady here with her new arrival."

Andrea dragged her feet, struggled, trying to free herself from Blessing's hold. It didn't work. He had her back with the others and back in the chain gang within a couple of minutes, once she'd worn herself out like a petulant child.

Warner stepped to the mother, who was lying on her back, a pack under her head, the child on her chest. The baby whimpered softly. It was naked against her, her hands covering its back and bottom.

"You gonna name her?" he asked and squatted on his heels by her head.

Startled, her eyes popped open and struggled to focus.

Before she could answer, he scratched his chin and offered a suggestion. "I wouldn't if it were me."

Her brow furrowed with confusion. Her grip on the child tightened almost imperceptibly, but Warner saw it.

"Wouldn't what?" she croaked, and cleared her throat.

"I wouldn't name the kid," Warner said. "It's like naming a prized pig or a heifer. You wouldn't do that now, would you?"

The woman inched away from him, her head as far from Warner as she could rest it without falling from the relative comfort of the pack underneath. She shifted the baby to the other side of her chest. Her spread fingers pushed into the child's pink flesh, blanching it where she maintained her hold.

"I see from that look on your face you don't quite catch my meaning," said Warner.

She didn't respond. Her expression tightened.

Warner rested his arms on his legs, like a baseball catcher would have done before the Scourge, and he used his hands as he spoke. A smile spread across his face. His black eyes almost sparkled within the shadow cast by the brim of the ball cap. He talked as if telling a magical bedtime story with a happy ending. It was anything but that.

"What most people are gonna do," he said, "at least what they did before the damn drought, was they'd find a pig farmer and they'd buy a weaner. Right? You ever raise a pig?"

The woman shook her head.

"Right. A weaner's a pig that's maybe a couple of months old and don't need its mother's milk anymore. You *could* raise pigs from scratch, but then you gotta deal with stags and gilts, mating them at the right times, castrating the stags, caring for the sows. A sow is a pregnant girl pig."

"I know what a sow is," said the woman.

Warner reached out and touched her arm. She recoiled. He kept his hand there.

"Good on you," he said. "Good for knowing that. I never castrated a stag. Wouldn't really have a desire to do that. But that's beside the point. The point is, you buy a little pig. It's cute and playful. Pigs are smart too. They know you. They recognize you. They greet you when you come calling to feed 'em."

She pulled away from his hand again. Warner moved his elbow back to his own leg.

"My dad was a drylands cotton farmer," he said. "We never had much use for pigs. But for FFA one year, I decided to raise one."

Warner looked away and checked the chain gang. They were standing now. Blessing had them in a line and was checking their binds one at a time. The children were cranky, the mothers exhausted.

Too bad, thought Warner. *We have time to make up.*

He looked back at the new mother. He had her full attention. "I named my pig. Dad warned me not to do it. He told me I'd live to regret it while my pig wouldn't. I was headstrong though, in the way that teenagers know everything and their parents are stupid. I ignored him. I named the pig."

He sat there watching her. Waiting.

"What did you name it?" she asked. She couldn't help herself.

The grin broadened on his face. "Old Major. Name mean anything to you?"

She shook her head. "No. Should it?"

"Probably not," said Warner. "We were reading a book called *Animal Farm* at the time. It was a short book, so I actually read it."

He chuckled. She didn't. The baby shifted against her body and whimpered.

"A dude named Orwell wrote it. The book was about this farm where the animals become human. That's an oversimplification of it. It's really about government oppression and such. But anyhow, there's this boar named Old Major."

Warner adjusted the cap on his head. The crackling fire drew his attention for a split second before he continued his story. "Old Major has this meeting of the animals at the farm. He tells them about this dream he had. There were no people around, only animals, and the animals had to work together to create a perfect society where everyone was equal. Therein lies the rub. Of course, not everyone's equal, even if they're animals, you know? Anyhow, I liked the book. I liked Old Major. So I named my weaner. Bad idea."

The baby stretched her legs. Her little fingers were balled into tight fists. She held one of them to her face like she was hitting herself in exasperation.

"When you've got a weaner, and you're raising one for show," said Warner, "you keep 'em for a few months while you're getting them up to slaughter weight. You know that's the goal. That's the reason you get up every morning, feed them, clean them, water them. That's the goal, fatten them for sale. The whole relationship, as it were, is predicated on that fact. You're raising the pig to kill it."

The woman's eyes widened with concern. She clearly knew where this story was headed. But what did it have to do with her baby?

Warner could see it on her face, that puzzled expression trying to fit the pieces together. A rush of electricity ran through his body. He liked it, the sense of control.

"See," he said, "I talked to my pig. I'd sing to him, tell him stories about me and my girl. He'd listen and I swear he'd sometimes nod in agreement. Pig was smart…"

The more of his story he told, the more of his west Texas vernacular, the twang and drawl in his voice, took hold. It was like he was back on the farm, chewing a weed, shoveling feed, brushing the pig's back.

"I loved that guy," he said. "All the time, in the back of my mind, I know there's gonna come a day when he's gonna be bacon and carnitas. Don't matter, though. I keep treating Old Major like family."

A child on the chain gang cried out and drew his attention. The mother put both of her hands on the boy's face, cradled it, and got close to him. Warner couldn't tell if she was comforting the kid or scolding him. Either way, as long as the boy shut up, it was all good.

"Then comes the show," he said. "Big one. Old Major looks great. Judges love him. He's reserve grand champion. Gets a blue ribbon. I get some scholarship money for college. Then the buyer takes him off."

There were tears in the new mother's eyes. They glistened in the firelight, pooling on her lids.

"You know the hardest part?" Warner asked rhetorically. "The hardest part wasn't that first cold morning in the fall, knowing that was the day they were gonna gut Old Major, trough him, use a razor to cut off his hair. It wasn't that."

Warner looked at the woman but didn't see her. He was

somewhere distant again, somewhere in his past.

"It was the empty stall where I kept him. It was still getting up in the morning at the ass-crack of dawn and going out there to feed him, forgetting he wasn't there. I'd call his name, not thinking about it. He wasn't there…" He snorted a chuckle. "Last time I named a pig."

Warner blinked back into focus. He jutted out his chin toward the baby. "That's why I wouldn't name the kid. 'Cause you're gonna wake up one morning and she won't be there. It'll be a lot easier without a name. But that's just me."

Warner rubbed his hands on his thighs and stood. His muscles protested for an instant, but he pushed past it and reached out his hands. "Hand me the baby."

The woman shook her head. The tears ran down her cheeks, the sides of her face.

"I'm not stealing her. I'm holding her so you can get up."

The woman lifted her head and kissed the baby's forehead. Hesitant at first, she lifted the infant from her body and held her out to Warner.

He leaned over, the small of his back tensing with pain, and took the child in his hands. "Hey, Blessing," he called loud enough for his partner to hear him. "Help this woman up, would you?"

Blessing marched over to them, squatted, and helped lift the woman into a sitting position. From there he stood, grabbed both of her hands in his, and pulled her up, steadying her when she wobbled.

Her dress was stained and filthy. It was rumpled at her knees, folded under itself.

"See if you can't get a woman to help her with her clothes," said Warner. "She needs underwear, maybe a clean dress or pants. See what people got."

Blessing took the woman by her arm and led her over to the chain gang. Warner followed them over to the fire and handed the baby to Andrea.

"Hold this for me," he said. "I got my hands full with other things."

Andrea looked at the baby, then Warner, then the baby again. She took the child and turned her to cradle the baby in her arms. "She needs a blanket or something."

"Blessing will get it," he said.

"What do you have on him?"

Warner raised an eyebrow. "What do you mean?"

"Why does he do everything you say?" asked Andrea. "I wouldn't."

He laughed. "You *don't*."

"Why does he?" she persisted.

"He just does," said Warner. It was none of her business why the partners were the way they were. And who was she to ask?

Andrea motioned toward the new mother with her head, holding the baby's head against her neck. "She can't go right now. You can't do this. Where are you taking us?"

Warner clenched his jaw. He tightened a fist at his side. He thought about ending her right here. But the baby inside her was worth something. He could tolerate her insolence for a while longer.

"You wanna know?" he asked. "You *really* wanna know?"

Andrea stiffened. "Yes."

"Okay," said Warner. "I'll ask you a question first."

She remained silent.

"You wanna put an end to the government?" he asked. "The government that doesn't want you having babies? The one that made you so desperate you hired a coyote?"

Her face twitched, a betrayal of her intended stoicism.

"I bet you do," said Warner. "I see it on you. You want to put an end to all of this. To the government, to me, to Blessing."

"You're scum. You're a bottom-feeding piece of—"

Warner raised his hand. "Hold up there, missy. We got mixed company present. No need for foul language."

Andrea grumbled and shifted the child to the other side, swaying.

"I'm giving you an opportunity to end it all," he said. "You'll be part of something bigger than yourself. Help take down the government."

"How is that?"

"I'm selling you to a tribe near Fort Worth," he said. "They pay really well for childbearing women and young children whose minds are moldable."

The disgust on her face softened and morphed into something else. Something like fear.

"They're building an army," he said. "They're big enough, these tribes, that the government don't mess with them. But they're small enough they can't initiate a fight. They can't take control of things."

Andrea's bitter defiance was wavering. "I don't understand." Her voice trembled.

"You don't have to understand. You just have to do what they tell you. Eventually your kids will be their army. Were you ever a fan of baseball?"

"Baseball?"

"Yeah. Pro teams had what was called a farm system. They grew their own talent. Young players would learn the system, get better, and if they were ready, they'd be the future for the big team. That's what the tribes are doing. They're growing their own talent."

"You're selling us into slavery?" she asked. "And then our children will be trained as soldiers?"

"The children you have, the ones you're about to have, and the ones you'll have down the road," said Warner. "It's genius, ain't it?"

"It's sick." Andrea *looked* sick. Even in the ambient, flickering glow of the flames, her color was sallow, almost green.

"It's business." Warner clapped his hands together and raised his voice loud enough for everyone to hear. "We need to hit the road."

Chapter 16

APRIL 18, 2054, 8:30 PM
SCOURGE +21 YEARS, 7 MONTHS
NEW ORLEANS, LOUISIANA

Marcus stood at the platform and watched the train rumble past. Its breeze cooled his face. Its power vibrated through his body. He craned his neck to one side and then the other, cracking the soreness from it.

"You get any sleep?" Dallas asked.

Marcus grabbed the top of his hat and pushed down on the crown, lowering it on his head. It was warmer here. The humidity thickened the air. "Some," he said.

"That's better than none."

"True," said Marcus. "C'mon, we gotta find a ride west."

Dallas shrugged his pack up onto his back and followed Marcus from the platform and into the terminal. It was busy but not crowded.

The mustard-colored terrazzo floor was pitted and chipped from wear. Sections of blue seats were bolted to the floor in rows. An analog clock built into one of the walls was missing the numbers two and nine. The minute hand was bent at an odd angle, like someone had tried to pry it from the wall.

Next to the clock was a schedule of trains. There were only two on the display. One was the train arriving from Birmingham and points north. The other was the train departing from Birmingham and points north. In a world where everything was backwards, where food was scarce, and the government punished pregnant women, the trains ran on time. Of course they did.

Marcus walked across the open expanse of the terminal, moving between two rows of chairs. A pile of blankets covered the set of chairs to his right. It shifted as he passed, and Marcus noticed the person sleeping underneath the pile. Then he smelled the person underneath the pile. He held his breath and walked toward the exit at the front of the terminal.

A sign above the doors indicated he could find private cars outside. Dallas told him it wasn't a remnant of the past, that there really were people who'd give rides for a fee. Marcus passed a couple sitting next to each other, sharing a sandwich. Or maybe it was two pieces of bread with nothing in them. They eyed him suspiciously and he looked away.

The lights overhead flickered and Marcus looked up in surprise. "Fluorescents. Didn't know they still made those."

Dallas was moving stride for stride with him. He looked at the ceiling. "I didn't notice that on my way north. Huh."

They pushed through a set of glass doors and back into the humid, oppressive air. Although the summers in Virginia could get humid, it was nothing like this. And it was only April. Lining the curb in front of the terminal were cars and trucks. Some were attended and running, others parked.

"Welcome to New Orleans," said a man who pronounced the name of the city the way natives said it. To Marcus, it sounded more like Nawlins than New Orleans, but he tipped his hat and smiled.

The man was smiling until he eyed the guns on the men's shoulders. His brow wrinkled. He stuffed his hands in his pockets. "You loaded for bear," said the man. He leaned against an older model F-150 pickup truck. "You hunting something or some*one*?"

His wizened eyes contrasted against his olive skin. The white in his beard and atop his head looked like a dusting of snow. He was tall and fit, his collared shirt frayed at the cuffs, though it was pressed and tucked into faded denim pants cinched too tightly at the waist. His boots were solid but worn.

Marcus scanned the surroundings. "Neither. We're headed to Texas."

The man chuckled. "So you're doing a little bit of everything, then, I reckon."

Marcus took a step forward and lowered his voice, making sure to keep his hands open and in front of him. "You wouldn't happen to know where I could find a ride west, would you?" he asked. "For a price."

The man's eyebrows arched. "How much of a price we talking about?"

"You tell me," said Marcus. "If you know someone who might have an inclination to make the trip."

Dallas stood next to Marcus, silently watching the exchange.

The man shrugged. "I might know someone."

"And that someone would be—"

"Sheesh," Dallas cut in. "Enough with the dance."

Marcus frowned at Dallas. The man grinned.

"We don't have time for this," said Dallas. "Sir, can you take us to Texas in your truck? My friend here and I assume that's why you're parked here. That's why you said hello. That's why—"

"Sure can," said the man. He extended a hand to Dallas. "Name's Doolittle."

"Like the doctor?" asked Marcus.

"Like the general," Doolittle clarified.

"You serve?" asked Marcus.

"Syria," said Doolittle. "You?"

"Same."

Doolittle offered his hand to Marcus and shook it. It was a firm shake, strong but not showy.

"Well, I'll be," said Doolittle, the grin broadening on his face. It revealed a smattering of teeth, some healthy, some not. "Mind you, I wasn't a general. Just a private first class doing my job. Working for a living."

"I'm Marcus. This is Dallas."

"Like the city?" asked Doolittle.

"Like the television show," said Marcus.

Marcus and Doolittle laughed. Dallas didn't.

A confused look crossed his expression. "What show?"

"Before your time," said Marcus. "Before my time too. I think I watched reruns on Netflix or Hulu before the world went to hell."

"I miss me some Netflix," said Doolittle. "And HBO."

"Enough reminiscing," said Dallas. "We can do this in the truck. We gotta hit the road if we're gonna do it."

"You can ride in the back," said Doolittle. "It'll be two hundred plus gas or a thousand plus gas and damages."

"What?" asked Dallas. "I don't—"

Marcus held up a hand to silence Dallas. "Two hundred gets us to the wall?" he asked. "A thousand gets us to wherever we're going?"

Doolittle winked and shook a finger at Marcus. "See? I knew a military man would catch on quick. What's it gonna be, fellas?"

"You can get us past the wall in a truck?" asked Marcus.

"That's where the damages come in," said Doolittle. "We might have to pay fines, you know?"

"Deal," said Marcus.

"Deal," said Doolittle. "Hop on in. Let me get you some water. I got a couple of canteens in the front seat. You'll get dehydrated down here without even knowing it. It's the humidity."

Doolittle moved to the passenger's door and stopped. He snapped his fingers and spun around. "I forgot. One little thing that's not so little."

"What's that?" asked Marcus.

"I need half up front."

"How about two hundred up front," Marcus countered. "Three hundred when we cross the wall, the rest on delivery?"

Doolittle bobbed his head, using the fingers on one hand to count on the other. Then his grin reappeared. "I can do that, but it'll be eleven hundred, plus gas, plus damages."

Marcus reached into a pocket on his pack. He pulled out a handful of bills, peeled four of them from the stack, and handed them to Doolittle.

Doolittle stuffed it into his pocket. "Let me get you that water."

Marcus walked around to the back of the truck, opened the tailgate, and removed his pack, tossing it into the bed. One at a time, he set the weapons in the bed next to his pack and slid them away from the tailgate.

Then he turned around and, with his palms flat on the bed, lifted himself into a seated position at the edge of the tailgate. His legs hung over the side and his boots hung in the air.

Dallas raised an eyebrow and smirked.

"What?" asked Marcus. "I'm not twenty anymore. I told you I ain't what I was. But you insisted."

"I did," said Dallas. "My bad."

He unloaded his gear next to Marcus and climbed in beside him. Doolittle appeared at the tailgate with two canteens and offered them to his new passengers. They thanked him and he shut the tailgate. The slam echoed across the front of the terminal.

"How often you do this?" asked Marcus.

Doolittle leaned on the tailgate, his hands resting on it. "Do what?"

"Give strangers rides for cash."

"All the time. It's how I make a living."

He slapped the tailgate and started around the driver's side. In a minute, they were on their way, maneuvering north on Earhart

Boulevard, directly beneath the Pontchartrain Expressway. It wasn't much of an expressway anymore, but the crumbling infrastructure still mostly stood in place.

There were tents lining the southern side of Earhart as they rode northwest. Metal trash cans doubled as firepits and lit the scene. Different colored pitches housed men and women huddled on the gravel and dirt. Children kicked a deflated ball around in a circle. Teenagers played cards or dominos or some weird combination of the two Marcus hadn't seen before.

It was easy to forget how many people lived like this now. Not everyone was lucky enough to find land, work it for food. Not everyone was self-sufficient. Not everyone wanted to be.

As was the case long before the Scourge, there were people who didn't want to help themselves. They were content to let others do it for them. They survived instead of living, stumbling from one day to the next without purpose.

Marcus looked off to his left as they sped up, not wanting to dwell on the tent city. A block away, a large rounded structure loomed against the dark sky beyond. The Superdome. It was still there. Somehow it hadn't collapsed.

"I heard there's death matches in there," said Dallas, like he was reading Marcus's mind. "It's chaos."

Marcus kept his eyes on the dome until it faded into the night as Earhart jogged west and underneath a spaghetti bowl of intersecting freeways above.

"Where'd you hear that?" he asked Dallas.

"People talk. Some guys on the train headed north had just come from there. They'd watched it, said it was brutal. Sounds unreal to me. I know the Romans did stuff like that. Lou told me she read about it in books. But in real life? I don't buy it."

"Why not?"

Dallas shrugged. "People are cruel, yes… But making men and women fight to the death for entertainment? That's too much.

Humans aren't savages."

Marcus's memory flashed to Lubbock, Texas, and Jones Stadium, and he wasn't in the truck anymore. He wasn't riding through New Orleans, he was blinking against a bright west Texas sun. It was a lifetime ago. Sixteen or seventeen years? He couldn't remember. The clear, pale blue morning and the high wispy clouds in an otherwise empty sky he did.

He didn't fear death then, like he didn't fear it now. The impending sense of doom, of pain, was something else altogether. One of twelve gladiators, the Cartel had forced him to fight for his life on the floor of a football arena.

The tattered remnants of artificial turf cushioned his feet. Brown turf, stained with the blood of those who'd come before him. There was the ripe, pungent aroma of body odor and urine.

He was there with Sawyer, Lola's son, when the fight began. There was Pico too, and Baadal the Dweller. All four of them fought side by side, back to back, arm in arm.

Pico died that day from a bullet to his back. Baadal was left at the wall after Lola kicked him unconscious, his nose and mouth soaked in his own blood. Sawyer died east of Rising Star at the foot of the treehouse.

Marcus squeezed his eyes shut, trying to burn the image of Sawyer's dead body in the tall, dry grass. He was back in the truck, bouncing in the bed next to Dallas as they passed what was once Xavier University and merged onto Interstate 10 due north.

"People *are* savages," Marcus said. "If you haven't learned that by now, Dallas, you haven't been paying attention. Or you chose to bury your head in the sand. One or the other. because there's no way you've lived a life like yours and not seen the worst of humanity."

Marcus considered the oxymoron of it, but didn't correct himself. He put a hand on the side of the bed and adjusted his back against the pack between his body and the exterior of the cab.

They were picking up speed now. The warm wind whipped around them.

"I've also seen the best," said Dallas.

"The best what?" Marcus said loudly over the wind.

"The best of humanity," said Dallas. "The best in people. People can do incredible things when they put their mind to it."

Marcus stared out the back of the truck, watching the asphalt fall away behind them into the darkness. The truck hit a pothole in the road and they bounced. Marcus almost bit his tongue.

"I don't have my head in the sand, Marcus," Dallas said. "I see clearly. I choose to see the good in people though, not the bad. That's the difference between you and me, I guess."

Marcus chuckled and shook his head. "Like the bandits on the train who robbed and killed? Like the coyotes who will sell you and your family down the river? Like the government taking children from their mothers and fathers? Like the Llano River Clan? Like the Dwellers? Like the Cartel?"

The truck slowed and sped up again, knocking a red gas container onto its side. Dallas righted it, moved a length of rope to one side, kicked a toolbox into the corner of the bed, and shook his head. "I'm not saying there aren't bad people, Marcus," he said above the roar of the wind.

Marcus raised his eyebrows. Dallas frowned.

"I'm not a moron," Dallas said. "You can't measure good without evil."

"How very Zen of you," said Marcus.

"I don't think that's Zen, but it doesn't matter. My point is there are plenty of good people too. Rudy, Norma, most everybody in Baird. Lou's the best person I've ever met. And you, you—"

Marcus shook his head. "Don't put me in the good category. There's nothing good about me, son."

"I'm sick of this notion that every stranger is bad. That everyone is out to get you. It's not that way. Most people are good. You included, Marcus. No matter what you think."

The truck hit another bump. Doolittle swerved but maintained his speed. Marcus glanced into the cab. The glow of the dash illuminated Doolittle's face in the rearview mirror. The man smiled and jutted his chin out in acknowledgment.

Dallas was wrong. Since his days in the military, Marcus had learned most people were prone to doing bad things. That was why laws existed. That was why morality existed. They were there to tell you what was right when nobody else was looking. Texas was living, breathing proof that people couldn't be trusted to do the right thing.

Marcus loved Texas. It was his true home. It was the place he'd chosen to raise a family. Twice. It was also the place that had taken everything from him. Twice. And for some damned, stupid reason, he was headed back.

Chapter 17

APRIL 18, 2054, 9:00 PM
SCOURGE +21 YEARS, 7 MONTHS
ATLANTA, GEORGIA

Sally gripped the sides of the toilet with trembling hands. The porcelain was cold against her palms. She wanted to press her sweaty face against the outside of the bowl, but knew better.

As poor as she felt, as loopy and confused as her mind was at the moment, this was a stranger's house. Lord only knew who or what had preceded her at the throne.

The third knock at the locked door behind her made her want to scream. If she had the energy, she would have screamed. She didn't. Instead she spat into the bowl. A thick trail of spit stuck to her lips, and she swiped at it with the back of a hand.

"You okay?" The question carried with it concern. The voice was sweet, sincere.

Another series of knocks. Harder this time. "If you need help—"

"I'm fine," Sally groaned. "I'm fine."

"Are you sure?"

"Yeah. Just not feeling good."

The woman on the other side of the door was named Gladys. Or at least, Gladys was the name she was using for Sally's benefit. Sally didn't give her a name. She told Gladys it didn't matter.

"Was it the food?"

Sally spat into the bowl again. "No, it wasn't the food."

She hadn't eaten the food. Gladys knew that. It was a bowl of broth. Simple, unlikely to upset her stomach, salty and hydrating. Good for her. But she hadn't even had a spoonful of it.

"You got anything for a headache?" asked Sally. "My head's pounding."

She turned back to the bowl and dipped her head inside, gagging. It was another dry heave.

Gladys tried the knob again. "I might," she said. "Are you sure you—"

"I've been through this before," said Sally. "It'll be a day or so. I'll be fine."

Sally let go of the toilet and slumped against the wall. The bathroom was only a toilet and a sink. She tried stretching out her legs, but her feet hit the other wall before she had them fully extended. She plucked at her shirt, sticky and heavy with sweat, and used it to fan her face.

All that did was bathe her in her own stink. Waves of garlic-tinged body odor filled her nostrils and she winced. Garlic? Why did she smell like garlic?

Another wiggle of the doorknob. Gladys was persistent if nothing else. The ball-shaped brass knob moved but didn't turn.

"I'll be out in a minute," Sally said. "I'll meet you in the kitchen."

Gladys hesitated. The shadows of her feet moved in the gap between the floor and the bottom of the door. "Okay. But if you're not there in a minute, I'll be back for you."

It was a promise more than a warning. Gladys did seem concerned. And if Sally rationalized it, it made total sense that the woman was on her like flies on stink.

This *was* her house, as far as Sally knew. Sally was a stranger who refused to offer a name, even a fake name. She refused to eat and was clearly in withdrawal. The sweats, the shakes, the nausea, the headache were all physical signs of an alcoholic coming down. Then she locked herself in a bathroom and refused to come out.

If this were Sally's house and Gladys was the addict, Sally admitted to herself she'd have kicked the woman to the curb.

Sally put her fingers to her neck. Her pulse was racing.

She used the wall to help herself stand and stood there for a moment, letting the wave of light-headedness wash through her. She puffed her cheeks and exhaled like she was blowing out a cake full of candles. Her vision focused on the sink, she stepped to it and turned on the water. A pitiful spitting trickle fell from the faucet and splashed into the bowl. The low pressure wasn't unusual in the city. Sally plugged the sink and let it fill halfway. Then she dipped her clammy hands into the room-temperature water and splashed it on her face.

With a towel she dragged from a hook next to her, she dabbed her face dry and stared at herself in the mirror. Her eyes welled as she took in her unfamiliar reflection.

In the dim light, and thank goodness the light was dim, there was a woman who only vaguely resembled the woman Sally remembered. How long had it been since she'd looked at herself in a mirror? Days? Weeks? Months?

She touched her face and traced the dark circles that framed the undersides of her eyes. She lightly pushed the puffy, tender spots and then ran her fingers down the deep lines that ran along the sides of her nose and framed her mouth. Her sharp cheekbones, more angular than she remembered, threatened to push through her pale skin.

Her lips were thin, and the dimple in her chin seemed deeper. The skin at her neck was like crepe paper. Her hair, thinner than the last time she studied it, was a mess, and there were the first hints of gray at her scalp and temples.

She looked so much older than her age. The work, the stress, the nightmares, and the alcohol had conspired to wreak havoc on her appearance.

Sally ran her fingers through her hair, wiggling them through the tangles, and wondered if the damage she could see in the mirror was a reflection of what she'd done to her insides too. She put the chances at eleven out of ten.

Her chest tightened when she thought about everything she'd done, what she'd given up to help nameless strangers. It had cost her. And now, after having done all she'd done, her bosses were kicking her to the proverbial curb.

Sick of looking at herself, she drained the sink and left the bathroom. It was a few short steps to the living room, where Gladys was awaiting her.

The room was best described as cozy. Bathed in warm incandescent yellow light, the walls were covered in whitewashed shiplap. Large gilded frames held replicas of renaissance paintings replete with cherubic angels and mourning disciples.

There was too much furniture for the space. At the center was a large square wooden table that looked reclaimed, something popular fifty years earlier. On one side of the table was a pair of overstuffed fabric chairs angled toward each other. On the opposite side was a sagging love seat that had seen better days, a crocheted yellow blanket draped across the back of it.

Gladys sat in a highjack armchair positioned between the overstuffed chairs and the love seat. She was ramrod straight with her shoulders back and her hands on her knees.

She reminded Sally of pictures she'd seen of early twentieth-century schoolmarms. Her facial expression was tight and judgmental. Her hair was pulled back into a tight bun that sat atop her oblong head, there were smudges of pink at her cheeks, a hint of lipstick, and gray eyeshadow highlighted her eyes.

Gladys motioned to the love seat. "Relax," she said, in contrast to what she appeared to be doing. "Have a seat."

Sally eyed the love seat, its depressed feather cushions, and stepped to the opposite side of the table. She plopped into the chair farthest from Gladys, sinking into the plush cushion.

On the table in front of her, a collection of tchotchkes cluttered the space. There were porcelain dogs, stacks of coasters with cork inserts, a brass lantern, and a fan of old housekeeping magazines with dates older than Sally.

"How are you?" asked Gladys.

"Meh," said Sally. "Been better."

"You like to feel sorry for yourself, don't you?" asked Gladys. "Throw little pity parties inside that head of yours?"

Sally bristled. Her stomach tightened, as did her fists. She hoped the scowl on her face answered the accusations.

"I've done this before," said Gladys. "I'm not an idiot."

Gladys fingered her high-colored blouse, stretching the fabric at her neck, her gaze focused intently on Sally.

Sally felt her eyes. It was like they could see through her, burning into her soul. It was more uncomfortable than clutching a stranger's toilet.

Sally looked away, resting her hands on the chair's wide arms. The chenille felt cool under her palms. "Done what?"

"This."

Sally rolled her eyes. Everything about the railroad was obtuse. *Nobody* could answer a question with a straight answer. It was part of what made the job so taxing. There were always more questions than answers. And usually an answer, or what served as one, only gave birth to more questions.

"By *this*," asked Sally, "you mean sitting in your living room with a stranger?" She shifted in the chair and pulled her bare feet up behind her. Tucking them under her rear, she leaned on the arm closer to Gladys.

"Or by *this*," she said, "do you mean you've gotten all high and mighty, judging aforementioned strangers sitting in said living room?"

Gladys pursed her lips. The red she'd painted on almost disappeared. She was otherwise unfazed. "Yes, all of it. I've done it all. But you're not really a stranger."

Sally raised one eyebrow, her expression doubtful. "Is that so?"

The schoolmarm nodded. She crossed her legs at her ankles and folded her hands in the lap of her full-length chambray skirt. "You think you're the first conductor the railroad has run over, left for dead on the tracks? You think the daily grind of trying to salvage lives against incredible odds hasn't done this to countless people before you?"

Sally hadn't thought about it. Why would she? She had enough to worry about, enough problems of her own that thinking about the trials of others wasn't even a blip. Still, she didn't like Gladys pegging her like this.

"Nice metaphor," Sally said. "You use that before? Or am I the first?"

Gladys sniffed. "You're not special; you're an addict. That makes you common."

"Thanks," Sally said, starting to stand. "I think I've heard enough. Where's the bedroom?"

Gladys held up a hand then motioned for Sally to stay. Her expression softened. "I'm sorry, let me clarify that. What you did *was* special. You risked yourself to help others, people you didn't know. That's commendable. And truly, it's remarkable in this hell our world has become."

Sally folded her arms across her chest. "I don't need your praise any more than I need your criticism. Both are worthless."

"I'm sure they are," said Gladys. "My point is that what you've done has made you who you are. Good and bad. My job is to help filter the bad out of your system."

Sally's brow furrowed, her mind racing.

"My job isn't only to give you a place to stay until you go out on your last mission for the railroad," said Gladys. "It's also to get you sober and functional."

"You're a shrink?"

Gladys smiled. It was the first hint of emotion she'd shown Sally since they'd met. The woman wasn't stone after all. "Not a shrink per se. More like a facilitator."

Sally smirked. "Facilitator of what?"

"Mostly sobriety."

"What else?"

Gladys waved her hand, sweeping it across the room. "You name it. I'm here to make sure that you leave here better than I found you. Your work is difficult. It takes its toll. It has on you. It has on others. It will on more."

Sally understood. This was a halfway house. It was a holding cell. It was purgatory.

"So how do you make me better?" she asked. She flexed her sweaty hands and balled them into fists.

"First," said Gladys, "you don't drink. If you did drugs, you don't do them either."

"I didn't do drugs," said Sally.

"Okay. Then this should be easier than it might otherwise have been."

"What else?"

"You talk to me," she said. "You tell me about what you've done. Who you've helped. Who you've hurt. Why you are the way you are."

Sally flexed her hands again and wiped her palms on the chair's arms. A rivulet of sweat traced her spine and joined the moisture at the small of her back. The nausea in her stomach swelled and subsided. It was like a wave pool in her gut, an undulating rise and fall of sickness.

Gladys held Sally's gaze, staring her down like a master might a dog. Sally stared back until a buzz in her head made her uncomfortable, and she flitted a glance at her lap, the floor, the wall opposite her. Gladys was boring a hole into her.

"What if I don't want to talk?" asked Sally.

"You don't have a choice," said Gladys. "You either do what's required and complete the final task that sets you free of the railroad, or you don't, and your journey ends abruptly."

Sally frowned and whipped her head toward Gladys. "What does that mean?"

Gladys blinked. A slow, thoughtful blink. Her expression flattened. "I think you know what that means. Don't make me spell it out for you. Do what's asked of you and your life will be better than you could have imagined."

Sally swallowed hard. "Okay. What do you want to know? What do you want me to say?"

Gladys brushed out the wrinkles in her skirt. "My father was a journalist. Before the Scourge, of course. Aside from every conversation with him being an interview of sorts, he was consistent in one thing."

Sally bit. "What was that?"

"He always wanted to know the who, what, where, why, and when," she said. "They were the cornerstone of good reporting, he told us. If you could include all of those questions, you had a great story. Without one or more, you didn't."

Gladys uncrossed her ankles and then crossed them again. The faintest hint of a smile twitched on her face. "That's not to say you had answers to all of them, it just means that you asked. You probed. You thought of everything. Sometimes the best stories were the ones with no answer to one of more of those questions. They led to follow-ups, to deep dives, to uncovering hidden truths."

"Where are you going with this?"

"I want you to answer those questions," said Gladys. "Who are you? What did you do? Where did you come from? Why are you here?"

"When?"

"When what?" asked Gladys.

"You left out when," said Sally. "Who, what, where, why, when."

"I'll get there. Let's begin with who you are."

Sally felt the bile rise in her throat. Her headache, which had drummed into the background, was pounding again. "That's not easy."

"Why?"

"Because after all I've done," Sally said through the throb of her headache and the acidic burn in her throat, "I don't really know the answer."

Chapter 18

APRIL 19, 2054, 3:30 AM
SCOURGE +21 YEARS, 7 MONTHS
THE WALL AT THE SABINE RIVER

The truck rumbled to a stop and jerked into park. Marcus opened his eyes and stared into the darkness. The deafening sound of cicadas and frogs chirped and croaked around them.

The driver's side door creaked open and slammed shut. Heavy footsteps crunched on the gravelly asphalt. Doolittle leaned against the truck. His voice was barely loud enough to hear above the din of insects and reptiles.

"We're here," he said. "Maybe a few hundred yards from the wall."

Marcus rubbed the sleep from his eyes. "What time is it?"

Doolittle shrugged. "After three in the morning. Close to four. We've been going nonstop since I picked you up. Surprisingly smooth sailing."

"How are you on gas?" asked Dallas. His voice had the rasp of someone still waking up.

"Good," said Doolittle. "Quarter of a tank still. This truck's modified. Gets good mileage."

"So what now?" asked Marcus. "Why'd we stop?"

Doolittle shifted from one foot to the other and looked west. After a heavy sigh and much visible consideration, he tucked his chin and said, "When I said I'd crossed the wall a bunch of times, I might have exaggerated a little."

Marcus sat up straight and exchanged glances with Dallas, then asked, "What's a little?"

Doolittle looked at the ground. "I haven't crossed it a whole bunch of times."

"How many times *have* you crossed it?" asked Dallas.

Doolittle shrugged. "I haven't."

"At all?"

Doolittle lifted his chin and shook his head.

Dallas cursed. Marcus put a hand on Dallas's arm to quiet him.

"There's nothing to be afraid of," said Marcus. "It ain't like it used to be. You can cross no problem, especially going into Texas."

"I know that," said Doolittle, an indignant tone creeping into his voice.

"Then what's the problem?" asked Dallas. "Why'd you tell us you've been a bunch of times?"

"I'm not afraid of crossing the wall," he said. "I'm afraid of what comes after it. I've heard all sorts of stories about tribes near the cities. They'll kill a man for looking funny. They steal women. It's like the dark ages or something. Medieval times."

None of the men spoke for a few seconds. The cacophony filled the air, echoing against itself.

Dallas cursed again. "I still don't get why we're stopped here."

"I don't think I can do it," said Doolittle. "I can't—"

Marcus held up a hand. "I get it. You want more money."

Doolittle scratched the top of his head.

A broad grin spread across Marcus's face. "I get it. It's a bait and switch. Happened to me in Syria. Maybe that's where you learned it, Doolittle."

"Bait and switch?" asked Dallas.

"Yeah," said Marcus. "Maybe not the exact right terminology, but it works. Basically you get someone, a local, to help you out. You know, like a fixer."

"I've heard of fixers," said Dallas.

"Right," said Marcus. "You agree on a price for what you need. It's all good until you get to a critical place or a tight spot. Then the price goes up, big time. You've got no choice but to pay it. Otherwise you're screwed."

Doolittle didn't argue, didn't dispute it. His expression tightened. He raised a pistol and leveled it at Marcus.

Marcus moved his arm to the sidewall of the bed. It was inches from Doolittle. He rapped his fingers on the metal.

"Slowly," said Doolittle, angling the barrel toward Marcus's chest.

"What's your new price, Private First Class Doolittle?" asked Marcus.

"Two thousand," he said. "Plus damages and gas."

Dallas cursed again. It was loud enough to silence the cicadas.

Marcus smiled. "Two thousand? That all? You got us stuck between a rock and a hard place here, Private First Class Doolittle. Why not ask for more?"

"Okay then," said Doolittle, his face hardening. "I'll take all you got."

"You're robbing us now?" asked Dallas.

Doolittle shrugged. "It's business," he said. "Nothing personal. You give me everything and I'll let you live. You can walk to the wall for all I care."

"We're not walking to the wall," said Marcus. "And we're not giving you everything we've got."

Doolittle snorted and barked a laugh. "Is that so, old man? You ain't got—"

In a swift move, with speed surprising even Marcus himself, he extended his arm and grabbed the back of Doolittle's neck with his hand. He shoved Doolittle's head down onto the metal side rail of the truck bed with such force the frame rattled and the gun fell into the bed.

Doolittle groaned and then slumped, falling to the road. His head hit it with a sickening smack. Marcus picked up the handgun and leaned over the side, aiming it at the heap beneath him. The injured man didn't move.

Dallas laughed. It was a nervous laugh. "Holy mother—"

"Watch your mouth," said Marcus. "And help me tie him up."

Marcus got to his knees, stood up with help from the side rail, and hopped over it. His knees screamed at him when he hit the ground next to an unconscious Doolittle.

Dallas followed him. The two stood in the road for a beat, and Marcus put his hands on his hips. He looked east from where they'd come, and west toward where they were headed.

The faint odor of rot danced in the air. They were near swampland. It was mostly mud now. There wasn't nearly the inland spread of water there'd once been. Bayous were less than streams now. Nonetheless, he could smell the vegetation.

"How'd you do that?" asked Dallas. "It was like a blur."

Marcus shrugged. "Honestly, I don't know. I think I got a surge of power or something because of the adrenaline. I don't like people trying to rip me off."

"I guess not."

"That, and I'm mad at myself for not seeing it, not sensing something was off with this guy."

"How would you know? He seemed legit."

"Most scammers do," said Marcus. "Otherwise they wouldn't be scammers."

"Good point," said Dallas. "So now what? We tie him up and leave him here?"

"Yep. Somebody will be along to help him eventually. We'll be long gone by then."

Dallas reached into the bed and pulled from it a length of rope. It was more like thick twine than rope, but it was plenty thick enough.

The two hog-tied Doolittle and hauled him to the side of the road. He was semiconscious by the time they'd finished the job. Marcus found a rag on the passenger's seat and shoved it into Doolittle's mouth.

Marcus patted him on the side of the face. "You've got quite a bruise there, Private First Class Doolittle. Probably gonna leave a mark. Good thing is, it's swelling. If it weren't, you'd probably have some brain problems pretty soon."

He winked at Doolittle. The man's eyes groggily opened and closed.

Marcus drummed the side of the bed with his hands and motioned for Dallas to join him in the cab. He swung open the driver's side door, which caught at the hinge and popped like it was about to break, and used it to help himself into the driver's seat.

The worn leather felt good against his legs and lower back. It was almost too comfortable. After spending the better part of the night in the back of the truck, Marcus was up for a nap in the cushy confines of the F-150's cab. As old as it was, it was better than the bed.

Marcus put his foot on the brake and hit the push-button ignition. The engine's electronics whirred and the engine cranked. The motor coughed and purred. The headlights offered a bright cone of light in front of them.

He shifted the automatic into gear and pushed the pedal. The truck jerked forward and he stepped on the brake.

"Put on your seatbelt, Dallas. It's been a while since I was behind the wheel."

Dallas pulled the belt across his chest, clicking it into place.

Marcus adjusted his own belt and eased his foot off the brake. The truck idled forward, and he slowly applied pressure to the gas pedal. The truck accelerated slowly, picking up speed, and Marcus aimed the truck along the center of the highway.

In the distance, beyond the horizon, a halo of hazy light rose above where Marcus knew the wall to be. His pulse quickened and a buzz of electricity ran up his spine. This was a place he was convinced he'd never go again.

As many good memories as Texas held for the man once known as Mad Max, there were bad ones that cast a pall over everything. Marcus checked the speedometer. He was cruising at thirty miles an hour. It wasn't fast, but it was fast enough. The truck rumbled against the uneven, neglected road and it vibrated through his body. He tightened his hands on the wheel and rubbed his thumbs against the leather wrap. Marcus thought about Doolittle and how their encounter could have gone a lot differently. He clenched his jaw against swelling anger.

"What were you saying about people being inherently good?" Marcus asked. "Benevolence and all that?"

Dallas sighed. "This doesn't change anything. One bad apple doesn't spoil the bunch."

Marcus chuckled derisively. "That's *exactly* what one bad apple does."

Dallas shrank in his seat and crossed his arms, tucking his hands under his armpits.

Marcus could tell the man-child was sulking. They drove another minute before Dallas sat up straight and stared at Marcus. The leather squeaked underneath the shift of his weight. "You always have to be right, don't you?" he fumed.

"I don't have to be," said Marcus. "Past experience tells me I'm not. I think your anger says more about you than it does about me."

Dallas snorted. "You're the doomsdayer who thinks the world is out to get you, and *I'm* the one with the problem. You're the self-pitying martyr who hid from the world, abandoned the people who loved you, who fought beside you, and *I'm* the one with the problem. You're the—"

Marcus slammed on the brakes. Hard. The tires screeched against the road. Dallas's momentum snapped him forward. The belt locked, holding him in his seat, and he threw out his hands to brace himself against the dash. Smoke from burning rubber lifted from the asphalt and surrounded the truck.

Marcus glared at Dallas, hoping it conveyed a rare combination of building rage and swelling disappointment. In the same moment he wanted to drop his head and sob, he wanted to throat punch the punk in his passenger's seat. Even if the kid had a point, Marcus didn't want to hear it. Not now. Not ever.

He gripped the steering wheel and swung toward Dallas. His fist balled, Dallas recoiled, backing into the corner of his seat where it met the passenger's door. Marcus didn't hit him. He aimed a rigid finger at him and jabbed it close to Dallas's face. It was close enough that every stab at the air made Dallas flinch.

"Enough," Marcus said through his teeth. "I know you blame me for hurting Lou. And you love her, so I hurt you. Get in line. My life is a trail of people I've disappointed, failed, abandoned."

Dallas's eyes were wide, his mouth open, slack with fear.

"But I don't need this crap," Marcus seethed. "Not from you. We're either on the same team or we're not."

Dallas had his hands at his chest. Fingers wrapped around the seatbelt, he gripped it like a security blanket.

"As for you"—Marcus jabbed a finger again—"either cut it out or get out."

Dallas's brow furrowed. "What?"

"Either stop with the arguing or get out. I'm not doing this with you. I've got a thick skin. I can take a lot. But I cannot handle the bickering with you when we've got a thousand things more important than allowing you your passive aggression."

Dallas started to speak. He didn't.

"So what is it?" Marcus said. "In or out?"

Dallas's eyes flitted across the cabin, landing everywhere but Marcus. Then he looked at him and nodded. "In."

"All right then," Marcus said. "Let's go cross the wall."

He patted Dallas on the thigh, and the kid jumped in his seat. Marcus laughed. This time it was genuine. He put the truck into gear and eased onto the gas pedal. The truck's engine responded and it accelerated.

"You thought I was gonna hit you?" asked Marcus, the angry tension in his voice having evaporated as quickly as it appeared. "Dude, I'm an old man."

Dallas adjusted himself in the seat. He faced forward and plucked at the seatbelt, loosening it before it snapped back against his chest. "Yeah," Dallas replied, his voice shaky, "but you're an old Marcus Battle, which isn't old."

They drove in silence until they reached the wall. The top of it rose above the horizon, as if lifting within the Earth. Even in the dark, with pale spotlights highlighting its stone facade, it looked to Marcus as it had the last time he'd crossed it more than a decade earlier.

Unlike his previous crossings, however, he was driving. And he was on a main thoroughfare that led straight through a protected opening. It wasn't a clear path though. There were large wooden structures flanking the road. More akin to shacks or sheds than full-fledged buildings, they looked like guardhouses. Armed men stood outside the one to the left.

Atop the wall there were a pair of snipers. One had his back turned to Marcus, appearing to scan the interior of the perimeter. The other had binoculars aimed at the truck. The guard dropped the binoculars to his chest and lifted a radio.

Marcus heard it squelch in the handheld transceiver of a man in front of him.

He took his foot off the accelerator. A pair of uniformed guards stood in the road between the truck and wall. The one with the radio said something and the other one leveled his rifle at Marcus. Then he flicked his hand, palm down, across his neck.

Marcus put the truck into park and killed the engine. The sound of cicadas and frogs bloomed in the air, adding a soundtrack to the building tension. Marcus kept his hands on the wheel, visible, as he had when he was a teenager and a state trooper pulled him over for speeding.

Marcus kept his eyes on the men as they approached. The one with the radio moved toward his side of the truck. The one with the rifle raised to his shoulder marched toward Dallas.

"Put your hands on the dash," Marcus said to Dallas.

"What?"

Marcus kept his eyes on the radio man. "Just do it, slowly."

Dallas slowly reached out and extended his arms. Keeping his fingers spread, he put his hands on the dash.

Both of the guards reached the truck at the same time. The one next to Marcus tapped the glass with the radio.

"Roll it down," he said. "Easy."

Marcus smiled. "Sure thing."

He found the control for the window and pushed it. It didn't work. He tried it again. Nothing happened.

"Truck has to be on," he said. "Can I start it?"

The radio man took a step back. He put the radio on his hip and lifted his sidearm. It was a nine millimeter. Taurus. Marcus hadn't seen one of those in ages.

"Careful," said the guard. "Don't put it in gear."

Marcus pushed the start button and the engine idled. He tapped the button and the window lowered; then he tapped the button for the passenger's side. It slid into the door. Marcus shut off the engine. The song of the cicadas was almost as deafening as it had been a couple of miles back.

The radio man stepped back to the window. He was young looking. His face was ruddy, his beard haphazard and blotchy. But his eyes still twinkled with the optimism of someone who hadn't lived long enough to lose it. They focused on Marcus, shot a look at Dallas, and moved back.

"Where are you headed?" asked the guard.

"Baird," Marcus answered.

"Why?"

"Does it matter?"

"It does," said the guard. "Why are you headed to Baird?"

Marcus aimed a thumb at Dallas. "His wife is there. I'm an old family friend. She asked me to visit, he came and got me, and we're headed back."

"What's the occasion?"

"Reunion," said Marcus. "I used to live near Rising Star, then settled in Baird. Moved north a while back. Live in Virginia now. I'm getting old. Wanted to spend some time together before it's too late for me."

"Where in Virginia?"

"Chatham."

Marcus knew the questions and answers were irrelevant to the guard. What mattered was the way Marcus spoke. It was his tone, his demeanor, the movement of his eyebrows, the twitch of his face.

When he'd been in the military, they'd learned techniques like this. It was the same sort of thing customs agents used to employ at the airport. They'd ask the same simple questions of everyone who came through.

Where are you headed? Business or pleasure? How long are you staying?

Marcus was impressed the technique was still in use. He tapped his fingers on the steering wheel. He wondered, though, if they'd have been better to try to sneak across or find a tunnel. He hadn't anticipated the twenty questions from an armed guard.

The guard glanced at Dallas and back at Marcus. Then he asked Dallas, "What's your wife's name?"

"Lou," said Dallas.

"Lou? That's a man's name."

"It's short for Louise," said Dallas. "But she doesn't like Louise."

Marcus chuckled. He dropped his chin and shook his head. The guard bristled.

"What's funny?" asked the guard.

"I'm just thinking about his wife," Marcus said. "She wouldn't like it if she heard you suggest her name was manly."

"That so?"

"Yep," said Marcus.

"Yep," said Dallas.

The guards exchanged glances through the cab of the truck, and the radio man nodded with his chin. The guard at the passenger's side backed away from the truck and lowered his weapon.

"All right," said the radio man, "move on, then. Approach slowly and they'll open the gate for you."

Marcus thanked the radio man, started the engine, and left the windows down. He pressed on the brake and shifted into gear, eased off the brake, and let the truck lurch forward.

As they neared the wall, one of the guards near the gate swung it open. The bottom of the gate scraped against the road. Marcus eyed the guard and nodded at him as they drove through the gate and under the wall. The guy couldn't have been more than twenty. He wasn't even alive when the Scourge hit. He probably didn't know a world without the wall. Marcus wished *he'd* never known one with it.

He pressed the accelerator and the truck responded. The engine rumbled. A warm breeze blew into the cab through the open windows. It smelled of dust and sweat.

Marcus Battle was back in Texas.

On the side of the road was a sign that told him Beaumont was thirty miles west and Houston was one hundred and eighteen. Baird had to be close to five hundred miles.

"There's no place like home," he said.

Chapter 19

APRIL 19, 2054, 7:00 AM
SCOURGE +21 YEARS, 7 MONTHS
RISING STAR, TEXAS

Lou sat with her back against the wall of the treehouse, her hands resting on her belly. Her attention was focused on the shafts of pink early morning light poking through the pine slats opposite her. She hadn't slept much. The cramping was gone, the labor pains likely false. That was something, at least. Still, they had a long day ahead of them. Maybe two.

David stirred and rolled onto his side to face her. "Momma, I gotta pee."

Lou smiled and put a hand on his head. She tousled his hair. "C'mon. Let's climb down. We need to hit the road anyhow."

After David took care of business, Lou watered the horse. Then she pulled out a package of jerky one of the Pop Guards had carried with him. Sitting on a stump, she unwrapped the brown paper, picked out a couple of the thicker pieces, and handed one to David.

"What is this?" he asked.

"Jerky."

"Jerky?"

Lou closed the package and stuffed it back into her pack. She held her piece between her fingers. Holding it up, she turned it over in her hands.

"Yeah," said Lou. She sniffed it and tore off a piece with her teeth. "It's meat. You cut off the fat and then dry it with salt."

David tentatively lifted his piece, studying it. "What kind of meat?"

Lou chewed. The jerky was sweet, a little gamey, and tasted something like venison but not quite. She tongued the jerky into her cheek and held it there, relishing the brine. "I don't know," she said, "but it tastes good and it's got protein. You're gonna need that today."

"Why?"

"Protein gives you energy. The salt will help you keep water in your body. That'll help with dehydration."

David sniffed the piece of jerky in his hand and wrinkled his nose. "I thought salt made you thirsty?"

Lou chewed and swallowed. "It does, but it also helps your body."

David put the jerky to his lips and sucked on it. Then he tore off a piece and chewed. The sour look on his face remained.

Lou chuckled. "Don't like it?" She took another bite.

David shrugged. He chewed and swallowed and tore off another bite.

Lou remembered how she'd been a picky eater before the Scourge. Her mom would fix the family a big meal or her dad would cook out on the grill in their backyard in Austin. Half the time, Lou wasn't interested in whatever her parents had made.

"There are starving kids in Syria," her dad would say, "and you're wasting food."

Lou would drag her fork across her full plate and eye him. Raising an eyebrow and smirking at her parents, she'd challenge, "Name three."

"Three what?" her mom would ask.

"Three starving kids in Syria."

That got a laugh and got them off her case. Then the Scourge killed most of the world, including her mother, and being picky wasn't an option. David was never picky. Even when he clearly didn't like the modest offerings on his plate, he would eat them without complaint. He was a good kid. He was too good for this world.

Lou swallowed another cheek full of jerky and blinked back a swell of tears. She popped the last of the jerky into her mouth and wiped her hands on her thighs. "All right, let's go, dude. Finish your jerky. We've got a lot of riding ahead of us today."

"My butt hurts," said David.

Lou smiled. "Mine too. I think we rode so much yesterday the baby is saddle sore."

David smiled. He tore off another piece of jerky and chewed.

Lou left him at the stump and moved back to the horse. It was tied off at the treehouse oak. She checked the rifle in the scabbard, made sure it was loaded, and pulled her knives from the saddlebag. She slid one into each of her boots, keeping the grips accessible, and slid a third into a sheath at the small of her back. It wasn't comfortable, especially given the constant ache along the base of her spine, but it was the best she could do.

Lou bloused the oversized coat Rudy had given her to wear and did her best to make sure the baby bump wasn't visible. Taking a swig from a canteen, she swished the warm water around in her mouth, freeing the bits of jerky stuck in her teeth.

To the east, the sun was above the horizon. The pink had given way to the pale blue of early morning. Thin, wispy clouds painted the low sky with wide brushstrokes.

To the west, the sky was still shades of purple where it met the uneven ground. Her eyes followed the hues until she was looking almost overhead. Inhaling deeply, Lou studied the heavens, deep in thought.

"I'm ready," said David.

Lou jumped. She hadn't noticed him sneak up on her. Startled, she put a hand to her chest. "All right," she said. "Let's do this."

She helped David into the saddle and climbed on behind him. The muscles in her back and thighs protested. They were sore and didn't like the familiar stress of riding a horse.

With a tug of the reins and kicks with her stirruped heels, Lou urged the horse forward. It loped at first but quickly found its stride. They reached the road and she guided the horse east. She glanced back at the treehouse and the piles of blackened char past it.

Lou was glad she'd found the place, that she'd taken the time to connect with Marcus. She was also profoundly sad. As much pain as she'd endured, as much as she'd lost, it was almost incomparable to what Marcus had managed to bear.

No wonder he is the way he is, she thought.

No wonder he'd been on a dark, vengeful quest when she met him at that gas station. No wonder he'd always carried something heavy, something invisible and burdensome. It was something she hadn't fully understood until she'd knelt in front of the five crude grave markers, until she'd spent the night with her child in the treehouse Marcus built for his.

They rode east and Lou tightened her hold on her son, feeling his back against her belly, as the horse moved at a good pace farther away from the place Marcus had called home. It wasn't long before David was leaning back against her, his head bobbing with sleep.

He reminded her so much of Dallas: thin, smart, sensitive. They were all good things, and they all had their drawbacks.

As her body swayed with the motion of the Appaloosa, she wondered how Dallas and Marcus were faring. She knew Dallas was angry and supposed Marcus wouldn't have it.

A smile crept across her face as she thought about the two of them arguing, about Dallas calling Marcus out for his absence, and Marcus telling Dallas he was a moron. She laughed out loud, envisioning their banter. It woke David. He sat up and rubbed his eyes.

"Sorry for waking you," she said. "You were out for a couple of hours."

David yawned. "It's okay," he said. He stretched his arms and then pointed into the distance.

Lou followed the direction of his finger. Before he said anything, she knew his next question. A cloud of dust bloomed like smoke a mile ahead of them. Then the question came.

"What's that?"

Lou narrowed her eyes, trying to focus on whatever was headed toward them. The plumes of dust rose higher into the sky, spread wider across the road. Her pulse quickened. Whatever it was, it was moving fast and headed straight toward them.

"Momma," said David, "what *is* that?"

"I don't know," she said.

"Good people or bad people?"

"I don't know."

"What do we do?"

The land on either side of the road stretched as far as she could see without any visible place to hide. Lou could go back, race toward Marcus's place. But that was more than two hours in the wrong direction.

She'd seen a ramshackle barn, collapsing under its own weight, maybe five or six miles back. But that might not be any better than standing in an open field of dead weeds and cracked earth.

"Momma?" David pressed. There was urgency and anxiety in the way he said her name.

"We're going to hide," she said. "Hang on."

Giving one last glance at the growing cloud of dust, she made out what looked like horses. Five or six horses, spreading beyond the edge of the narrow road. There might be more than a half dozen. She couldn't see from this distance. But they were closing, and there was a good chance they could see her.

Lou yanked the reins and spun the horse one hundred eighty

degrees. She drove her heels into its sides, and it reared its head before accelerating into a gallop. The Appaloosa was fast, faster than she'd expected, and the warm breeze on her face felt good. It blew her hair from her face and dried the sweat at her brow and on her neck behind her ears.

Clinging to David with one hand, they bounced in the saddle. Lou tightened her legs, bracing them against the up and down of the gallop. Her thighs burned, her back ached, but she urged the horse faster.

She checked. The cloud wasn't closer to them. If anything, they might have lost ground. Up ahead, the crumbling barn leaned toward them. Lou slowed the horse and guided it off the road and onto the dirt. It trotted the rest of the distance and, after dismounting, she tied it to the back side of the barn. It was the least visible spot from the road.

The barn, or shed, was built on a concrete foundation. A long forking crack that reminded Lou of a lightning bolt stretched across the gray and brown expanse. There was a rough-hewn cedar pole in the center of the space that reached up to a lattice of beams forming a false ceiling beneath what was left of the peaked roof. The beam was bolted into the concrete floor at its center but leaned at a slight angle where two of the bolts were loose from their hold.

Standing inside a gaping hole, which might have once been the doorway to the barn, Lou told David to stay put. She hustled, as best she could, back outside and loosened the Appaloosa's tie. She walked the horse inside the structure and affixed the lead to the center pole.

A trio of large cockroaches skittered across the floor and disappeared under a haphazard pile of cut wood in one corner of the barn. Lou followed them and then scanned the rest of the space.

The interior was bathed in arcs of early midmorning light. Angled shafts beamed through the wide holes in the roof and the spaces between the gray boarded walls. Dust danced and spiraled in the light. Lou tasted it in her mouth. She coughed and cleared her throat.

On the wall closest to the road there was a large box or piece of equipment covered in a dust-covered tarp. There was a stack of four or five chairs. A rusted spike aerator was parked along the adjoining wall, its hitch pointed diagonally upward. Leaning against the wall was a piece of sheet metal. It was jagged on one end and peppered with rust spots, giving it a burnt orange hue.

Directly behind Lou was a wooden A-frame ladder. It was collapsed and lying flat on the concrete. Lou took a couple of steps toward it, studied it, and then looked up at the beams overhead.

Outside, the rumble of hooves grew louder. Lou smiled at David, told him to be quiet, and moved to the wall facing the road, squeezing herself between the chairs and the tarp. Through a gap, she could see the narrow highway in front of her and the flat expanse on the other side. Dead trees dotted the landscape, their bare limbs stretching out as if reaching for water.

There was no sign of the approaching horses, but she could hear them. The rhythm of their gallop masked their numbers. Lou wiggled her way back from the wall, leaned on the stack of chairs for balance, and moved to the wall facing northeast.

She found a narrow gap and pressed against it. Narrowing her gaze to adjust for the brighter light, she saw the coming threat. Eight horses, eight men.

"Pop Guard," she muttered. They were perhaps five hundred yards away.

"What?" asked David, and Lou jumped again. He'd ignored her and was at her side. The kid was sneaky quiet.

"Sheesh, dude," she said. "You can't *do* that."

She noticed the abject fear on her child's face, his wide, watery eyes and wrinkled brow. His chin trembled and his little hands were clenched into fists.

Lou crouched down to his level, put her hands on his shoulders, and locked eyes with him. "Sorry," she said, softening her tone. "I'm not mad at you. You're just so good at sneaking up on me that sometimes it frightens me."

"What's wrong, Momma? Who's coming?"

"Bad guys," Lou said. "So I need you to do exactly as I say."

David nodded.

Lou hugged him, kissed the top of his head, inhaled the sweaty stink of his hair, and stood up, wincing at the sting of pain in her back. It ran down her leg and made the back of her thigh burn.

She moved over to the tarp and pulled it back. Dust clouded around her and she fanned it from her face. Once she'd rubbed her eyes, she saw what the tarp was hiding.

"Perfect," she said and waved David toward her.

A large metal tool chest, the kind mechanics used to have in their garages, sat mostly intact. To the left was a large cabinet. Lou slid her fingers into the molded grip at its side and pulled. The door swung open with a loud whine. The space inside was empty other than a collection of dead insects and wisps of spiderwebs.

"I need you to get inside, David. It's like hide-and-seek and the quiet game mixed together."

David eyed the dark cabinet with suspicion. "There are bugs."

"Don't worry," she said, forcing a smile, "you won't scare them."

David frowned.

"They're all dead. They won't hurt you. And it's only until the bad guys are gone."

David drew his hands to his face and scratched his cheeks.

"C'mon, David. We don't have time."

David nodded and crawled into the space. It was large enough for him to fit but too small to be comfortable.

"I love you," she said. "I'm going to close the door and cover it up. It's going to be dark. Try to nap."

David closed his eyes and huffed, blowing out a worried breath. Lou closed the door.

Outside, the Pop Guard was much closer. She could hear individual gallops now. It was less rhythmic and more haphazard. She grabbed both sides of the sheet metal and picked it up. Heavier than she expected it to be, she dropped it with a warbling clang. Lou winced at the vibrating noise she was sure echoed beyond the porous walls of the ramshackle barn.

"What's that?" David's muffled voice came from inside the cabinet. "Momma?"

Lou grunted and bent her knees to try again. "It's okay," she said to reassure her son. "I dropped something."

"I love you, Momma," he said, his sweet voice tearing at Lou's chest.

Lou heaved the sheet metal to the tool chest and laid it against the cabinet, repositioning it to cover the door.

Quickly, she replaced the tarp. "I love you too," she said. "Very much."

She held the underside of her belly and hustled to the horse, withdrew the rifle from the scabbard, and crossed the space to the ladder.

It took her a minute to lift and open the A-frame. Although her back and thighs protested, she managed. The ladder was tall enough she could reach the overhead framework.

With the rifle in one hand and her other on the ladder, she climbed it one rung at a time. The ladder was rough, the hinges were loose, and her movements were unsteady. More than once, she wavered, her balance in jeopardy.

At the top rung, Lou reached over her head and raised the rifle toward the lattice of cedar beams. She rested it on a joint where two beams connected and then lifted herself to the top of the ladder. With what strength she could muster, she pulled up on a beam and lifted one leg, then the other.

Out of breath, she lay still for a moment, acutely aware of her pulse in her neck and chest. Outside she heard voices. The clop of horses had slowed. Quickly and quietly, she repositioned herself in the rafters and shouldered the rifle.

She leaned on one side, unable to aim from a true prone position because of the baby. Lou remembered what her father had taught her a lifetime ago and controlled her breathing to slow her pulse.

Women were better shots, he told her. They could slow their heart rate and steady themselves better than men.

"I could swear I saw something," said one of the voices. It was a high-pitched voice, nasal-infused. "Right around here."

"I don't see anything," said another voice, deeper and more resonant.

"Maybe there ain't nothing," said a third, thick with a Southern twang.

"We gotta head west," said the deeper voice. "We don't have time for this."

Lou had thirty rounds in the fully loaded magazine, she had three knives, and she had the high ground. She exhaled slowly, hoping she wouldn't need any of them.

"Nope," said the first voice, "I see some tracks. Right here. They're leading to the barn."

"Where?" asked a fourth voice.

"Here." Then the first of the men appeared at the barn's entry.

Lou cursed to herself as a second man materialized. Then a third and a fourth. All of them stood in the daylight outside the barn. Two of them had pistols drawn. One shouldered a rifle like the one through which she targeted him. The fourth started to move inside the barn.

"If there's a horse," he said, "there's bound to be—"

Lou didn't wait. There was no point. She applied pressure to the trigger, and the rifle punched a round into the man's chest. The crack pierced the dry air before she fired another round that found the target's stomach. The man clutched his gut and staggered backward. Without waiting for him to hit the ground, she pivoted and fired a trio of rounds into the man with the rifle. Then she drilled a pair into one of the other two guards and then a single shot into the other.

One of the downed targets squirmed on the floor, kicking his legs, his arms reaching for the sky. Lou sighted the man's head and plunked a single shot into his temple. He stopped moving.

Her eyes darted across the floor at the motionless quartet of bodies. A sticky web brushed against her forehead. She dipped her chin and used her shoulder to wipe it free. Her pulse thumped against her neck, her chest, her temples. Perspiration formed on her cheeks, the back of her neck, the small of her back.

She glanced at the tarp under which her son hid. It was undisturbed. Again, she swept the barn with her eyes and found the bodies near the entrance. Four down, four to go.

She kept her aim at the opening. Nobody appeared. The adrenaline spread through her, reaching her fingers and her toes. She was hyperaware now. Her senses tingled. Time stretched, Any second now, a barrage of gunfire would erupt at the opening. She'd be ready. What felt like minutes was only a few seconds.

But when the return fire exploded, it didn't come from the doorway. It was all around her.

Daylight sparked through the holes in the wooden walls. It was coming from everywhere, a deafening barrage that engulfed the barn in a hail of hot metal projectiles that splintered wood, clanged off metal, and produced clouds of debris and shrapnel. The entirety of the space bloomed with dust. The Appaloosa whinnied, tugging at its line. It shook its head wildly. It kicked, and then it dropped, falling to its side.

Instinctively Lou buried her head and squeezed her eyes closed. She wanted to curl into a ball against the relentless onslaught. She let go of the rifle with one hand and used it to strengthen her hold on the rafter upon which she was precariously perched. She felt the percussive cracks in her body, vibrating through the cedar as the barn somehow withstood the attack.

Then it was over. The gunfire stopped abruptly. The barn groaned, a prolonged creak signaling the weakness of its structure.

She opened her eyes and squinted against the brightness of the light that filled the space.

Lou wiped the dust from her face and took hold of the rifle, settling herself. Her finger found the comfortable curve of the trigger, and she readied her aim. Then, from behind her, a stuttering creak blossomed as part of the wall collapsed and she was bathed in light.

Two figures were climbing through the large gap. They didn't seem to notice her, their rifles sweeping the room. She wasn't in a position to fire, unable to shift her aim or her body without making too much noise. Lou waited.

The men crossed the space cautiously, the weapons' aim following their eyes as they moved toward the collection of bodies near the entrance into the barn. One of them stood watch while the other knelt to check on the dead men.

That man was in her sights now, but the other was directly beneath her. If she opened fire, he'd have a clear shot. And there were two more men whose position she didn't know.

Lou held her breath, unaware she was doing it until her lungs burned. Slowly, she let it out through her nostrils.

A third man appeared at the entry. He said something she couldn't hear, her ears still muted and ringing from the gunfire moments earlier. Then he saw her.

His eyes locked on her like an animal about to pounce. Before he could alert the others, Lou put two quick shots in his chest. The man stumbled backward, dropping his semiautomatic rifle.

Lou trained the rifle on the squatting man at the bodies. A single shot to his head snapped his neck sideways, and blood sprayed out the back. He toppled onto the body next to him, his eyes wide, his feet twitching.

The man beneath her looked up and pointed his rifle at her. She met his gaze and saw his true aim and his finger already on the trigger. Time slowed again. Her mind raced with memories and questions.

David. Dallas. Marcus. Rudy. Norma. Her father. Her mother. A funeral pyre. A library. The feel of a blade in her hand. The power of it hitting a target. A house on a river. The baby growing inside her. Her Astros ball cap. Rudy's dog Fifty. Dallas. Her boy inside the cabinet. Trapped maybe. Who would find him? What would happen? How could this be how it ends?

Lou was frozen. She couldn't move. Not with the rifle in her hands. Not with her belly. Her focus narrowed on the end of the man's barrel as he squeezed the trigger. Lou braced herself.

Click.

She took the rifle and threw it at the guard. Its butt hit him in the shoulder and staggered him. He dropped his rifle and reached for the handgun at his hip. It was holstered and he struggled with it, giving Lou the time she needed.

She reached the small of her back and found the single throwing knife. In a fluid motion, she grabbed the handle, withdrew the blade from its sheath, rolled onto her side for momentum, and rolled back as she shot the knife at her target.

The weapon spun twice end over end, whipping across the short distance and accelerating with gravity. It drove hard into the man's neck where it met his shoulders. He cried out in pain, shrieked, and flailed, grabbing for the blade.

Lou drew her knee up and pulled a second blade from her boot. As the man dropped to one knee and turned, she flung the knife at him. The flat throw drove the knife between his shoulder blades.

He shrieked again, his back arched, and he lost his balance, falling back. He hit the concrete, the force of his fall driving the blade deeper into his back. He gargled something as he looked blankly up at Lou. Blood leaked from the corners of his mouth and trickled from his nose as his last gasp rattled from his throat.

Lou looked behind her, through the gap in the wall, then snapped back to face the barn's opening. There was still one man alive. She didn't see him. Unarmed aside from her one remaining knife, she couldn't stay exposed on the rafter. As quickly as her body allowed, she swung herself from the rafter onto the A-frame ladder. Incredibly it still stood despite the hail of gunfire that had shattered much of the place.

She slid down the rungs, and her boots hit the concrete. The solid connection shot through her legs and lower back. Lou winced with pain. Then a cramp swelled low in her body. It tightened, sending waves of clenching pain through her gut and back.

She doubled over in pain, sweat dripping into her eyes.

Lou grunted and grabbed at the underside of her belly. "Now?" she growled. "Are you kidding me?"

As inconvenient as the cramps had been at Marcus's place the night before, this was absurd. It was as if karma was telling her something.

Lou staggered forward and bent over to pull the knife from the dead man in front of her. Instead, though, she took his handgun from the brown leather holster at his hip. His dead eyes stared at her as she freed the weapon and checked the magazine.

Where is the eighth man?

Lou stood against the undulating tension that pulsed through her body. Gripping the gun with both trembling hands, she stalked the empty space. The carnage in front of her was still. There was no breeze. The smell of cedar and dust was pungent, and Lou coughed against the particulate in the air, moving forward one careful step at a time.

Splinters of wood crunched and dust slid under her boots as she moved. The handgun trembled in her hand as she struggled to keep it leveled in front of her. The swells of pain threatened to drop her to her knees. She swung from one side to the other, trying not to leave herself exposed.

From the corner of her vision, she caught movement. Whirling in that direction, she saw another flash on the outside of the barn. It moved beyond the gaps and holes in the standing wall, the shadow of its figure blocking out the light as it passed from one space to the next.

Lou tracked it with the gun. Her finger on the trigger, she steadied herself until another tsunami of contracting agony forced a grunt from her throat, and the weapon wavered. She backed up. Her vision blurred and she tightened her jaw. Teeth digging into her cheek until she tasted blood, Lou kept her composure and silence until the wave subsided.

The release of pain was almost as jarring as its sudden arrival. It was as if someone holding her up had let go. Her knees weakened and she stumbled as the eighth man stepped into view.

Lou fired a shot before he saw her. Then a second. She missed both times. The first drilled into the edge of the opening, ringing off a metal hinge. The second zipped between the doorframe and the hostile.

The man had his rifle at his shoulder, a hunter stalking prey, and swung to face the source of the incoming fire. He shifted to avoid her errant shots and lowered the rifle for an instant. His finger was on the trigger, and the crack of his rifle rode on the echo of her twin shots. The thick sound of metal on metal thunked behind her.

It barked twice and Lou felt a punch to her leg. The hit was followed by searing heat. She cried out and returned fire before losing her balance.

This time her aim was on target. A quartet of shots hit the man one after the other. It was a wide pattern, but it was enough. He popped off another series of rounds that sprayed wildly into the air as he fell.

Lou was on the ground, the hard concrete jabbed at her hip, and she watched the man stagger forward and drop. His was the last of the eight lives she'd ended single-handedly.

She needed to get to David. He was still in the cabinet. Alone and likely frightened.

"David?" she called.

No answer. A thick lump caught in her throat.

"David?" she called, recognizing the tremor in her voice.

Lou rolled onto her back, not wanting to look at her injury. The heat gave way to a bruising ache that took her breath away. She sat up on her elbows and prepared herself for the worst.

A smile twitched at the corners of her mouth when she saw the bloodstain at the outside edge of her thigh and the torn fabric at its center. Lou tugged at her pants and saw the wound was a nick. She was grazed at her thigh. A small chunk of flesh was gone. She needed to stop the bleeding, but it was minor. A bandage and some painkillers would do the trick.

"David?" she called again. "Are you okay?"

Convinced she could stand, Lou struggled to her feet and tested her injured leg. It hurt, but she could put weight on it. Limping, she made her way to the tarp. The barn was spinning. Her balance was off. Her heart pounded.

"David?" The worry was panic now. Her hands trembled as she tugged free the tarp. It pillowed, floated, and drifted to the ground as her eyes fell to the sheet metal. Her heart nearly stopped.

It was pockmarked with bullet holes. Lou counted five of them.

"David?" Panic was abject fear now.

Lou ignored the pain, adrenaline coursing through her as she flung back the metal plate. It slapped against the concrete, forcing up a cloud of dust. Lou coughed against it, dropped to both knees, wincing against the explosion of pain in her thigh, pulled open the door, and looked inside the small space. Her vision blurred, and she nearly lost consciousness.

David was inside. His eyes were closed, his body pulled into a tight ball, his hands pressed against his ears.

"David!" Lou shouted, reaching for his arm.

He opened his eyes and dropped his hands, diving at his mother with wide arms. She enveloped him in hers.

Both of them cried, sobbing, as they embraced. Lou kissed his head again and again. She inhaled the stink on his head, laughing at it through her veil of tears.

Lou pulled back and grabbed both sides of his face, cupping his cheeks with her sweaty palms. Her eyes studied him. He was okay. No injuries, no scratches, no blood.

The surge of adrenaline that had powered her through the violent encounter and the uneven stagger to free her son faded. Instantly, exhaustion washed over her, and she wanted to collapse on the floor, her son in her arms.

"You're okay," she said finally. The words came like hiccups. "You're not hurt."

David wiped his nose with the back of his hand.

Lou swiped his hair from his forehead. "But you didn't answer me when I called you," Lou said softly. "I was so scared."

"It was too loud," David said. "I covered my ears. I tried to pretend I was somewhere else. I closed my eyes and pretended."

Lou's heart sank. David's innocence was gone. There was no avoiding it. Being a child was tough enough in a drought-ravaged existence. Add to that the violence he'd witnessed over the past few days, and his childhood was evaporating before her eyes.

Tears streamed down her cheeks, streaking clean the dust and dirt that covered her face. Lou forced a flat smile and leaned in to kiss his forehead again.

"What happened?" he asked. "Are all the bad guys gone?"

Lou nodded. "They are. I want you to close your eyes again. Take my hand. I'll take you back to the horses."

"What about our horse?"

Lou shook her head. "I think we need a new one."

David stood, reaching for his mother's hand. He found one and laced his fingers between hers.

Lou stood unsteadily, using the tool chest to support her weight. She grimaced against the dull throb at the outside of her thigh and led David through the mess of bodies. As they passed the Appaloosa, Lou checked to make sure the poor animal was out of its misery. It was. Still and silent, the horse somehow retained its majesty even in death.

Lou bit into her cheek and led David out into the daylight. Each step sparked a bolt of pain in her leg, but she managed to get him outside and to the collection of eight horses standing at the edge of the road, picking at weeds and desert brush with their teeth. They swatted at the odd fly with their tails.

"Okay," said Lou. "You can open your eyes. It's bright out here though, so open them slowly."

David let go of his mother's hand and shielded his eyes from the sunlight. He surveyed the horses and glanced back at the barn. His face was contemplative, but he didn't speak.

"All right, David, pick a horse. Whichever is your favorite, that's the one we'll take. I'm going to get the rest of our stuff from inside the barn. Okay?"

David nodded. He stepped back and then glanced at his mother's leg. The boy did a double take and frowned. "Momma, you're bleeding."

Lou looked down at her leg. Her pants were soaked with blood now. It leeched across her thigh toward her crotch and down below her knee. "I'm okay. I'll clean it up in a second."

David focused on the wound. "It doesn't look okay."

"It's okay," she said. "It's a flesh wound. It nicked me. Looks worse than it is."

David locked eyes with her and then looked again at her leg dubiously, but he nodded and didn't say anything else.

Lou turned on her good leg and limped back toward the barn. As she rounded the corner to walk inside, she glanced back at her son. He was studying the horses with his hands on his hips.

She checked the road, the horizon, looking for any threats. Seeing none, she dipped back into the barn.

It already smelled different. The strong scent of cedar was mixed with blood and death and excrement.

Lou crinkled her nose at the odor and maneuvered her way across the bodies toward her horse. The large beast was on its side, its legs awkwardly tucked underneath its body.

Thankfully her pack was next to it and not trapped on the underside of the Appaloosa's frame. But its strap was stuck, still attached to the saddle.

Lou limped the few steps to the man whose body still held two of her knives. She put her boot on his shoulder and used the leverage to pull free the one in his neck. She wiped the blood clean from the blade on the man's shirt and used the blade to cut the strap from the pack. That freed the bag and she yanked it loose. She dragged the bag back to the dead man closest to her. Her third blade was still in his back.

Lou dropped to her knees, withstanding the pain in her thigh, and reached across the man to pull his arm over his chest. She sat back and pulled on his arm, rolling him onto his side. The dead weight was heavy. It tugged at her lower back, which ached from the pressure of the pregnancy and was additionally sore from the contractions she'd endured.

Lou freed the knife and wiped it clean on his arm. She slid the pack next to her and used the blade to cut away the fabric at her thigh. She set the knife beside her and tugged at the fabric, tearing it wide enough to reveal the full wound.

Bile rose in her throat as she looked at the damage to her leg. Swallowing it, she unzipped the pack and found the first aid kit. She cleaned the wound and dressed it, wrapping an Ace bandage around the circumference of her thigh. It held both the dressing and the torn pants in place.

She'd lost a lot of blood. That contributed to her exhaustion, she was sure. But there was no rest for the weary. They had miles to go before it got dark again. So she pressed forward.

Hero

Scavenging what she could from the dead men in the barn, Lou slung an overstuffed pack and a pair of fully loaded rifles from the barn and went back to the road. David was sitting in the dirt, feeding a horse weeds from his palm. He was smiling.

"C'mon," she called out to him. "Let's gear up and head out, dude. We're behind schedule."

Chapter 20

APRIL 19, 2054, NOON
SCOURGE +21 YEARS, 7 MONTHS
DALBY SPRINGS, TEXAS

Andrea's jaw clenched. A wave of anger surged through her as rivulets of sweat dripped from her face. She balled her hands into fists.

"We're going to leave her," said Warner. "Cut her free, Blessing."

Andrea strained against her binds. The chains clanged. She spat when she snapped at her captors. "You can't do this," she said. "You can't leave her."

Warner raised an eyebrow and glanced back at her. He said nothing, turned, and jutted his chin toward the new mother. "Take the kid," he said to Blessing. "Cut her free."

The sun was high overhead. It beat down on the chain gang as they stood in the middle of the highway.

The new mother refused to let go of the child at first. She held the baby tight to her chest. Her fingers wrapped the back of her head, underneath her fleshy thighs.

Even a gun to her temple wasn't enough to make her let go of the baby, so Blessing pressed the barrel against the forehead of the woman next to her.

Hero

Warner put his hands on his hips and winked. "I'd go ahead and do what I asked. Every minute that passes and you don't, we're gonna kill another one of your lady friends. Then we'll start shooting other children. Even your older one. You might be the last one standing. Then we'll shoot you."

She wavered but tightened her grip. Her chin quivered. Her shoulders shuddered.

"Then all of this was for nothing," said Warner. "'Cause you could hand over the baby now and avoid everyone else getting plugged."

She kissed the baby on the forehead and offered it to Blessing. He shook his head and motioned to the woman at whom he'd been aiming his pistol.

The woman took the child and cradled it, mouthing her apologies to the new mother, who now had her trembling hands over her mouth, suppressing her sobs. Her eyes were wide with pain. Her legs were bloody and her chest heaved.

Blessing began his work on her binds while Warner stalked the chain gang like an officer inspecting his troops. His boots scraped along the asphalt. There was a hitch in his walk, a limp still evident from the blow Andrea had struck in the jail.

"We're way behind schedule, ladies," he said. "What should have taken us seven hours has taken us ten. At this rate, we're never going to reach Fort Worth. Or if we do, a good half of you will be carrying babies in your arms instead of your bellies."

The women were all crying now, as if the new mother's sobs were infectious. Andrea suppressed her sadness underneath the building rage, her eyes glassy with tears she refused to release. Her narrow gaze was locked on Warner as he moved past her and continued babbling another soliloquy. She was convinced the man was a sadist, not just because of his violence, but because of his insistence in making other people listen to him speak.

"We need to move faster," he said. "We have places to be and people to see. I don't think you understand the urgency of this, the necessity of being on time."

He reached the end of the chain gang and paused. His arms were behind his back, one hand holding onto the opposite wrist. Warner lifted his chin and spun on his boot heels, the leather grinding against the asphalt, and started back along the line.

"There is a weak link," he said. "We have to get rid of it."

The new mother wailed through her cupped hands. Saliva seeped through her fingers, and sticky threads of it hung from her chin. It was the most pitiful and gut-wrenching thing Andrea had ever seen. And that was saying something.

"So," Warner dragged out the word for effect and took a long stride to match it, "we're providing incentive for the rest of you to move with purpose. That's what this is. At its core, it's an incentive."

"You can't do this," Andrea said over the wails of the other women and the whimpers of the children. "You can't leave her here. She'll die. There's no water, no food, nowhere to sleep. You're killing her."

Warner took two steps toward Andrea and leaned in with a hardened expression. His eyes were obsidian pools that absorbed light. Black holes.

She didn't flinch. "You're killing her," she repeated, the venom oozing as she spoke.

"She's killing herself," Warner said. He jabbed a finger at her. "And I heard enough outta you."

"The children are slower than the adults," said Andrea. "The fastest child can't keep up with the slowest women. You're being cruel."

Warner lowered his hand and shifted his weight from one leg to the other. His expression softened, his eyes remaining black holes, sucking in the light around them. Adjusting the cap on his head, he took a deep breath and held it.

"I'm being practical," said Warner. A grin twitched. "Maybe this will be an incentive for the kids too."

Andrea lunged at him, but she couldn't reach him. Her chain snapped taut. Then she turned on the chain gang. "Are none of you going to stop him?" she cried. "Are you just going to sit there and take this? You're going to let them take our children from us and lead us to slaughter? Or worse?"

The other women averted their eyes, their shoulders hunched with despair. Tears rolled down their cheeks. They wrung their hands or held their children or rubbed their bellies. None of them said anything.

Warner scanned the chain gang. He snorted a laugh and took a step close enough to Andrea that she could smell his sweat and his hot, fetid breath. She wrinkled her nose as he moved to within inches of her.

"Looks like you're on an island, chickadee," he whispered. "Might be best you keep your musings to yourself."

Andrea drew a flood of saliva into her mouth and spat, hitting Warner in his left eye. He flinched and stepped back. His grin broadened and he wiped the spit with his thumb and walked away.

"Let's move," he said to Blessing.

The new mother was free of her binds. She was off the road, in the dirt next to a wiry shrub. She was on her knees, hands out in front of her clasped in prayer. Her body trembled.

Blessing held the woman's older child by the hand, another woman held the baby, and the chain gang began to move. They shuffled slowly away from the woman.

Warner stepped away from the line and handed the woman a canteen and some rations.

Andrea watched this and considered stopping. She could sit in the road and refuse to move. Then they couldn't leave the woman behind.

Yet that wouldn't do any good. They'd hurt her or Javier. They'd leave her to die. There was no point in it. She had to keep walking. Keep walking.

Andrea glanced at the woman in the dirt, the new mother who'd never know her child. "Walk," she called out to her. "Walk with us. Keep walking with us."

A murmur rippled through the chain gang, as if nobody had even considered this as a possibility. There was nothing to keep the woman from walking alongside them. They could help her. She could keep up.

Craning her neck to see behind her, Andrea called again. This time louder and with more command. "Get up! Walk with us."

The woman stood, collecting the canteen and the package of food. She scrambled from the dirt and onto the road. Stumbling awkwardly, she followed the chain gang.

Warner said nothing at first. He marched ahead, leading the gang toward their destination. Then he hung back, trailing the caravan of women and children, occasionally glancing back at the new mother struggling to keep pace.

After an hour, Warner pulled even with Andrea. He pulled off his cap and raked his fingers through his greasy hair. The sound of his fingers scratching his scalp made Andrea shudder. He wiped his brow and replaced the cap.

Andrea kept her eyes forward, watching him in her peripheral vision but not giving him the satisfaction of thinking she paid him any attention. She braced for another diatribe. Instead he offered seven words.

"You only made it worse for her," he said.

Andrea clopped forward. Her ankles raw, every step burning against the blisters that had formed, burst, and formed again, she kept moving. The new mother was staggering now. She was fifty yards behind them and losing ground.

Andrea wanted to run back and help the woman along. She flexed her hands in and out and shook them at her sides. Her exhaustion gave way to anxiety when Warner tipped his cap to her and stopped walking.

Hero

He stood in the middle of the road, staring at her as the chain gang kept its pace. Andrea kept checking at decreasing intervals. She tripped once, but the woman behind her caught her arm before she fell.

Still, Andrea didn't want to take her eyes from Warner. Her stomach twisted. Her throat tightened. She shortened her steps to a shuffle so she could keep pace and her balance.

Warner stood in the road, unmoving, growing smaller the farther Andrea got from him. He stared at her. Even at a distance she could feel it, the tractor beam of mass in his eyes.

Then he turned and slowly walked, sauntered really, toward the new mother, who was barely able to stand. She appeared drunk on the road, woozily moving from one side to the other.

Andrea was far enough away now that she couldn't see. She couldn't turn her neck far enough to tell what was happening. She didn't need to see it. Her gut, her roiling gut, told her what was coming next. Andrea didn't want to believe it. She wanted to tell herself Warner would give her more water and tell her to rest. She hoped he'd launch into another speech that he gave as if it held some philosophical meaning, when in reality it was dime-store nonsense.

The pop that cracked through the air, its echo that hung behind them and above them and around them, told her Warner hadn't helped her. He hadn't offered water or advice or anything other than a bullet.

Andrea's body shuddered with the pop. She wanted to puke, but there was nothing left. A ripple of muffled cries worked its way through the chain gang. They all knew what had happened.

They all knew there were two orphans now traveling with them. Andrea steeled herself, tightened her grip on Javier's hand, and told herself it was for the best. If they were all going to die or be slaves to a tribe, a quick shot to the head might be the most merciful thing for which any of them could hope. Warner did her a favor.

Andrea shook the thought from her mind and chastised herself for having thought it. This wasn't the end. She would not be a slave. Nobody would take her children from her. Andrea convinced herself she would find a way out. One way or the other, she would escape, she would free the others, and she would kill Warner.

Chapter 21

APRIL 19, 2054, 3:00 PM
SCOURGE +21 YEARS, 7 MONTHS
ATLANTA, GEORGIA

Sally couldn't sit still. She paced restlessly, rubbing her hands together. A glaze of sweat covered her face, her bare shoulders, her neck.

Gladys sat in her chair, her hands folded in her lap. Her flat expression was unchanged from the last half hour of the session with Sally.

"You already know all of this," said Sally. "Why do I need to tell you? Why me? You've said repeatedly I'm not special, that you've done this before. I'm sure other unremarkable people have shared with you everything. Ev-er-y-thing."

"They have," Gladys conceded.

Sally stopped pacing, frozen in place by the surprisingly candid response. She motioned toward Gladys with her hands. "See? You admit it. So we're done. Can I get a cigarette?" Her eyes flitted across the room. She started to pace again.

"I don't have any," Gladys said. "And I didn't think you smoked."

"I didn't. I think I need to start."

Gladys's expression softened, and the faintest hint of a smile formed at the edges of her lips. It flashed and disappeared. "Have a seat. It may be that I know the origin of things, the progression of them. But I need to hear them from your perspective. More importantly, you need to hear it. You need to hear yourself say it aloud."

Sally plopped into the armchair she'd claimed as her own on that first night and lolled her head back dramatically. She rolled her eyes and slapped her hands on the plush fabric arms of the chair.

"How did you find out about the railroad?"

Sally rapped her fingers on the chair. "When is my next job going to get here?" she asked. "Any update?"

"They're here when they're here," said Gladys. "How did you find out about the railroad?"

Sally lowered an ear toward her shoulder until her neck popped; then she did the other side. "A friend of a friend," she said. "I was looking for work. For a place to stay. I got approached. I'd been hassled a lot by the government, and this was my chance to get back at them."

"So you were angry?"

Sally exhaled audibly and nodded. "Yes. I mean, who isn't angry? This world sucks. I was a kid when the Scourge happened. I don't really even remember it that well. I remember a lot of crying, a lot of moving around, a lot of hunger."

"You lost your home?"

"I don't know if we lost it or it was taken from us. It's blurry and I don't really like to think about it. My father and older brother died. It was me and my mom."

"What happened to her?"

"What happened to a lot of women after the Scourge?" Sally asked. "She worked. She did what she could to provide. But there was no economy, not for years. And once it got going again, she was worn out. I found her in bed."

"She died," said Gladys. "And you found her."

"She was a drunk. Took pills too. So I was on my own. Then the drought takes hold and look where we are."

"You're from Atlanta?"

Sally shook her head. "Florida. Orlando. We ended up here."

"Why were you recruited for the railroad?"

Sally shrugged. She plucked at her shirt and fanned herself with it. "It's hot in here," she said. "Is it hot in here? Are you hot?"

Gladys shook her head. She crossed her legs at the ankles and pressed the wrinkles from her long skirt.

"I think they recruited me because I was good at sneaking around."

"How so?" Gladys pointed at the cluttered coffee table. "There's a glass of water if you're thirsty."

Sally scooted to the edge of the wide seat and took the glass. She gulped it like a child, tendrils of water leaking from the sides of the glass. The glass was empty in a matter of seconds, but Sally kept it in her hands. Leaning back in the seat, her toes touching the floor en pointe, she rubbed the glass with her thumbs like it was a totem. "I was good at finding things that belonged to other people, and taking them for myself or others."

"You were a thief."

Sally frowned. She glanced at Gladys then focused on the glass in her hands. "I liked to think of myself as Robin Hood. You know the old story about the guy who took from the rich and gave to the poor?"

Gladys blinked but remained silent. She uncrossed her legs and folded her hands in her lap, her silence prodding Sally for more.

"Yes," Sally acknowledged with an eye roll. "I was a thief. But I took from people who had more than enough, and I shared it with people who had little."

"How did the railroad find out?"

"I took from someone with the railroad," she said. "I got caught. Instead of ratting me out to the government, I was offered a job."

Gladys raised an eyebrow. "Conductor."

Sally nodded. She slid a finger inside her shirt collar and tugged it, stretching it along her neck.

"Then what?" Gladys prompted.

"I didn't want the job, but I didn't have a choice. And to be honest, it was a pretty sweet deal. They gave me a place to stay, they fed me, and I was doing something good with my sneakiness."

Gladys tilted her head to one side. "Something good," she said. It was both a statement and a question.

"I knew about the quotas," said Sally. "That women couldn't have more than one kid, and if they did, the government took the kid from her. That wasn't right. The railroad told me I could do good."

"And you did good," said Gladys. Again, a statement rolled into a question.

Sally shrugged. "I guess. They told me I was one of their best. They'd recruited a lot of people from Texas, but said I was as good as any of them."

Gladys put her elbow on the arm of her chair and set her chin in her hand. "Why?"

"Why was I good?"

"Why Texas?"

"Because Texas was full of people doing weird things," said Sally. "They've got the wall, so people were always trying to move across it one way or the other. There were different smugglers. The Cartel, I think. Then there were the canyon people."

"The Dwellers."

Sally snapped her fingers and pointed at Gladys. "Yeah, them. Plus there were a bunch of gangs. It seemed like ever since the Scourge, people in Texas were forced to run or hide from something. Took a generation, but they got good at it. So the railroad made friends down there. Hired people away."

"But you were as good as them," said Gladys. "Then what happened?"

Sally inhaled through her nose and exhaled through her pursed lips. She rubbed the glass with her thumbs. "I think I saved more than five hundred women and their babies. Five hundred. I calculated that's a thousand people now. At least. Then if they have kids and they have kids, that's tens of thousands of people I saved."

Sally looked up from the glass. The sweat had dried on her forehead and cheeks. Her neck was cooler now too. The trembling in her hands had subsided.

"Tens of thousands of people," she said. "That's entire towns. Whole cities. All because I was good at sneaking around without getting caught."

"Then what happened?"

"It got harder," Sally said. "Sometimes I couldn't get to the women in time. Or they wouldn't follow me exactly. They'd get caught. Their kids would get caught. I'd watch it happen. From a dark corner or alley, maybe from a window. I'd see it. I'd think about running to them and doing something."

Sally was still looking at Gladys, but her vision was focused elsewhere. She was in another place and time. Tears formed and her eyes glistened.

"I told myself I couldn't risk getting caught. If I did, then there would be others I couldn't help. That's what I told myself. I was helping more people by letting a few end up…"

The first of the tears rolled down her cheeks. Her chin quivered. She wiped her nose with the back of her hand.

"Is that what haunts you?"

Sally spoke without thinking about it. She said what floated to the surface, what she'd submerged for so long. "That, and the isolation. The loneliness of it all."

"Loneliness?"

Sally knuckled the corners of her eyes. She sniffed, wrinkling her nose. "The railroad shouldn't be called a railroad. In a railroad, all of the cars are connected." She lifted her arms and laced her fingers, her hands in front of her. "Everything is moving in the same direction together. All advancing as one singular thing. What we do is different. It's like all of the cars are headed in the same direction, but every car is on a different track."

Gladys appeared truly interested in what Sally was telling her.

"You know how it works," Sally said, counting off on her fingers as she explained. "The passenger contacts somebody. That person lets ticketing know what's what. Ticketing tells the porters. The porters tell the conductors. Each conductor takes a leg. They never know each other. I mean, maybe you recognize someone, vaguely, but you don't know them. The passengers keep switching conductors until they get to wherever it is they're going. Sometimes it's family; sometimes it's a safe house. Sometimes it's the Harbor, I guess."

"You guess?"

Sally raised her shoulders in a shrug and held them there. "Until recently I didn't know it was a real thing."

"It's a real thing," said Gladys. "And I think it'll be good for you."

Sally shifted in the chair, turning her body toward Gladys. Now she was the one truly interested in the conversation. She sniffed back the last of the tears and blinked a couple of times to clear her vision. "What do you know about the Harbor?"

A smile stretched across her face, changing Gladys's appearance. Her back straightened and her shoulders squared. Gladys carried the stature of someone who'd done something so big that the mere mention of it made them glow.

"I built it," she said. "From the ground up."

Chapter 22

APRIL 19, 2054, 7:10 PM
SCOURGE +21 YEARS, 7 MONTHS
EAST OF BAIRD, TEXAS

The sun was blinding. It was a bright orange-yellow disk that hung above the horizon. Heat warbled around it, and vapor rose from the asphalt. Even with the visor down, Marcus had to shield his eyes with one hand as he drove west on Interstate 20.

"Why does the sun get bigger when it sets?" asked Dallas. "It's so small up in the sky around noon, but at sunset sometimes it's huge."

Marcus glanced at the man-child in the passenger's seat. He considered saying something sarcastic. He was sure Lou would have said something biting. Dallas might expect that. But it was an honest question from a child of the apocalypse without real schooling. Deciding against derision, no matter how much fun it might be, Marcus offered an honest answer.

"It doesn't actually get bigger," said Marcus. "It's a trick your mind plays on you."

"Trick?"

"Some people think it's what's called the Ponzo illusion," Marcus explained. "It's about the perspective of things. You take two lines of the same size and put one against objects that look smaller, it's gonna look bigger."

Marcus glanced again at Dallas, seeing he was trying to process it. Dallas frowned. Marcus pointed over the dash and wiggled his index finger.

"Look at the road ahead," he said. "See how the road looks like it gets smaller?"

Dallas nodded. "Yeah."

"Now take your finger and hold it horizontally in front of you and up above the edge of the dash."

Dallas complied. "Okay."

"See? It's one size compared to the road. Now lift it higher and squint your eyes to compare it to the size of the road in the distance. See?"

Dallas grinned with understanding. "Ahhh, I get it. So what's the other idea?"

"Other idea?"

"You said some people believed it was Ponzi's illusion."

"Ponzo."

"Ponzo," Dallas echoed.

"Other people think it's the shape of the sky," said Marcus. "We see the sky as a flattened dome, with the zenith nearby and the horizon far away. Take the moon or the sun and move them along that flattened dome and they get bigger as they move toward the ends of the dome."

"Huh," said Dallas. "That makes sense too."

The truck hit a pothole and bounced. The tailpipe rattled against the undercarriage. Other than the occasional pothole, divot, or forced detour, they hadn't encountered much in the way of obstacles on their way west. Marcus kept expecting the bottom to fall out. Nothing should be as easy as their five-hundred-mile trek had been.

"How come you know so much?" asked Dallas. "Lou says you know everything."

"I don't know how to throw knives."

Dallas laughed. "Seriously, how do you know so much?"

"I don't really," said Marcus. "I know a little bit about a lot of things. It makes me seem a lot smarter than I am."

"Maybe. But Lou said you survived a war before the Scourge. Then you lived through that. You built some super compound; you rescued people, including Norma. They called you Mad Max, right?"

"Sounds like some dude in a dime-store novel, doesn't it?" Marcus joked. "Like some pulp fiction writer made up some unkillable soldier type, dunked him into one horrible situation after another, and the dude survives against all odds. Like the trials of Job but worse. Makes you wonder what hell I've got in front of me."

"One question," said Dallas.

"What's that?"

"What's a dime store?"

Marcus shook his head and chuckled. "A store that sells cheap things."

Dallas nodded and then did a double take at the road ahead. He extended his arm and pointed ahead, toward the south side of the highway.

"We're getting close," he said. "The place is only about a mile up here. You can turn off at the next exit."

Marcus shielded his eyes with a flat salute and scanned the road ahead. It was still an hour before sundown. That would give them a little bit of daylight when they arrived at the house. They'd get a half-decent night's sleep before leaving in the morning.

Dallas had taken off his seatbelt. He was sitting on the edge of his seat, his hands on the dash, fingers tapping nervously on the hard plastic. "You think we've got enough gas?"

Marcus checked the gauge. The tank was half full. "I thought you said it was a mile from here."

Dallas tapped his fingers on the dash. "No, I mean do we have enough to drive all the way back to the wall?"

Marcus glanced in the rearview mirror. "Maybe. We've got the half tank here and another twenty gallons in the bed. It'll be close. It definitely won't get us all the way to Atlanta. We're probably going to—"

"Turn here," Dallas said. "This exit."

Marcus eased the truck toward the exit and slowed as he navigated around a large crumbling hole in the middle of the road. Dallas sat back in his seat, then leaned forward again. The kid reminded Marcus of a dog at a window, watching squirrels run around outside the glass, who couldn't sit still.

"You gotta take a leak?" asked Marcus.

He navigated another pothole and drove off the edge of the exit ramp. Dirt and rocks crunched under the tires and he accelerated back onto the asphalt. Swinging the wheel left, he tapped the brake, drove under the overpass, and punched the gas again.

"No," said Dallas. "I'm just excited to see my wife. And maybe my new kid."

Marcus understood that. He envied it. His mind drifted to the day he and Sylvia brought Wes home from the hospital. It was the happiest day of his life, next to the day they'd gotten married, and the day he left Syrian soil for the last time.

Wes was a good kid. He slept a full eight hours the second night they had him home. Marcus said it was a blessing. Sylvia worried something was wrong.

"Babies don't do that," she said. "They don't sleep through the night that fast."

They stood over the crib at one o'clock in the morning, whispering to each other and watching him as he slept. Marcus had never seen anything so peaceful as the look on his son's face. His pale, smooth skin almost glowed in the shaft of moonlight that shone through the white sheers that decorated the window in his bedroom.

Marcus stood behind Sylvia and wrapped his arms around her. He lowered his head, resting his chin on her shoulder. "I think he's sleeping through the night so we'll have a second one."

Sylvia slapped his hands then rubbed her thumb on his wrist. She giggled softly. "Hush. We barely have one and you're ready for a second? You didn't have to carry that bowling ball around inside you for nine months."

"It was only a bowling ball for the last trimester," he said, nuzzling her. "And my point is that if he didn't sleep through the night, we wouldn't want another one. The less this one exhausts us, the more likely we are to want another one."

Sylvia sighed. It was a contented sigh, one that told Marcus everything was right with the world.

They were together. They were a family. They had a lifetime ahead of them.

Until they didn't.

Until the world ended and he found himself the hero of a fiction too fantastic to be real. Until he was in a truck going back to a place he said he'd never go again. Until the road ahead was as uncertain as anything had ever been.

His stomach lurched and a sour taste filled his mouth. Marcus exhaled slowly, bringing himself back to the present.

"Make another left," said Dallas. "Here."

Marcus swung the wheel with one hand and slowed into the turn. They were running east now, away from the sun. He felt it on his neck as he accelerated again. Dead trees and barely living shrubs cast long shadows on the dirt and the asphalt. The lines that divided the lanes were virtually gone, barely visible. Not that it mattered. Marcus figured there wasn't much vehicular traffic outside Baird, Texas.

There was horse traffic, though. Fresh mounds of manure dotted the road in front of them, on the shoulders. There was a lot of it, the product of several horses. And it was a couple of days old at most. Flies swarmed the piles.

"Lot of horses around here?" asked Marcus as they motored closer to the house.

"Not really," Dallas replied. "Other than ours. We've got a couple. Why?"

"No reason," said Marcus. "Just curious."

Dallas appeared ready to jump from the truck. He couldn't sit still.

"We might want to stop the truck before we get to the property," said Marcus. "Make sure we're ready."

Dallas looked at him quizzically. "What do you mean?"

"Check the weapons."

He eased the truck to a stop, slipped it into park, but kept the engine idling. The two of them hopped out and moved to opposite sides of the truck's bed. The stale of odor of manure hung in the air.

"Somebody on horseback was here," Marcus said, making sure he had a round chambered in the rifle. "Several somebodies, I think. Yesterday or the day before. You know who it could be?"

Dallas stood with one hand on the truck and the other on his head. He looked toward the house and shook his head. When he turned back to Marcus, his expression had morphed from nervous excitement to concern.

"I can't be sure," he said. "But it could be the Pop Guard."

Marcus raised an eyebrow. "They ride horseback? They're government. Why would they do that?"

Dallas checked a rifle. "They like the flexibility of the horses. They can get to places fast and quiet that a truck wouldn't allow, and they don't have to worry about gasoline. They can cover a lot of ground looking for babies. Then when they find them, they've got room for them on any of the horses. A truck's only got so much room for extras."

Marcus studied the ground for tracks, but there wasn't much evidence other than a few random horseshoe prints in the sandy dirt. The sun was behind him. His own shadow stretched in front of him on the asphalt. It was tall and lean. For a moment, it reminded Marcus of the man he used to be.

"How about you hop in the bed," said Marcus. "I'll drive."

Dallas swallowed hard. Deep wrinkles dug across his forehead. "How come?"

"Two reasons," said Marcus. "If there is an army there, you're already in a position to fire on them. If there isn't anybody there, this truck isn't going to look familiar. We don't want Rudy, Norma, and Lou thinking we're attacking them or something. They'll see you in the bed. We'll be fine."

With the rifle in one hand, Dallas moved to the tailgate, flipped it down, and climbed into the bed. He stepped around the gas cans and stood behind the cab, leaning on its top with the rifle aimed straight ahead. He glanced down at Marcus. "What are we waiting for? Let's do this."

Marcus heaved himself back into the driver's seat. He laid the rifle on the passenger's seat next to him. The truck in gear, Marcus accelerated slowly at first and then found his cruising speed.

He drove on a narrow road, south of a lake, and past a rickety deer stand. Ahead, beyond the lake, he saw a collection of buildings. At the center of them, and out front, was what appeared to be the main house. It was two stories with a wraparound porch. Behind the house he could see other, smaller buildings, one of which was a barn.

There was no sign of any intruders. There were a couple of large horses grazing at the weed-infused dirt. Marcus recognized them as Appaloosas.

Two bangs on the roof of the cab startled him and he jerked the wheel. Another pair of hits and Marcus slowed the truck to a stop. Dallas leapt from the bed. Marcus lowered his window.

"Those aren't our horses," Dallas said breathlessly. "I don't recognize them."

Marcus put the truck in park and shut off the engine. He grabbed his rifle and joined Dallas on a driveway. His knees and hips ached, his neck was stiff, and his lower back ached. He flexed his fingers on his right hand. The knuckles hitched and popped.

Road trips weren't good for an old man's joints. He eyed the horses and wondered how far he could make it in the saddle. It had been years since he'd ridden any distance on horseback.

"You were right," said Dallas. "Somebody's been here. Looks like they're still here."

"What are those buildings?" Marcus asked, gesturing with his chin at the barn and the buildings past it.

"Barn, our place, and storage," Dallas said. "It's possible Lou and David are in the barn. That was part of the plan if the Pop Guard showed up."

"If the Pop Guard showed up, they've been here a while."

Dallas frowned. His attention darted across the yard, as if he'd forgotten something and was trying to remember where he'd last seen it.

Marcus raised his rifle to his shoulder. He used two fingers to point to the left; then he motioned to the right.

Dallas nodded his understanding and moved to the left, his rifle leveled and scanning the yard for any threats. Marcus moved to the right, scanning the buildings and the dead trees beyond them. Despite their lack of foliage, the trees could hide hostiles looking for a perch.

He swept his eyes across the trees, the tops of the outbuildings, and the roof of the main house. He didn't see anything that set off alarms. He deliberately moved forward, closing the distance between himself and the barn. He'd check there first. But he didn't get more than a half dozen steps before a voice told him to stop moving and lower his weapon. It was behind him.

"Hold it right there," came a woman's voice. "Don't move or I'll put a bullet in your head."

Marcus didn't move. He kept the rifle pointed toward the barn. His knee throbbed, but he kept his weight on it.

"What do you want?" she asked.

"I'm looking for Lou," he said. "Her kid, David, and—"

"She's not here. Who are—"

"Norma?" Marcus's back was still to her. How had she gotten the drop on him without Dallas seeing her? He started to turn to face her.

"Stop," she ordered. "Who are you?"

"It's me, Mar—"

Then Dallas called from the other side of the yard. "Norma, we're back. Are you okay? Where's Lou?"

"Dallas?" she said, confused.

Dallas's boots crunched on the dirt as he ran toward them. Marcus could hear his hurried steps, his breathy questions.

"We made it back," he said. "Long couple of days."

Marcus slowly turned to see a woman he hardly recognized. The look on her face told him she didn't truly recognize him either.

Dallas reached her and threw his arms around her. In the embrace, Norma stared at Marcus. Her wide eyes and open mouth gave her the appearance of someone who'd seen a ghost and couldn't process whether it was real or a figment of her imagination.

Marcus lowered his rifle and offered a smile. He tried to smile. He wasn't sure if it was actually a smile or more of a constipated grimace. "Norma."

"Marcus?"

He offered a hand. She looked at it before taking it in hers.

"Good lord," she said. "You're old."

Marcus chuckled. "And you haven't changed a bit."

"Liar," she said.

"Maybe."

"Where's Lou? David?" Dallas interjected. "What's with the horses?"

Norma lowered her gaze to the ground and sighed.

"What happened?" Dallas asked, tears forming in his eyes. "Where are they?"

"They're not here, Dallas. The Pop Guard came and—"

"They took her?" The pain in Dallas's voice was heartbreaking.

Marcus winced at it. His grip tightened around the rifle he held at his side. His eyes searched the property beyond Dallas and toward the lake and the Appaloosas.

"They didn't take her," Marcus said. "She left."

Norma and Dallas gaped at Marcus. Dallas's eyes darted between the two of them before settling on Norma.

"That's right," said Norma. "But how did you know?"

Marcus jutted his chin toward the horses. "The Appaloosas. They're not yours. If the Pop Guard had taken Lou, they wouldn't have left them behind. My guess is you stopped them, but you're afraid they're coming back."

Both of them looked at him, dumfounded. Norma nodded slowly.

"I'm old," said Marcus, "but not stupid."

Dallas glanced at the horses. "Where did she go?"

"Where's Rudy?" asked Marcus.

"Come with me," Norma said. "Let's get inside and I'll tell you everything."

She set off toward the main house, followed by the two men. Marcus inhaled slowly as his joints creaked. The smell of dust and ozone was comforting. It was like walking into his home after having been away, smells that were at once familiar and foreign.

"Lou and David are okay," she said. "I know where they're headed. You can meet them there. So don't worry, Dallas."

"What about Rudy?" asked Marcus.

"He's hurt. It was a tough fight when they showed up."

Marcus noticed Norma's gait had changed. It was slower, uneven, and she favored her right side now. While she still carried the confidence of a woman who'd survived more than most and come out the other side stronger than she'd been before, there was something aged in the way she moved, a hitch, a caution. He knew his own swagger was less Texan than it had been.

Norma stepped onto the porch and paused, glancing at Marcus. "He'll be so happy to see you," she said. "He missed you."

Hero

"Me too," said Marcus.

Norma raised an eyebrow. "Really?"

It was judgmental. Questioning. Doubting.

Marcus didn't blame her. He stepped onto the porch. A dark smear of blood stained the deck. He walked around it and into the house.

Norma led them straight through the house toward the kitchen. More bloodstains marked the floors and walls. It looked like a house of horrors. He could smell the death.

"They got in the house?" Marcus asked when they reached the kitchen. He laid his rifle on the counter without asking permission.

Norma leaned against the sink. She turned on the water and it trickled from the faucet. "Well's running dry," she said, running her hands under the pitiful stream. She ignored his question, rubbing the dirt from her fingernails.

"Where did Lou go?" asked Dallas. "She's okay? When did she leave?"

"She's headed toward Fort Worth," said Norma. "The railroad has a contact there."

"Fort Worth?" Dallas's voice rose an octave. Or three. "That's tribal territory. Why would she go there? Why wouldn't she wait here? Or go somewhere less…tribal?"

Norma turned off the water and shook the water from her hands, then wiped them on the front of her jeans. "She couldn't stay here, Dallas," she said flatly. "You know that. Once the guard came, the chance was too great they'd show up again. Especially after what we did to them. I didn't say she was going to Fort Worth. I said toward it. She'll steer clear of the tribes."

Her eyes flitted to the hallway and then to Marcus. Clearing her throat, she moved to the counter where Marcus had put his rifle. Hers was next to it. Dallas still held his in both hands.

"I couldn't be sure you'd make it back," she said. "And if you did, I had no way of knowing if you'd have Marcus with you. It was better to send her to get help, start the journey without you. You can catch up. She's only got a day's head start. With that truck you've got, you'll close the gap quickly. Where *did* you get that truck?"

"Did she have the baby?" asked Dallas.

"A generous benefactor gave us the truck," said Marcus.

"You stole it?" Norma asked.

"Not really."

"No on the baby," Norma said to Dallas. "Not when she left."

"What happened here?" Marcus asked.

The conversation was frenetic. All three of them had questions that were connected but had nothing to do with one another. It was like two children trying to share the highlights of their day with a parent, simultaneously providing information while asking for it. Nobody finished a sentence or a thought, because all of their minds were racing toward whatever it was that interested them.

Marcus wasn't sure who the children were, but he was pretty sure Dallas wasn't the adult. He was fidgety, unable to stand still. He tugged at his hair, the exasperation on his face evident.

Norma ran her fingers along the creases framing her cheeks that ran from the edges of her nose to the outsides of her lips. Her eyes misted and tears pooled in their corners. When she lowered her hands and folded her arms across her chest, she appeared more worn than she had a few minutes earlier. She was looking through the men even as her gaze settled on them. Her silence, and her emotion, calmed the room.

"The Pop Guard showed up. We saw them coming," said Norma. "We got Lou and David into the barn. Rudy and I were on the porch. Everything was fine. Tense but fine. Then they searched the house and found a wooden toy."

"The horse?" asked Dallas.

Norma nodded, her chin quivering.

"What does that matter?" asked Marcus. "People can have toys. They can have one child. Why would that—"

"They knew we lied to them," said Norma. "Everything exploded."

"Why didn't you take them out before they could get too close?" Marcus asked. "Pick them off on horseback one by one?"

Norma's eyes darkened. Her jaw clenched, the muscles flexing as she glared.

Marcus immediately regretted having questioned their tactics. He started to apologize when Norma turned her back on him. She started out of the kitchen toward the hallway and called after him, "I have to check on Rudy. You can say hello if you want."

Dallas was the first out of the room, following Norma closely up the stairs. He was asking her about Lou and David. She answered him in hushed tones Marcus couldn't hear.

"Great," Marcus grumbled. He moved toward the hallway, his knee aching, his ankles stiff. He twisted his neck to one side and then the other. It cracked and felt good.

Despite the dim lighting in the hallway and the shadows that cast odd shapes onto the walls and floor, Marcus saw more bloodstains. Blotches of dried, dark liquid leached across the floor. His boots were sticky with it as he reached the stairs.

He ascended the steps one at a time, each push burning his knees. The smell of dust was thicker on the second floor. It was warmer too. The air was dense, almost stale.

The boards creaked under his weight, and he followed the low drone of conversation toward the end of the hall to the right. The door was open, and flickering candlelight spilled into the hall.

Marcus moved to the doorway and stood at the threshold. Norma sat on the edge of the bed, her feet planted on the floor. She was wringing a rag free of excess water, the drippings clinking against the metal bowl on the bedside table.

Dallas stood back, watching Norma. Then she turned and looked at him. Her eyes washed over him with a mixture of what Marcus recognized as disgust and disappointment.

Those two feelings were cousins often joined at the hip. Marcus knew them well. He'd gotten to know them in the two decades since the Scourge took his wife and his son.

When Norma moved, Rudy appeared behind her. His head was propped on a trio of saggy pillows, their white cases stained yellow from sweat and pink from blood.

His eyes were closed. His skin sallow, almost translucent, he appeared weak and racked with exhaustion. But as Marcus stepped closer, Rudy somehow looked as he had years ago. Despite the wounds, he looked young. Time hadn't aged him as it had others.

A floorboard creaked, drawing Rudy's attention. His eyes opened, if only a little, and he turned his head toward Marcus.

"Marcus?" he asked. "You're here? Dallas told me you came. I said I wouldn't buy it unless I saw you standing in front of me. And I'll be, you're in front of me."

"Seeing is believing," said Marcus, unsure of what to say at first. He exchanged a quick glance with Norma and then focused on Rudy and smiled.

"Damn, you're old," said Rudy. His voice was raspy but strong enough. "I know we all age, but damn, Marcus. It's like the years took you out back and put a whooping on you. Like you looked at Methuselah and said, 'Hey, brother, hold my beer.' It's as though—"

Marcus waved his hands in surrender. "I get it, I get it," he said, still smiling.

Rudy laughed until he coughed.

"Take it easy," Norma warned him and blotted the damp rag on his forehead. She looked again at Marcus. "He's had a fever on and off. I'm trying to keep it at bay."

"You have antibiotics?"

"Yes. They're old," she said. "Not sure how effective they are."

"I've got some honey out in my pack," Marcus said. "I can give you some to put on his wounds. It can't hurt. It's not medical grade, but it's from my bees, so…"

"Your bees?" asked Rudy. "You have bees?"

Marcus nodded. "I do. They keep me company."

Marcus regretted his words the moment he said them. Judging from the six eyes drilling into him and the shift in the air, he wished he could pull them back, delete them. It was too late.

"No offense, Marcus," said Rudy, "but that's offensive. No need for you to be alone like that. You did it to yourself. You hurt a lot of people."

Marcus looked at his boots. They were caked with dust and grime. His pants were gathered at the cuffs, wrinkled and coated in a layer of the same dirt on his boots. "You mean I hurt *Lou*," he said. "It couldn't be that I hurt y'all. You're the ones who wanted me to leave. You're the ones who, rightfully so, suggested all of the bloodshed in Baird, or anywhere I go, is my fault. I bring it with me like I'm carrying a plague."

Rudy coughed again and licked the spit from his lower lip. Norma put a hand on his chest and urged him to rest. He shook his head. "We didn't ask you to excommunicate yourself, Marcus," he said. "You did that on your own."

"Let's put this behind us," Norma said. "Or at least bury it for now."

Marcus tensed at her choice of words. Images of roughly carved tombstones, of crudely wrapped bodies wearily dragged into shallow graves, flipped in his mind. It was a macabre slideshow reminding him of his failures, of the others in his life whom he'd irreparably hurt.

His bones ached. The muscles in his neck stiffened, and sparks of pain shot from the base of his skull to his shoulders. "I'm good with that," he said. "We can revisit my failings once everybody is where they need to be."

Agreement was exchanged with subtle nods and juts of chins.

Marcus shifted his weight and the floor creaked. "How are we to manage this?"

"How so?" asked Norma.

"The two of you," said Marcus. "We've got a truck that could hold all of us. We could put a mattress in the bed for Rudy and—"

Norma shook her head and laughed. It was the kind of laugh that was born not of humor but of disbelief. "That's not happening," she said, the condescending chuckle clinging to her declaration. "He's not going anywhere, so I'm not going anywhere. The two of you are on your own. I'll point you in the right direction, give you the contact information."

"Wait, what?" Dallas said. "You can't stay here. The Pop Guard will be back. You'll be defenseless."

Norma's expression was somewhere between resignation and defiance. Marcus couldn't figure out which was more represented as she pulled back her shoulders and lifted her chin.

"I'm not leaving my husband," she said. "That's final. And as for being defenseless? I think that's not giving me enough credit, Dallas."

Marcus thought of the woman who'd stood in the middle of Baird's main street, a hostile force descending on the town. She'd been brave. She'd readied herself for a fight. That was when Marcus decided the look on her face, the shift in her posture, was defiance. There was nothing resigned about Norma Gallardo.

"Rudy will heal," she said. "He'll get better a lot faster here in bed than he will on the road in the back of a pickup truck. And he'll be here to help me should we need it."

Rudy reached up and put his hand on his wife's shoulder. He winced as he did it, but his touch softened her. She took his hand from her arm, holding it in both of hers.

"Can I at least set you up?" Marcus asked. "Ready some defenses for you before we head out in the morning?"

Norma smiled. It was a straight line smile, but it was kind. Her sharp edges dulled a bit; she nodded and thanked him. "Of course," she said. "You can do whatever you want, old man."

Chapter 23

APRIL 20, 2054, 2:00 PM
SCOURGE +21 YEARS, 7 MONTHS
GUN BARREL CITY, TEXAS

Lou sat outside the Moorhead Epps Funeral Home on the eastern edge of Gun Barrel City. She looked south toward what was left of a reservoir that stretched around the city in a way that made it a peninsula in the middle of the oblong body of water.

There was a portico that covered the front entrance to the long ago abandoned brick building, which gave enough shade to make the wait palatable. Lou leaned against the brick, her hands cupping the underside of her belly. David was squatting in the large parking lot, drawing pictures on the asphalt with a large rock he'd found.

Five horses were tied to a leaning telephone pole set in the middle of a weedy dirt plot that separated the property from its frontage on East Main Street. Main Street was also Texas Highway 334, a little-used road that kept Lou from encountering any additional threats.

Norma had suggested the route, which she'd learned of from a friend who worked at the railroad. It was warm, the air thick with dust and grime. Lou could taste it on her tongue.

Watching David be a child for a few stolen moments, she was thankful that she hadn't had any more cramping since the barn and the deadly encounter with the traveling Pop Guard. She was not thankful that she'd been sitting at the funeral home awaiting her contact for three hours.

Lou arched her sore back and picked up the canteen next to her on the concrete. She shook it, and the remains swished around inside, telling her it was virtually empty.

Rolling onto her side, she managed to get to her feet using the wall. The brick was rough on her fingers and rubbed against the raw flesh worn from holding reins for the last two days. The insides of her thighs and her tailbone ached. She sighed.

"Hey," she said to David. "Let's walk down to the water and fill our bottles."

David looked up from his drawings and nodded. Then he returned to his handiwork and scraped out a couple of additional flourishes before he dropped the rock and stood. He slapped the dust from his hands and then rubbed his palms on his shirt.

Lou made her way to the parking lot and sidestepped her son's artwork. She stood there for a moment, taking his hand. "It's beautiful," she said, her eyes sweeping across the white collection of scratches on the fading, cracked asphalt.

It was pitted and crumbling in spots. David managed to find a wide, unscathed area that provided a suitable canvas.

"You like it?" he asked. "I drew it for you."

The drawing was a line of stick figures. Some of them were tall with hats. Others were smaller or wore triangular dresses to indicate they were women or girls.

"Who's who?" she asked.

David pointed at the smallest figure on the right. "That's the baby. I don't know whether it's a boy or a girl, so I made it neither. It's just a baby."

Lou let go of his hand and put hers on the top of his head, tousling his hair. She smiled. "Your idea was perfect."

"That's me," he said, pointing to the left. "I put a hat on my head even though I don't have one. I like hats though, so I drew it."

The hat was a square with a line that separated it from David's imperfectly oval head. He wore a smile on his face, curving up beneath the single dot nose and twin circle eyes.

"Next to me is Norma," he said. "She takes care of me when you can't, like a grandma. That's why I put her there."

The triangle dress Norma wore was decorated with dots. She wore boots. Her hair was long.

"She looks lovely," said Lou. "Is that Rudy next to her?"

David nodded, waving his hand across the drawing like a magician. As if the movement gave his creation life, he wiggled his fingers. "He's not hurt here. This is before he was hurt. That's why he's standing up. Do you think he can stand now?"

David glanced up at her as her fingers ran through his hair, her nails scraping gently against his scalp. He squinted against the sun, blinking rapidly.

"I think so," Lou said, hoping her tone was convincing. "Rudy is a strong man who can overcome about anything. Plus he's got Norma nursing him back to health. I bet she'll have him doing chores around the house in no time."

David appeared to like that. He chuckled and agreed. Norma could be a taskmaster, but in a good way. Someone had to run things on the property, and she was the best to do it.

"That's you, Momma," he said, squatting and tracing the outline of her shape on the ground. "I tried to make you as beautiful as you are."

"You flatter me," she said, "and I think the drawing makes me look prettier than I am."

She made a silly face, crossing her eyes and puffing out her cheeks. David's hand was at his forehead, shielding his eyes from the sun. He chuckled again. This time it was closer to a belly laugh.

Lou studied the drawing of herself. He'd made her tall and slender and had dressed her in a long, narrow skirt, and there was what looked like a sideways-turned baseball cap on her head. There was a star with the letter H in the center of the cap. One hand, though, was markedly longer than the other.

"What's that?" she asked.

"What?"

"My hand," she said. "The right one."

David clucked. "Really, Momma?" he asked, his mouth twisting to the side with disappointment. "That's your knife. One of them anyways."

Lou wasn't sure how to feel about it. Sure, she always carried a knife. It was habit. It was religion. But that her son would make sure to include it as part of her said something that maybe she wasn't willing to admit.

Violence, or the threat of it, had always been a part of his life. Nothing she did could have saved him from that. And in so many ways, she believed the threat of violence, the preparation for it, and the stress surrounding its possibility were more harmful than the violence itself. She'd done him no favors in that regard. But what choice did she have?

As her father had prepared her for the inevitable, didn't she bear that same obligation, same responsibility? Of course she did. She cleared her throat and motioned toward the stick figure next to her. "Is that your dad?"

"Yes. He's taller than you. He's taller than everyone."

There was one more figure to the far left of the rogues' gallery. That figure loomed over the others. It was the tallest, the broadest. It wore a cowboy hat on its head and boots on its feet. Extending from each hand was the crude but unmistakable shape of handguns. Although Lou knew the answer to her question, she asked it regardless.

"The one on the end is the tallest. Who is that? Who's taller than your dad?"

David pivoted in his squat, his shoes crunching on the asphalt. He glanced at the figure on the left and then used his fingers to push himself up. He stood at his mother's side, using her body to shield him from the sun. "That's Marcus Battle, Momma. You said he was a hero. I figured I'd make him big. All heroes are big, right?"

A lump swelled in Lou's throat. She swallowed against it, her eyes stinging from pooling tears she was trying to keep at bay. She cleared her throat and forced a weak smile. "No, heroes don't have to be big. They come in all sizes. You're a hero, dude. No doubt."

David squinted, though it was evident, as he stood in the shade she created for him, that it wasn't because of sunlight. It was confusion. He frowned and scratched his cheek, leaving a smudge of white dust on his face. "Me?" he asked. "A hero?"

"Of course." Lou winked at him. "You're my son. How could you be anything but a hero?"

A broad grin brightened his face. His cheeks flushed beneath the pale smudge.

"C'mon," she said, "let's go get some water."

Slung over her shoulder, connected by a strand of leather bootlace, were two canteens. She carried a third in her hand. Motioning for David to join her, Lou started the walk south toward the dry, caked edge of the reservoir.

They stepped onto East Main Street without checking either direction. There was no point given the absolute absence of traffic.

The only sounds, at first, were their steps on the hard surface of the state highway and the distant chirps of birds. Once they'd crossed the highway, they were in a neighborhood. A street sign, bent and almost illegible, told them they were on Overlook Trail. Both sides of the narrow pitted road were lined with dead trees. Lou thought it might have been beautiful at one time, before the drought took hold. There were homes on either side of the road. Some of them were built on concrete foundations that sat above the ground; others were mobile homes in severe disrepair, their skirts bent or missing, the cinderblocks on which they stood visible from the road. Plumbing, where people hadn't salvaged it, hung in mazelike tangles stretched between the ground and the underbellies of the homes.

They followed the road south, past an intersection that would have taken them west, and another that would have turned them north again. After a few minutes, they reached a clearing devoid of silvery tree trunks or developed property. To the west, the land sloped gently downward toward a sea of dried mud veined with cracks that gave it the appearance of shattered clay pieced back together but not yet glued.

They walked a hundred yards before the land dropped. On both sides of them, stretching like fingers out across the dried mud plain, were wooden piers that ended with ragged docks and modest boat houses. There weren't any boats, and many of the long piers were missing planks. In some cases, posts were missing and the remaining planks hung precariously.

Between the piers there were charred remains of what must have been campfires. Desperate people needing warmth or something over which to cook food had used the available wood as a resource.

David walked alongside Lou in contemplative silence. She glanced at him and saw the concentration on his face, the wonderment at what they were seeing.

It was like walking across an abandoned planet, alien and new. Lou noticed David was looking at his feet now, trying to avoid the cracks in the ground as he walked. He hopped and skipped, as if playing a game, but kept pace with her as they moved farther from what had once been the shore.

Ahead of them and somewhat south, the sunlight glinted off the remains of the reservoir. The water was bright, reflecting the noon light like a mirror or a precious stone. Despite the evaporation of most of the reservoir, there was still plenty of water. Something between a small lake and large pond remained. It looked to Lou like an oasis in the middle of a desert, though the dried mud darkened the closer they got to what was now the bank.

Lou was sweating, her shirt clinging to her skin, as they reached the water's edge. It was still. There was a thin film on its surface that gave Lou pause. She scanned the water, which stretched a quarter mile across. Farther down the bank, the water appeared to move. It wasn't stagnant.

She lowered herself to the ground and started working at her boots. David watched her quizzically.

"I'm going to wade out there a little bit," she said. "I think the water is better, less gross. Even with the filters, I'd rather have that water out there."

After she removed her boots, she rolled her pant legs up to above her knees.

"Can I go in?" asked David.

"No. You can't swim. I don't know how deep it is. I won't be long."

David plopped down onto the ground. It was softer here and he ran his hands across its surface, like he was making a dirt angel.

Lou kissed him on the top of his head and stood. She stepped into the water, expecting it to be cool. It wasn't. At its edges it bordered on hot, its shallow depth cooking in the daylight.

As she inched farther out into the water, the film parting around her as she moved, her toes sank into the crispy mud at the bottom. The water cooled the farther she went. When the water reached the bottom of her protruding belly, she turned to spot David.

She was much farther out into the water than she'd expected. David was where she'd left him, but she was a good fifty yards from him if not farther. It was difficult to judge. From her spot in the water, the edges of the reservoir blended into the light brown clay at its banks.

"David?" she called. "You good?"

David raised his arm high, stretching it skyward, and raised a thumb.

Lou cupped her hands around her mouth and called out to him, "Love you."

He mimicked her. "Love you."

Lou offered a thumbs-up before turning in the water and taking a couple more steps. Once the water was cool at her feet, she uncapped the canteen in her hand and dipped it beneath the surface. The water gurgled and bubbled as the canteen filled with water.

Once it was full, she capped it and let it float on the surface. She slid her thumb under the leather lace on her shoulder and filled the connected canteens one at a time. When they were full, she draped the leather over her neck, resting the canteens on her chest, and fished the other from the water nearby.

She turned and waved to David. He waved back. She was focused squarely on him as she waded back toward the embankment. Then something caught her attention. The edge of her vision saw movement in the distance. She squinted and drew a wet hand to her forehead to shield the sunlight. It wasn't there at first, but she swept the landscape, searching for movement. Then she saw it. A cloud of dust plumed on the far edge of the reservoir's desert.

Lou's pulse accelerated. Her chest tightened and her eyes flitted from the dust to her son and back. She pushed herself through the water, which seemed to bear more resistance than before. Her feet slipped in the mud, the sticky cake squeezing between her toes, as she trudged in long strides, working her hips and elbows to maintain her balance.

She started to call her son's name again, but knew it wouldn't do any good. There was nothing he could do without her help. It was better not to frighten him.

The dust cloud was a brown mist, lifting from the desert toward the pale blue sky. In it now, through the splashes of water in front of her, she could see dark figures moving. At first it looked like a single person; then it shifted and there were several shapes. Three, four, maybe a dozen of them. They were too small to be vehicles or horses, and the dust cloud was too small to be from anything but people on foot.

The water was ankle deep and warmer now. She was almost to the embankment. David sat there, oblivious to anything but his finger drawings in the moist earth.

Breathless, Lou stepped from the water and joined him on dry ground. With one hand she cupped the underside of her belly, her wet shirt sticking to her skin. She extended her other hand holding the canteen to David.

"C'mon," she said, her attention split between him and the approaching threat. "We need to move."

David took the canteen. His hands were caked with mud, as were his cheeks and forehead. His shirt was streaked with the reddish brown color of the reservoir's bed.

"Everything okay?" he asked.

"Yes, but we need to get back to the horses. I'm sure they're lonely over there across the road."

David hopped to his feet. "Can I water them?" he asked. "I like doing that."

Lou nodded and swallowed. She'd caught her breath, but her heart was pounding in her chest, in her neck, at her temples. She stuffed her socks in her boots and picked them up as a pair in one hand. Then she ushered David toward the houses and dead trees to the northwest.

"Aren't you going to wear your boots?" David asked, carrying the canteen against his chest. "You're barefoot."

Lou was walking in short strides, her hips swinging like a race walker as she led her son away from the water. She didn't answer him at first. He was jogging to keep up with her.

"Momma, did you hear me?"

To the right, east of them, the dust was a translucent brown fog. The figures were bigger now. There were people of varying heights. They moved in unison like troops marching toward battle. They were too far away for Lou to know if they were armed. She assumed they were and turned her attention back to her son.

"I'll put them on when we get to the horses," she said.

"Why aren't you wearing them?" David was breathless now, his little legs working to keep pace.

Lou slowed a beat, still hustling but easing up for David's sake. "I wanted my feet to dry."

David didn't speak again until they'd reached the road called Overlook Trail. The worn road was rough on Lou's feet. Stray pebbles and crumbs of asphalt caught on the soft part of her low arch, jabbing the calloused pads beneath her toes.

Wincing, she had her hand on David's shoulder as they hurried north. Glancing back, she could distinctly see the line of people. They were spaced evenly as they moved; two of them were armed. The others didn't appear to be. Lou did a double take and stopped. David kept walking, unaware she'd turned her attention back toward the water.

"Hold up, David," she said. "I'm looking at something."

"The people?" asked David. He had seen them.

Lou stared at him for a moment, studying his expression. He wasn't frightened, didn't sense the possible threat. That was good. Or it was bad. Maybe he hadn't lost all of his innocence yet. That was good. However, being too innocent in this world was not.

"Yes," she said. "The people. I'm trying to figure out what's going on with them."

They were standing on the road, a cluster of trunks and a mobile home giving them cover. Lou narrowed her gaze, focusing on the group one person at a time.

They were still at a distance, and the sun darkened their features enough that she couldn't make out anything other than size. Though from the way they walked, she figured the taller one at the front of the line was a man and so was the tall one at the back of the line. Both of them were armed. No doubt now. The people in the middle looked to be women and children. They shuffled where the men strode, hung their heads where the men held their shoulders back, their chins up. Lou scanned the line again and saw the familiar curve of a pregnant woman's body on one, then two, then almost all of the women.

She knew what this was. Norma had warned her. This was why she hadn't used a coyote, why she'd waited for Marcus to help her and Dallas move north. These were men selling women to a tribe.

Lou's mind raced. The closest cities were Dallas and Fort Worth. They were north and west of Gun Barrel City, not too far. In a day or two these women would be slaves, their children raised to be soldiers. Lou glanced down at her son and then back at the women. It was then she saw the dust rising from between the women as they walked. Were those chains linking them together?

Lou's grip on her boots tightened. She clenched her jaw, anger swelling in her gut. The fear and apprehension that had hustled her from the water was boiling rage now. She had to do something.

With her free hand she took David by his upper arm and pulled. Tugging him gently toward East Main Street, she formulated a plan that would free the women and keep her boy safe.

"David," she said when they'd safely crossed the highway and reached their horses, "I'm going to help those people at the water."

David offered his dirty hand to one of the Appaloosas. It sniffed and nuzzled his palm. "What am I going to do?" he asked, his attention on the horse.

Lou took the canteens from around her neck and looped them over the horn on the Appaloosa's saddle. She ran her hand along its mane and faced her son. "I need you to stay here with four of the horses," she said. "I'm taking one of them."

David frowned. "Is that what heroes do?" he asked. "Stay with the horses?"

"Heroes do all kinds of things. And if you give these horses water and keep them company, you'll be their hero."

Lou knew leaving her son in the parking lot of a funeral home at the edge of an abandoned town wasn't the maternal thing to do. And as she described to him his role, pangs of guilt gnawed at her. She thought better of it. "Change of plan," she said. "Come with me."

She led David across the parking lot and around the side of the funeral home. At the back was a low, glassless window. She stopped there and peered inside, grabbing the lower edge of the wooden casement to lift herself onto the tiptoes of her bare feet.

It was dark inside the building, bars of light filtering into the space through the open holes where glass used to protect the interior from the elements. It wasn't ideal, but it would do.

"All right," said Lou. "I need you to stay inside the building."

David didn't ask her why or complain about the task. Both the interrogative and declarative resistance to her request were obvious.

"Remember the loud noises, the gunfire, at the barn?" she asked.

He nodded.

"There could be more of that," she said. "And I want you safe. You're safer in the building than you'd be in the parking lot with the horses."

David's eyes flitted toward the front parking lot where the horses were. He couldn't actually see them from where they stood, but Lou imagined he could envision them clustered around the phone pole.

"What about the horses, Momma?" he asked. "I was gonna water them."

"You can do that when I come back."

He drew in a deep breath through his nose and let it out. It was the sigh of a tired child, the kind of thing that reminded Lou how young her son was, how much she was asking of him.

His expression relaxed and his mouth curled into a disappointed frown. "How long?"

"How long what?"

He rolled his eyes. That was a new thing. He'd clearly learned it from her. Or it could be Dallas. Lou rode her husband hard, she knew that, and it wouldn't surprise her if, behind her back, her doting husband occasionally protested her demands with the silent protest of an eye roll.

"How long do I have to stay in there?" he asked.

"A few minutes. Less than the length of a bedtime story. I won't be long."

Lou hoped that was the truth. There was no telling how long she'd be. And what if she didn't come back at all? She was a pregnant woman, alone, taking on what she supposed was a skilled pair of coyotes. They were men who bartered in flesh and would have no compunction about killing her or, worse still, enslaving her. Then what would David do?

Lou reconsidered her plan. How could she risk her son's life for the lives of strangers? Did that make her a horrible mother? Probably. But what if they'd seen her and David moving toward the funeral home? What if they had binoculars and had seen she was pregnant? What if they came after her, got the drop on her before she knew what hit her? She couldn't risk that possibility. Better to be the attacker than the victim. Nonetheless, the risk was certain if she attacked. It wasn't if she waited and moved along. On horseback, she could run from them if need be, galloping away before they could ensnare her. Her mind raced. She could run now.

Yet she couldn't live with herself knowing she had the chance to save others and did nothing about it. She remembered something her father had once read to her when they were holed up in a library, surviving the apocalypse. It was from a collection of essays and speeches her father said were the work of a great leader in the second half of the twentieth century. He'd been a preacher and a man who advocated peaceful protest. He was beloved, and then a man shot and killed him at a hotel in Tennessee.

Her father had read to her, his feet propped on the long study table, and she sat next to him with her head resting on his shoulder, listening intently, reading along with him, following his finger as it underlined the words on the page.

Sometimes she'd ask him to read a passage again and again so she could commit it to memory. This was one of those passages, and it bloomed in her mind as she thought about what she had to do.

"Human progress is neither automatic nor inevitable… Every step toward the goal of justice requires sacrifice, suffering, and struggle; the tireless exertions and passionate concern of dedicated individuals."

Sacrifice for human progress. Could she sacrifice herself, possibly her son, for the betterment of society? Of course she could, although it pained her to do it. A thick knot twisted in her stomach as she hoisted her son onto the sill and into the dusty, dark innards of the funeral home.

She reached to the small of her back and withdrew a knife, flipped it over in her hand, and then reached across the sill. "Take this. You know what to do with it if you need it."

David took the knife by the hilt and measured its weight in his hand. He turned it over and the blade glinted in the faint light that found its way into the building. He nodded. "Like you taught me?"

"Like I taught you." A knot in Lou's throat joined the one in her gut. "I love you. Stay quiet." Then she left him alone in the relative dark.

Lou plucked at the front of her shirt as she moved toward the horses. She could feel the sweat under her arms, in the small of her back, under her breasts. Cupping the underside of her belly as she moved, adrenaline filtered through her body and replaced the exhaustion that threatened to overwhelm her. This would not be easy. She cursed at herself and twice stopped, started back toward her son, and decided against it.

She unthreaded the lead that held her horse to the pole. She rubbed his flank and then managed, with difficulty, to hoist herself into the saddle. Her thighs and butt immediately protested. The familiarity of the position exacerbated the soreness that had only gotten worse during the course of their long ride. She regretted not having spent more time on the horses at home in Baird. She'd left the task of running them to Dallas.

Lou checked the positions of her knives at the tops of her boots. She removed the magazine from a nine millimeter and replaced it, slapping it into the grip and chambering the first round. She slid the weapon into a handgun holster on the side of the saddle.

From a brown leather scabbard, she withdrew a semiautomatic rifle. Checking the position of the safety, she set it to semiautomatic and laid it across the saddle between her belly and the horn. She was ready.

Lou backed the horse from the others and it nickered. She soothed it, leaning as far forward as she could to tell the Appaloosa everything was okay and she'd take care of him.

The horse neighed, shook its head as if it understood her, and then trotted forward onto East Main Street. Lou kicked her heels into the horse to pick up the pace.

Within two minutes they were back on the cracked earth desert that marked the evaporated reservoir. When they hit the dry ground, moving past the sloped edge and onto the flat open expanse, she urged the horse to a gallop. It obliged immediately and its force pushed Lou back in the saddle.

She hung onto the reins wrapped tightly around her left palm, and leaned into the wind, her hair blowing into and out of her eyes. Guiding the horse directly toward the water's edge, she saw the men and women already there. Some were sitting, others standing, and a couple were in the water up to their ankles. The men with guns stood watch, but they weren't at the ready.

Lou bounced in the saddle, her toes turned outward against the stirrups, her heels kicking into the horse as it took her closer to her targets. She lifted the rifle as she neared the water.

The targets were coming into focus. She saw the men clearly now. One of them wore a green ball cap. There were children with the women. And yes, they were chained together.

Lou clenched her jaw. Time slowed. Maintaining her hold on the reins in her left hand, she gripped the underside of the barrel and settled the stock into her shoulder. Her right hand found the trigger guard and then the trigger itself. She tilted her head to the right and sighted the first of the targets. She pulled the trigger.

***

Warner heard the approaching horse before he saw it. He stood at the edge of the water, his eyes squarely on Andrea and her boy, Javier, as they washed themselves and filled their canteens. In the distance, above the splash of water, he heard the rhythmic thump. It was more like a drumbeat.

He adjusted the bill of his cap and saw a horse barreling toward them, a wake of dust pluming around and behind it, curling skyward.

Aboard the horse was a single rider. Warner couldn't tell if the rider was a man or a woman, but the slight build and long hair whipping gave him the impression it was a woman or teenage boy.

He didn't notice the rifle until the muzzle flashed and Blessing grunted in pain. A second flash popped before Warner turned to see his partner stagger, a hand at his chest.

Blessing held his rifle in the other hand until he dropped to his knees. A burst of red sprayed from his back an instant before the echo of a third shot, a crack barely louder than the mix of water and hooves, reached Warner's ears.

Screams filled his ears. Women dove to the ground, into the water, the chains that bound them stretching and tugging. Warner spun fully toward the rider and lifted the rifle to his shoulder. He sighted the target and fired two quick shots.

But the rider had turned the horse, running parallel to the water's edge. The twin rifle shots missed, zipping behind the rider and the horse. It was now he could see the rider was a woman. And in profile, realized she was pregnant.

Warner dropped to one knee to steady himself and tracked the rider with his rifle. He took another shot and missed as the rider cut back to the left. He cursed her, flipped his hat from his head, and took aim again.

The horse turned toward the water and was coming straight at him. He had her in his sights now. Even a sudden move to either direction would result in a hit. Warner applied pressure to the trigger just as something heavy and hard knocked him off balance, sending the shot wide of its mark.

His face slapped against the cake-batter-like ground, jarring his neck, and his shoulder slammed into it. A jolt of pain ran along his spine and in the joint connecting his arm to the rest of his body. Then thick jabs punched at his ribs and back.

Warner still had his rifle, and he tried to use it to free himself from his pinned position on the ground. It took him a couple of seconds, which felt like minutes, to get his wits about him. It was then he understood Andrea was on top of him, trying to pummel him.

***

Andrea saw the horse before she heard it. It was a large horse, the kind she recognized belonged to the Pop Guard. It picked up speed on the flat ground that separated clusters of dead trees and low-slung buildings from the water's edge. The dust plumed skyward, like smoke from a truck's exhaust, as it galloped toward them.

Andrea opened her mouth to say something, thinking they were under attack, but thought better of it. If it was a lone soldier of the Pop Guard, maybe it would be better to deal with him than her captors. She'd let him ride, approach without warning, and deal with the consequences. Nothing the Pop Guard could do to her and her children would be worse than what a tribe would inflict.

So she kept a wary eye on the rider as she filled her water bottle. The canteen gurgled on the water's surface as it filled. Light trails of film were sucked into the container's mouth, and the canteen grew heavier.

Javier splashed in the water next to her. He made puttering sounds and created waves that crested and fell as he twirled in the water. His shirt clung to his body, and Andrea tensed at how thin he'd become. The wet fabric traced his ribs, and through it she could see the flutter of his heartbeat. The horror of it almost drew her complete attention, for an instant redirecting her from the approaching horseman. She blinked past it and stole another look at the rider at the moment a bright light flashed from what Andrea recognized as a rifle. She also saw the long hair whipping around the rider's face. It was a woman. A woman was coming for them.

She knew it when the first shot, and then the second, hit Blessing. He grunted. His mouth agape, a wide-eyed look of disbelief and surprise dominating his expression, he staggered back to the water's edge. Then his body jerked and he dropped his weapon onto the dirt.

Blessing was on his knees, grasping at his body as if trying to pull off his clothing. He was clawing at himself when another spasm rocked his body, and he collapsed face-first onto the dirt, water lapping at his boots. All of this happened in seconds. It was so fast, Andrea noticed that Warner didn't have time to react.

He was taken off guard by the lone attacker. By the time he raised his rifle to fire, she'd turned her horse away from his aim and circled back. Andrea's eyes flitted repeatedly between Warner and the rider.

The women around her screamed in fear and dove to the ground, covering their children and holding their bellies with both arms. They struggled against their binds. The woman connected to Andrea started moving from the water, dragging Andrea with her. The tug against her ankle dug the metal cuff into the back of her leg and she winced. But she moved with the woman, taking Javier with her, and decided as Warner took a knee, she would use her momentum and her window of opportunity to help the mystery rider in her quest.

He took two more shots as the rider adjusted her path and came straight at them. Warner had a bead on the rider. Andrea did the only thing she could. She dove straight into him, toppling him as he fired an errant shot. The crack of the rifle was next to her ear. A deafening ring disoriented her as they fell to the ground, but she swung wildly at Warner, driving her tightly balled fists into him again and again.

She vaguely heard Javier's cries behind her. They were muffled and muted underneath the loud ringing in her ear, but it was there.

"Mami!" he called. "Mami!"

Andrea ignored his cries and kept punching. She was on top of Warner. His hat was gone and he was on his side, the rifle still in his hand. He grunted. He cursed. His body shifted underneath hers, and then he freed his rifle and jabbed the butt upward. It connected with her side underneath her rib cage.

He hadn't gotten a clean hit, but the blunt force of the butt knocked the wind from her, and she toppled from him. Momentarily paralyzed, gasping for air that didn't come, she lay on her back in the dirt. The bright sun above blinded her and she closed her eyes. Javier was on top of her now, his little hands on either side of her face.

She opened her eyes and the dark shape of his head blocked the sunlight. His fingers raked at her cheeks. He called her name over and over. She couldn't breathe. She couldn't move.

***

Lou saw the woman on her back, a child on top of her. Next to them, the rifleman coyote was finding purchase on the ground. But they were too close together for Lou to risk a shot. If she missed, she could hit the mother or the child, whose movements were wild and unpredictable.

She was close enough now to see the man's eyes. They were black. The sneer on his face was pure hatred. It sent a shudder along Lou's spine even as she steadied herself in the saddle and tossed the rifle. It spun from her hand and landed behind her in the dirt.

The man was wobbly, disoriented. Lou could see that as he groped, struggling to find his rifle. It was inches from his hand.

Lou was twenty feet from him now, closer still to the screaming women, the crying children, and the dead coyote. He reached the rifle and quickly pulled it up to take aim.

She reached into her right boot at the same moment she jerked the horse to the right. As the man with the black eyes lifted his rifle, finger already on the trigger, Lou flung a knife at him. End over end it flipped, zipping the distance between them until it found its mark, and the blade drove deep into his chest beneath his neck.

Still, he managed a shot and the horse jerked wildly, unexpectedly, and tossed Lou from the saddle. The earth and sky spun, flipping positions, one over the other and then under, until she hit the ground with a thick sucking sound. She was at the edge of the water on her back. Her head cracked against the ground, dizzying her. Her vision sparked with stars, and bolts of electric pain shot through her hip and the back of her shoulder.

If she hadn't landed at the edge of the water, she'd be unconscious or worse. The spongy ground at the water's edge cushioned her violent fall enough to lessen the damage.

Immediately, and despite her confusion, her hands went to her belly. She felt herself, as if she'd find something there that told her she'd hurt the baby. But there was no pain, no cramping. She felt her crotch and then raised her hand toward her eyes. She tried to focus but couldn't. Nonetheless, she knew her hands were dry as she rubbed her thumbs across her fingers and palms. There was no bleeding. That was something.

Lou lay there for long minutes before she managed to struggle to her feet. In front of her was the dead man she'd shot three times. He was facedown, his feet in the water, his hands caught underneath his motionless body. Splotches of dark red stained his back where the rounds had exited. Lou kicked him. His body jiggled but didn't otherwise move.

Hero

She winced at the pain in her hip and shifted her weight to the other leg. She limped past the whimpering women and children, who said nothing, but whose expressions told Lou they were confused and frightened.

Lou cleared her throat and tried to speak. At first all she managed was a squeak. Then the words came. They were breathless but intelligible.

"I'm here to help you," she said to the women. "Don't worry. You're safe now."

The women's expressions didn't change. The fear lingered, as if painted indelibly on their tired, pallid faces.

Then one of them, the one who'd dived onto the second coyote, buying her the time she needed, lifted an arm from her prone position and pointed at her. She said something Lou couldn't hear, so she limped forward, the pain lessening with every step.

Lou stood at the other coyote's head now. He was on his back. His eyes were open, no more lifeless than they'd appeared moments earlier when he'd stared into her soul. The knife was buried in him to the hilt. Its blade had found the soft spot above the collarbone to the side of his neck. Blood leaked from his nose and mouth.

She bent down to pull the knife from his neck when she realized the woman on her back wasn't pointing at her. She was pointing past her, behind her.

With her hand still on the knife's grip, Lou looked over her shoulder to see six men on horseback racing toward them. They'd come from the highway and were closing in on them quickly. Pop Guard.

"This is not happening," Lou muttered. "Not happening."

Her mind flashed to David alone in the dark funeral home. She'd told him she'd be back soon. It had already been ten minutes if not more. And now she had an unwinnable fight on her hands. The Pop Guard would be on them in less than five minutes.

She turned to the woman on her back. "Keys," she said. "To the chains."

The woman pointed at the dead man at Lou's feet. Lou fished through his pockets until she found a set of keys. She leaned across the body and unlocked the cuff at the boy's foot. Then she did the same for the woman.

"Can you move?" asked Lou.

The woman nodded. "I think so," she said, her voice airy, the sound of someone who'd just caught her breath.

"Unlock your friends. Quickly. And can you fire a weapon?"

The woman nodded again. "Yes."

"Take his," she said. "There's another one over by the other dead guy. Give it to someone who can use it."

"I'm Andrea," said the woman. *"Muchas gracias por su ayuda.* Thank you for your help."

"De nada," said Lou. "I'm Lou."

"You speak Spanish?" the woman asked once on her feet.

"Nope," said Lou. "That was the extent of it."

The woman tried to smile. It looked more like a nervous twitch.

"Get to work," said Lou. "We've got a minute or two at most. Then we've traded one evil for the other."

Lou wiped both sides of the blade on the dead man's shirt. His black eyes gave her the impression he was still alive, like a dead fish staring at her unblinkingly. She swallowed hard and got to her feet.

She turned from the dead man and scanned her surroundings. The horse was alive, on its side and struggling. It made sounds that forced Lou to cringe. As she approached it, walking as quickly as her throbbing hip would allow, she saw the rifle she'd tossed to the ground.

She redirected herself, heading straight for the weapon. Reaching it, she checked the horizon and saw the oncoming threats, the dust like a tornado roaring toward them.

Lou moved the distance to the horse and checked the progress of the chained women. Two more of them were free of their binds. They appeared confused, their shoulders hunched, stature diminished by whatever torture their captors had forced them to endure. One woman was on her knees, pounding her fists against the back of the dead coyote facedown at the water's edge. She was screaming something at him. Another woman was tugging at her, unsuccessfully trying to pull her away from the corpse.

Lou reached the horse and found the nine millimeter in its holster. She sighed with relief that the horse had fallen on this side and not the other. She got the pistol. A moment later, the beautiful, powerful horse was no longer in pain. Lou wanted to puke. She dry heaved, bending over at her waist, spittle trailing a line from her lips toward the ground. She quickly checked the progress of the advancing soldiers and cursed under her breath.

Spinning around, her free hand pressing against the underside of her belly, she waved Andrea forward.

"You!" she shouted. "Get over here. Use the horse as cover and get ready to fire."

Andrea did as she was told, bringing Javier with her. They hurried toward the horse and found a spot up against its saddle.

Lou scanned the collection of women and children and found the other one holding a rifle. She called out to her and checked the advancing troops.

"You too," she said. "C'mon. Get next to…"

"Andrea," said the woman already staking her position behind the horse.

Lou flashed a smile at Andrea, her son, and then shot a solid look at the other woman. She aggressively waved her to a spot next to Andrea. She spun back to the others.

"Stay low," she said. "There's going to be a lot of gunfire. I don't want you getting hit. Might even be best if you scatter a little. Head out into the water if you can."

The women looked at each other, paralyzed. Lou balled one hand into a fist and tightened her grip on the handgun with the other.

"Now!" she bellowed.

That shook the others into action. Lou counted them quickly. There were five women, six children, and one infant. They were up against six armed men. Lou didn't love the odds, given their lack of firepower. It would have to do. She took her place by the horse's head, stroked its mane, and dropped to one knee.

"All right," she said to the women beside her at the horse. "When I tell you, I want you to pull those triggers. Keep pulling them until they're empty."

The women nodded. The one named Andrea looked more confident. She squared her shoulders. Her finger found the trigger.

Lou wrapped both hands around the pistol. She exhaled and leveled the weapon. The horsemen were close enough now she could see all but one of them had rifles up and ready to shoot.

Lou thought they'd be slow to open fire. Their first goal was to take pregnant women alive. She figured dead women didn't do them any good until after they'd given birth. She was wrong.

No sooner had the woman next to her settled into her position than her head snapped back and she fell to the ground. An instant later, the crack of the rifle that fired the deadly shot reached Lou. One shot, one dead woman.

Lou exchanged a look of surprise with Andrea, and then both of them found their resolve. Andrea tightened her hold on her rifle and returned fire. Hot casings spit from the side of the rifle, clinking as they flipped from the weapon and bounced.

Lou tucked the handgun at her aching hip and took the rifle from the dead woman beside her. She pulled it to her shoulder, found the trigger, and pulled.

The men were almost on top of them now. Six of them. Then five of them. Four now.

Lou ignored the shrieks and cries behind her. She shifted positions, targeting the men atop their galloping Appaloosas. Next to her Andrea yelled something about being out of ammunition at the moment the remaining three horsemen peeled away, turning around to race away from them.

One of the felled men got up. He picked up his rifle and set up behind another dead horse. He didn't take aim. He was hiding.

Three men on horses and one with a position. Lou liked the numbers much better now. Especially since it appeared the three riding away weren't coming back yet. Still, with the man behind the horse, they weren't in the clear. He could pick them off one by one.

Lou took her finger from the trigger, and the echo of gunfire quieted. She checked with Andrea. "You okay?"

Andrea looked over the rifle. She still had it aimed downrange despite being out of ammunition. Her voice trembled when she spoke. "Yes," she said, "I'm okay. You?"

Lou winced at the pain in her hip and she shifted her weight. "Yeah. Your boy?"

Andrea moved the rifle and looked at her son. Javier had his back pressed against the saddle, his knees to his chin, eyes closed, hands pressed to his ears. The boy had made himself as small and insulated from the violence around him as he could. Andrea reached out and touched him, startling him. He jerked away from her before relaxing. His eyes opened and he flung his arms around his mother's side.

Lou's eyes welled. She shouldn't be here. She should be with David. How long had she left him now? Could he hear the gunfire from inside the funeral home? How scared he must be. How alone.

"Hey!" called the Pop Guard soldier from his covered position twenty feet from Lou. "We've got more men coming. You're done for. You're *so* done." The man's voice was trembling with pain. It cracked and pitched as he spoke. "You should give up."

It was a plea as much as it was counsel, Lou thought. She couldn't see him behind the dead horse Andrea must have accidentally shot. Or maybe she intentionally shot it. Lou couldn't know for sure. Neither of them had been expert shots. They'd unloaded countless rounds and only taken out three of the men.

"You should drop your weapons and raise your hands," the soldier said, his voice warbling. He grunted. "Otherwise they're gonna come in hot and take down all of you. Don't matter if you're pregnant or not."

In her peripheral vision she saw shades of movement. She swung to her right and saw three women moving forward, away from the water. Two of them had one hand raised and the other gripping a child. The third had a child beside her and an infant in her arms. The women were soaking wet. Their dresses or shirts clung to their distended bellies, accentuating their pregnancies. Lou watched them and unconsciously touched her own belly. The baby kicked underneath her hand.

"We'll give up," said one of the women, exhaustion threading her voice. "We don't want to die. We're giving up."

Lou clenched her jaw. She and Andrea exchanged another glance.

"Please don't shoot us," said the woman with the infant in her arms.

On the horizon, the three horsemen had disappeared. They'd found the highway and bolted, she supposed.

"He's bluffing," she said. "They're not coming back. They're gone."

"No, I'm not," he said. "I'm not bluffing."

The woman with the infant looked toward the man and back at Lou.

Lou shook her head. "Nobody's coming for him. He's buying himself time."

"They're coming," the man insisted. "A bunch more. They're at the funeral home."

Lou's stomach twisted.

"One of you is named Lou, right?"

Her head swam. She was nauseated. Bile rose in her throat, and her tongue was suddenly thick in her mouth. Cold sweat beaded on her forehead. How could he—

"We've got your kid," said the man. "David. Now they're coming back for you."

Chapter 24

APRIL 20, 2054, 3:00 PM
SCOURGE +21 YEARS, 7 MONTHS
GUN BARREL CITY, TEXAS

David stood in the parking lot, a soldier gripping his arm. Another stood across from them holding a bloody knife, shaking it as he appeared to chastise the boy. He spat as he spoke. His face and neck were red; a large blood vessel strained against the skin along the side of his neck.

There were four horses tied to a telephone pole, their saddles empty. Another five were closer to the front of the funeral home. Two of them had riders. Pop Guard soldiers. Armed. Impatient looks on their scowling faces.

Three more horses appeared from the opposite side of the highway. They were galloping. The men atop them looked shaken. Ashen.

The red-faced man with the bloody knife turned his attention to them. He shouted something and started pointing the knife at various horses and men.

The soldier holding David by the arm yanked him toward the four horses at the telephone pole, almost dragging him across the lot. The boy trudged and tripped alongside his captor.

"What do we do?" Dallas asked from the passenger seat of the truck. He looked ready to jump out of his skin, one hand white-knuckling the dash. "What do we do, Marcus? They've got my boy."

Marcus took the binoculars from Dallas and rubbed the scruff on his chin. The stubble was rougher, coarser since he'd gone gray.

"Be patient," he said to Dallas. "I know it's tough. But give it a second."

"Where the hell is Lou? What happened to her? She would never leave David alone."

Dallas turned to Marcus, his eyes glistening, his chin quivering. He wanted reassurance that wasn't coming. Marcus wasn't one to paint a rosy picture or even offer a best-case scenario. It was better to have low expectations and exceed them than to expect the best and fall short.

"They don't see us," Marcus said. "We've got the advantage. They're not gonna hurt your boy, I don't think. There's no advantage to that. They'll conscript him or sell him."

"That's Lou's knife," said Dallas. "The bloody one. This isn't good. It's not good, Marcus. We shouldn't have spent the night at home. We should've come straight here."

Marcus watched the men mount their horses. The four at the telephone pole stayed there, where they had tied David. He struggled, protesting, to no avail.

"Who ties a kid to a pole?" Dallas spat.

Marcus noticed that of the five horses not tied to the pole, only four had riders. Then there were the three who'd arrived moments earlier. Seven men, twelve horses. Something didn't add up.

"I think your boy got the best of one of them," said Marcus. "He know how to use that knife?"

Dallas nodded. "Yeah. He can throw better than me."

"I'm pretty sure that blood isn't Lou's. Now just hang back a second. Wait for them to leave. Then we'll grab David."

Marcus raised and lowered the binoculars again. They were a

hundred yards from the parking lot on the north side of the highway. They'd rolled slowly through the town, cruising above an idle, when they'd heard the echo of gunshots. Marcus recognized it as semiautomatic rifle fire. There was a brief firefight closer to the reservoir, so they'd headed that way. Marcus stopped the truck behind an old gas station and turned it off when he saw the collection of large horses he'd learned were standard issue for Pop Guard.

Now all but one of the soldiers took off, south, across the highway toward the reservoir. The lone man left behind was on his horse, keeping an eye on David.

"All right," said Marcus. "Let's go get your boy."

"How are we doing this?" asked Dallas.

"I don't know. But why don't you hide in the back. I don't want David recognizing you and ruining the surprise."

Dallas flashed a concerned look at Marcus but obliged. He shouldered his way from the truck, closed the door as quietly as possible, and climbed into the bed. Marcus motioned for him to lie down. He did.

Marcus pushed the ignition and started the truck. Shifting into gear, he pushed down on the gas pedal and eased onto the highway. In less than thirty seconds they were pulling into the parking lot. He rolled down the window and waved with his left hand. His left knee guided the wheel as he braked to a stop.

The soldier had his rifle raised, aiming it through the open window as he walked his horse a safe distance from the truck. He scowled. Despite the seriousness on his face, the hardened jaw and angry eyes, Marcus could see the soldier was young. The kid couldn't be more than nineteen or twenty. He had his finger on the trigger.

Marcus smiled broadly, faking an affable grin. Of all the things that described him, affable was not one of them.

"Howdy," he said, using the greeting he'd heard so many Texas Aggies use before the Scourge. "Need some help?"

"No," the soldier snapped. "You'd best mind your own business."

Marcus winked and pointed at David. The kid was crying, his lips red and pouty, his shoulders shuddering.

"No problem," he said. "Just passing through. But I saw the boy and thought you might need some help. Kids can be a handful. I could pay you for him."

The soldier's expression was unchanged. He motioned toward the highway, jerking the barrel to the east. "I said mind your business. Otherwise I'm gonna be—"

The guard didn't see Dallas until after he'd pulled the trigger. By then it was too late to do anything about it. The first shot hit his hand and kicked the rifle from his grip. The second drilled into his shoulder and jerked him in the saddle. The third, from the gun in Marcus's right hand, tore through his chest.

Stunned and still trying to finish his sentence, the soldier wobbled before slumping forward. His face smacked against the saddle as the spooked horse took off in a sprint. The kid fell to the side, his foot caught in the stirrup. The Appaloosa dragged him across the highway and out of sight within seconds.

Dallas jumped from the back of the truck and sprinted the short distance to his son. He hugged him, kissed his head, and wiped his tears.

Marcus stepped from the cab and took a couple of steps toward the two. David looked just like Lou. Dark skin, piercing eyes.

"Best untie him," said Marcus.

Dallas furrowed his brow with confusion, then nodded and worked at the binds on his son's wrists. He squatted on his heels, freed his son, and took him by the shoulders. "You're okay?" he asked. "They hurt you?"

David shook his head. He was still crying, snot leaking from his nose.

"Where's your mom?" Dallas asked. "What happened?"

David pointed with a shaking finger across the highway, then buried his head in his father's neck.

Marcus backed away, moving toward the truck. "You stay with the boy," he said. "I'll go get Lou."

Dallas wrapped his arms around David and closed his eyes.

Marcus climbed into the cab and had the truck in gear before he'd shut the driver's side door. He pressed the gas pedal to the floorboard, and the truck's tires squealed against the asphalt. Smoke poured from the burning rubber, an acrid odor filled the cab, and the truck jerked forward. Marcus spun the wheel and bounced across both lanes of the highway.

He drove straight across the road to one extending south toward the reservoir. Marcus had both hands on the wheel, almost standing on the pedal. The engine roared and the truck accelerated as he steered it onto the dirt, past a clump of dead trees, and down a slope onto an expansive clearing.

It reminded Marcus of the Middle East, the barren wastelands of sand and dust bathed in bright sunshine. The truck bounced him in his seat, and his hands guided the wheel. Ahead of him he could see the seven horsemen riding toward the water's edge. At the water there were two large dark figures and a collection of smaller ones.

"C'mon," Marcus urged the truck faster and faster along the flat stretch of dry lake bed. "C'mon."

The speedometer told him he was doing fifty. Then fifty-five. It didn't feel fast enough. The horsemen were too close to the figures at the water's edge. One of them, he assumed, was Lou.

He laid on the horn, pressing it again and again. His palm pressed hard into the center of the wheel.

Two of the seven horses peeled away and started riding toward him. Marcus bore down on them, aiming for them. A flash of light from one of them preceded a pop in his windshield. A crack spidered vertically. A second flash and a second pop.

This time the windshield exploded, shards of glass splintered from the large pieces of glass that hung together from the frame at its edges.

Marcus took his foot off the accelerator and pressed the brake. As the truck slowed, he steered hard to the right. The rear tires spun and the truck drifted. Marcus's driver's side window faced the oncoming horsemen now. He was within forty feet of them when he leveled his weapon and pulled the trigger, aiming at one and then the other.

In the distance, near the water, he was vaguely aware of more flashes of light as he repeatedly fired his weapon. Errant rifle shots clunked against the truck. One hit a tire and Marcus felt the truck rock, shift, and tilt. But his aim was truer than the riflemen on horseback.

Both the men dropped from their saddles and hit the dirt with sickening slaps. Their necks and arms twisted oddly when they landed. Blood leached onto the clay-closed dirt, draining into the cracks that made the ground look like someone had twisted an ice tray, loosening the pieces but leaving them in place.

The truck came to a stop and Marcus put it into park. He jumped from the cab, his knee screaming at him when he landed, and hobbled to the horses feet from him. He grabbed a rifle and swung himself into a saddle, kicked his heels into the horse's sides, and rode toward the strobing flashes of gunfire at the water's edge some hundred yards away.

***

Lou grimaced. She twisted the knife before pulling it out of the guard's neck. Blood drained from him as he slumped to the dirt. She'd attacked him, using the surrendering women as a distraction as she crossed the distance between the two dead horses and then dove over the soldier's cover. She drove the blade hard, coming in high and from the side. He grabbed at her hand, struggling for a few seconds before he spasmed and went limp. His words rang in Lou's ears.

"We've got your kid, David. And now they're coming back for you."

Lou grabbed the soldier's rifle and hopped to the other side of the horse before crouch running back to Andrea's side. She tried focusing on the coming threat now, saving her fire until they were closer. She didn't know how many rounds she had left. The one she'd given to Andrea wasn't fully loaded either.

She could see seven horses racing toward them now. There was no way they could kill all of them. No way.

"You're gonna get us killed!" cried the woman holding the infant. "Stop it. Stop it! You're going to get our children killed! We have babies!"

Lou checked with Andrea. "You good?"

Andrea nodded. "Thank you. No matter what happens, thank you."

Lou didn't know what to say. *You're welcome? No problem? Sure thing? Any time?* None of those rang true. She regretted what she'd done. The woman with the infant was probably right. She was going to get them all killed. And now they had her son.

She'd been foolish. This was not what Martin Luther King Junior meant about sacrifice. It couldn't be. Not even Marcus Battle would do what she'd done, leaving her child behind to go help strangers. But there was no going back now. She couldn't undo it. The best she could do was try to salvage an untenable situation.

Lou peered over the top of the horse's body again and counted five horses. Where were the other—?

Then she saw the truck speeding across the flat. Two of the horses were riding toward the truck.

"Now," Lou said, staring at the five horses approaching her. "We're better to do it now than wait."

She leaned against the horse, her belly straining against her shirt, the child sitting low against her pelvis. A shot of pain ran down her leg. She winced, gritted her teeth, and took aim.

The rifle kicked against her shoulder. Hot casings pinged to the ground beside her. Smoke drifted from the end of the barrel. Andrea joined in, and together they unloaded their weapons at the advancing hostiles. Two of them went down. Three left, plus the two taking aim at the truck.

Who was in the truck? Was it her meet? The tardy conductor who was supposed to house her until Marcus and Dallas arrived or until she was out of time and had to move again?

The three horsemen were closing in. To her left, Lou heard screaming. In front of her, the dead horse shifted with the thump of incoming fire.

Lou pressed the trigger again. It clicked. She was out of ammunition. Glancing to her left, she saw Andrea hunkered down, holding her boy, the rifle on the ground next to them. Lou reached across them and picked up the weapon. Leveling it at the horses now only twenty feet from her, she pulled the trigger. A round zipped by her head. Her weapon clicked.

Lou tossed it aside and slid down behind the horse. The gunfire stopped for an instant, and she reached for the handgun at her waist. She turned back and saw the horses were no longer coming for her. They'd turned and were bolting for a fourth horse.

The trailing soldier was close enough that she took a single shot with the handgun. She targeted his back, lifted the barrel slightly, and applied pressure to the trigger. It hit the rider between his shoulder blades. He was thirty yards from her when he arched, grabbed at his back as if stung, and then fell awkwardly from his ride.

There were two horsemen headed for the lone stranger. Lou stood from behind the dead horse. A sudden wave of tension clutched her body, and she dropped back onto a knee, balancing herself on the still-warm hide of the dead horse.

She groaned through clenched teeth and held her belly low, the gun still in her hand. The pressure intensified, sharpening and stealing her breath.

"You okay?" asked Andrea. She reached a hand toward Lou, touching her leg.

Lou winced again, breathing shallowly. She clutched the damp underside of her belly and grabbed a handful of shirt.

Andrea's eyes widened with a realization. "Are you in labor?"

"I don't know," said Lou. "I hope not."

***

Marcus held his knees tight against the saddle, keeping himself balanced and upright. He held a rifle with both hands. The butt to his shoulder, his stiff finger on the trigger, he took his first shot. It missed.

The two riders were close now. Marcus saw their eyes. He saw the sweat on their brows. Both had their weapons raised. They had a bead on him. Without his hands on the reins, he couldn't adjust course. One of them fired. Then the other. The first round zipped past him. The second grazed his arm. The sting was hot against his flesh, like someone had run a burning ember across his bicep. He flinched but held his aim and targeted the rider closer to him as they rode past each other.

The rider's eyes went wide and he reached for his side and lost his balance, dropping his weapon as he steadied himself. Marcus couldn't see him as he rode away from them, but he knew he'd hit him.

Marcus lowered his weapon and grabbed the reins with his left hand. He jerked the horse to the right, back toward the water, and headed for the women and children.

As he sped back, the horse kicking up dust and dirt, the sun shining down on him, Marcus stole a glance to his right. Only one soldier remained on his horse. The other was slumped in the saddle.

Marcus kicked his heels into the horse and closed the distance between his horse and the water's edge. He counted a half dozen women. There were children too. One woman held a bundle in her arms by her neck. An infant?

Marcus pulled back on the reins and slowed the horse. He raised his weapon and scanned the women with it. "Lou?" he shouted. "Louise? Are you there?"

None of the women responded. He stopped the horse, rifle in hand, and dismounted. He marched toward the water, conscious of the soldier still approaching on his horse.

"Lou?" he shouted again. No response.

Then an arm shot up from behind a dead horse, the middle finger raised. The skin was brown. Marcus's chest swelled. His heart pounded in his ears and he limped as fast as he could toward her. Then he stopped, feet from the horse. He could see her legs splayed on the ground, peeking out from the horse's body. A shot zipped past him, the crack echoing in the dry air. Marcus whirled around, pushing his weight on the better of his two legs, raised the rifle, and tracked the approaching horseman. He pulled the trigger and the weapon barked. Two. Three. Four rounds. At least one of them hit the rider, and he lifted from the saddle before sinking back down. He clutched at his gut with one hand and tried to fire off a shot with the other, but he couldn't and lost the rifle before Marcus hit him with another skillful shot. The horse bucked its head and changed course, racing off toward the abandoned neighborhood to the west.

Marcus lowered his rifle. Limping, his knuckles throbbing, his back aching, he inched toward Lou. Ignoring the cries and complaints of the other women and their children, he moved past the horse, and a simpering, sweating, much older Lou came into view.

For the first time in a very long time, tears formed in his eyes. He didn't even know he could cry anymore. He thought he was out of tears. He blinked past the blur, conscious of the wet drops streaking down his cheeks. He stopped, standing feet from her. His chin twitched, not quite quivering.

He cleared his throat. "Lou?" he asked, as if he didn't know.

Through pained breaths and winces, she locked eyes with him. The faintest hint of a smile edged the corner of her mouth. "Dorothy, I almost didn't recognize you. You look older than dirt."

He laughed. It was genuine. "I know."

"I don't even think the wizard can help you," she said.

"Maybe not."

"Brains, heart, and courage are one thing. A whole new face is something else."

"Okay, I get it. But seriously, you're gonna criticize me? You've gained a lot of weight. And that's not easy in a drought. I think you need to go vegan."

Lou's hint of a smile spread into a grin. Tears welled and she half laughed, half cried. A bubble formed in her mouth and popped.

Marcus tossed the weapon to the dirt and took another couple of steps toward her. Gingerly, and with considerable pain, he lowered himself onto his good knee. He reached out a hand to her. She took it and he pulled her toward him.

They embraced. Marcus wasn't sure if the sobbing was hers or his own. As they held each other, he whispered to her, "Dallas has David. He's okay. I mean he's safe. He's not okay. You gave him a stupid middle name. He'll never be okay."

Lou slapped his back and squeezed again before pulling back. She blinked at him and wiped the tears from her face with the back of a grimy hand. Then she glanced at his arm. "You're bleeding."

"Grazed," said Marcus. "I'll be fine."

"But never okay," she said.

"True."

She ran her fingers along the side of his face, tracing the deep creases. Like a child studying a father's face, she ran her thumb on his white stubble. "I'm not kidding," she said. "You do look old."

"You don't look so good yourself," he said, inching back from her. "And I'm serious. You're pale. Your heart is pounding. You're clammy."

"I might be in labor. I'm not sure. I've had a couple of contractions over the past few days since I left the house."

She shifted against the horse and put both hands on her belly, motioning with her head toward the woman next to her. "This is Andrea," she said. "She and the other women were going to be sold."

Marcus surveyed the carnage at the water's edge and beyond it the women with their children. Some of them stood. Others sat. All of them had vacant, bewildered looks on their drawn faces. A couple of them rocked with children in their laps. His attention turned back to Andrea. "Coyotes?"

"Worse," said Andrea. "Most of us paid coyotes to get us to safe places so the Pop Guard wouldn't take our kids. The coyotes sold us out to these two. They're brokers. They sell women and kids to the tribes."

Marcus looked at the woman's boy. He was curled against her as if he couldn't get closer to his mother.

She pointed at the man's body closest to them. "That one was pure evil," she said. "Pure evil. He was sadistic. Heartless. He killed a woman who couldn't keep up. Shot her. She'd just given birth on the highway. She had a newborn and he shot and killed her."

Andrea's face widened with the horror of what she'd seen. Deep lines creased her face. They weren't from age, Marcus reckoned. They were sun-aggravated stress lines.

"Lou helped us," she said. "If it hadn't been for her, we'd be on our way to slaughter."

Marcus looked at Lou. She was navel-gazing, rubbing her belly. The sweat had matted her hair to the sides of her face.

He could still see the little girl in her, the feral creature who'd flung knives at him outside an abandoned gas station near a Dairy Queen on Highway 36 outside Rising Star. He remembered the Astros ball cap sideways on her head.

She'd stood across from him, her fingers wiggling at her side and her head tilting to both sides as she cracked her neck. Her glare, he recalled, was the nastiest thing he'd seen on any person before or since.

Lou had been a gangly preteen who hadn't grown into her body or her enormous feet. She'd flung the blade at him so quickly, he hadn't seen her produce it. So much had happened since then.

"I'm sorry," he said to her.

Lou looked up. "For what?"

"Everything."

"Huh," she said. "Anything specific?"

Marcus grinned. "I'm sure there is. Too much for now. I can run down the list later. Let's get you back to your husband and son. And I guess we need to figure out what to do with these folks."

"Marcus?" Lou said.

"Yeah?"

Her eyes glistened; her chin quivered. "Thanks for coming for me."

Marcus didn't know what to say. It wasn't for a lack of words, it was the overabundance of them. A thousand things flooded his mind, and none of them captured how he felt. None of them was good enough, so he didn't say anything. He took a deep breath and blew it out.

They were together again.

He'd come so far. He had so much farther to go.

CHAPTER 25

APRIL 20, 2054, 3:20 PM
SCOURGE +21 YEARS, 7 MONTHS
BAIRD, TEXAS

Norma stepped into the barn and slid the wide door closed behind her. Rudy was sleeping soundly for the first time since the attack on their property. This was her first opportunity to slip away. Thankfully it fit with the prearranged time she'd agreed to be here.

The smell of sawdust and hay comforted her, drawing a dim smile, and she crossed the barn to the large wooden table pressed against the wall. On the table was a collection of electronic boxes and wires. They were powered by a lone solar cell purchased on the black market and affixed to the barn's roof. It produced enough electricity to charge a bunch of golf cart batteries they'd wired together to run the electronics and spin a lone fan hanging from the barn's roof.

The electronics were, more specifically, radios. Rudy had helped Norma cobble together a functional and, given their circumstances, impressive high frequency transceiver that provided communication with the outside world. On a good night, Norma could talk to people in Mexico, Canada, and both coasts of the North American continent. She'd once connected with someone who claimed to be in Havana, Cuba. Another instance had her talking with a soldier in

Cayenne, French Guiana.

The high frequency radio transmitted on all bands from 80 meters, all the way up to the 6 meter band. In the summertime, in the middle of the day, she got the best distance. Winter time at night was the worst for trying to reach far off ham operators.

Late afternoon in April, with the temperatures as warm as they were, should provide her enough of a push to find the person for whom she was searching. She hoped so. It was critically important. Especially given the change of plans.

Norma didn't have a license to use the radio. Most people didn't anymore. There wasn't an agency to test or enforce whether or not a given operator knew the rules of the road for short- or long-distance communication. She did, however, know enough about her equipment to get by and to have productive conversations.

One by one, she flipped the switches and dials to their respective positions. She made certain the antenna was matched to the transceiver, and initiated the call, pressing the mic key.

"Hello, this is NGBTX1," she said, identifying herself with a nonregulation call sign. "Is the frequency busy?"

She waited a moment. No response.

"Hello," she repeated. "This is NGBTX1. Is this frequency busy?"

Silence. Then a crackle and a high-pitched noise.

One more time, Norma checked for traffic. Finally, she got a response. A woman's voice came through the speaker.

"GA, NGBTX1, I hear you. GA. This is GFAGA5. I hear you. QRO?"

"Good afternoon," said Norma. "No, your signal is good. No need to increase power. Nice to talk with you."

Norma understood most of the Q signals and CW abbreviations ham radio operators commonly used in their transmissions, but she didn't use them much. It was like understanding a foreign language without the ability to recall it quickly enough to speak it.

Even though she recognized the woman's voice on the other end of the line, she had to be sure it was her and that nobody was listening. They had a code for this. The Pop Guard, and the government in general, regularly monitored amateur radio. They'd use the information they gleaned in various oppressive operations.

"Been a long time since San Angelo," said Norma. "I hear it's changed."

Norma took her finger off the mic key and waited for the reply. She held her breath.

"Especially Pearl on the Concho," the woman responded. *"The river is dry."*

She exhaled. A dry river meant all was clear. A flooded river meant there were problems.

"Good to hear," said Norma. "How is your guest? Doing well, I hope?"

"Yes," said the woman. *"She's doing well and should be ready for your arrival. Bags are packed."*

Norma adjusted the volume on the speaker and decided to plug in a headset. Uncoiling the cable, she plugged the quarter-inch pin into the transceiver. The external speaker went mute, and she slipped on the large over-the-ear headset. The cushions had cracked, and foam poked through, scratching her ears, but this was safer than using the external speaker should someone show up unannounced. Not that she expected any visitors. But there was a good chance the Pop Guard would come back looking for their dead compadres.

Norma checked over one shoulder and then the other. Her pulse quickened. She pressed the mic key again and leaned into the microphone to lower her voice. "We are delayed," she said. "Complications changed the departure and the route."

There was a pause. In her mind, Norma could see the woman on the other end of the line. She imagined the lines of consternation deepen on her face. Of course, the version of the woman Norma imagined was younger than in reality. It had been years since they'd seen each other face-to-face.

"We'll adjust," said the woman. "Not a problem. I've heard from our Gun Barrel friend. She is aware. How many travelers?"

The woman's voice was so much stronger, more confident than it had been when the two of them spent so much time together. Then, she was quiet, reserved, introverted. Now she had the command of a general.

Norma pressed the mic. "It's good to know Gun Barrel shared with you. At least two passengers," she said. "As many as five."

"As we planned, then. That's good."

"Yes," said Norma. "At least that's good."

In truth, both of the women knew there was a possibility that Lou, David, Marcus, and Dallas would never reach their contact beyond the wall. They knew the wilds of Texas were nearly as dangerous as they'd been under Cartel rule, under the hand of the Dwellers, and under the lawless outlaws known as the Llano River Clan, the LRC.

It was the LRC that had brought them together almost twelve years earlier. It was the fall of 2042. Both of them were kidnapped, enslaved, and held prisoner in what had been the Pearl of the Concho Hotel on the banks of the Concho River in San Angelo.

The hotel was a base for the gang. Norma and her friend had endured, catching occasional glimpses of one another during their captivity. Then Rudy, Marcus, and Lou had rescued them, freed them from their bonds.

"Is he one of the five?" asked the woman, her call sparking with static. "Mad Max?"

Norma blinked. She hadn't expected that question. Not this call. She pressed the key and spoke softly.

"Yes," she said. "Mad Max would be among the five."

Another pause. Both women felt the same way about Marcus. After their rescue, all of them had come back to Baird. Like Marcus and Lou, the woman had nowhere else to go, so she and her sister had come to live on Norma and Rudy's property. They lived in a guesthouse and, in exchange for free room and board, they cooked meals and sometimes cleaned.

Like Norma, the woman came to believe that Marcus brought about as much violence as he staved off. He was a magnet for it. And as much as his presence might comfort, it also threatened to ruin the town of Baird. She'd pushed Norma to urge Marcus to find a new home, a place where he couldn't hurt people simply by being present. Norma didn't want to talk about it.

The man they'd both decided was too dangerous to live near them was now the man upon whom Lou had called for help. Norma had tried to dissuade her. But given that she refused to allow Rudy to make the trip, that Dallas wasn't the fiercest warrior, and that they couldn't risk a conductor coming anywhere near Baird, Marcus was the choice.

"Tell me about your guest," she said, asking about the person who would help Lou on the final leg of her journey. "Is she up to it?"

"Yes, she is. Mended and good as new."

In the years after Marcus left Baird, the drought took hold. The Pop Guard was born and raids started. The government took mothers, stole babies, and murdered fathers, all in the name of state security and the preservation of resources.

Nobody believed that was the real reason. It was an excuse. But it didn't matter. When the woman's sister gave birth to a second child, she and Norma conspired to find a safe place, a way to help her get there, and a future where the sister, her children, and her husband could live together for the rest of their lives. The underground railroad was born.

Years later, the railroad stretched across the country with all paths leading through Atlanta and one of five so-called harbors. The West Coast was still in its infancy. It was too far a distance, and the railroad's influence hadn't rooted as it had east of Texas.

East of Texas it worked. There were hundreds of families living in harbors. They struggled at times, keeping the Pop Guard at bay, but they managed. All of it was thanks to the ingenuity of Norma and her friend.

Norma had remained in Texas, content to anonymously run the operation inside the wall. The Pop Guard had become so much more aggressive in Texas. Getting out of the territory was the hardest part. And Norma didn't want to leave Baird, her home. The friend, who was the first conductor, took her sister as far as Atlanta. She'd stayed there and set up shop right under the nose of the government and the Pop Guard, hiding in plain sight.

"Good," Norma said. "Talk again in twenty-four hours. By then we should have the latest from Gun Barrel."

"Yes," said the woman. *"CL."*

"CL," said Norma, ending her conversation with the woman now known to most people as Gladys, mother of the underground railroad.

CONTINUE THE ADVENTURE WITH
HARBOR
THE HIGH-OCTANE CONCLUSION TO THE TRAVELER

Acknowledgments

I have to begin by thanking you, the readers and fans of Marcus Battle. What began as a little story set in rural Texas turned into so much more during the three and a half years since HOME hit shelves in December 2015.

Hundreds of thousands of you have followed his journey, and mine, as he battled the Cartel, The Dwellers, The LRC, the new government, and his own demons. I hope you found his arc satisfying and you're happy that Marcus has found peace at long last.

Now it's on to other adventures and I hope you'll take the trip with me as I explore new people, places, and events that shape imaginary and speculative worlds. Again, thank you for your loyalty, your praise, your messages of encouragement, and your embrace.

Thanks also to the team of people who help me unleash these stories on the world. Felicia Sullivan is a crack editor. Pauline Nolet and Patricia Wilson cross every T and dot every I. Hristo Kovatliev is a master cover artist who captures the essence of every story in a drawing. And Stef McDaid at Write Into Print makes the books, digital and print, look beautiful with his expert formatting. And Steve Kremer is the finest of beta readers. He fixes the things I break.

Also thanks to two fellow writers; Steve Konkoly and Murray McDonald. The two of them encouraged me to write in the Post-Apocalyptic genre and to self-publish these stories. I owe both of them a debt I can't repay. The result of their gentle prodding was life-altering.

Lastly, and most importantly, I thank my family. Courtney, Luke, and Sam are the best of agents and managers who are honest critics and unrelenting advocates. I love you all immeasurably. And to my parents, my siblings, and my in-laws, you are always my best marketers. Now on to the next big adventure…wherever and whenever it might be.

Made in United States
North Haven, CT
15 April 2023